# DARLING DESCENT

## LEIGHANN HART

First paperback edition April 2022

Images © DepositPhotos – Photo_life
Cover Design @ Books and Moods

Copy Edits by Justin Williams

ISBN 978-1-7376130-4-6

# PLAYLIST

I Wanna Get Better - Bleachers
My Body - Young the Giant
Mountain Sound - Of Monsters and Men
Trouble - Cage the Elephant
Simple Song - The Shins
Kick Drum Heart - The Avett Brothers
Lost in You - Three Days Grace
I Will Possess Your Heart - Death Cab for Cutie
Animals - Living in Fiction
Hate Me - Blue October
Shake It Out - Florence + The Machine
Savior - Rise Against
Feeling Good - Muse
Come As You Are - Imaginary Future
The Cure - Lady Gaga
Awake My Soul - Mumford & Sons
Blank Space - Our Last Night
Woke the F*ck Up - Jon Bellion
Elastic Heart - Written by Wolves
I Knew You Were Trouble - The Animal in Me
Heart-Shaped Box - Andie Case
Power & Control - MARINA
Dreams - Mateo Oxley
Don't You (Forget About Me) - Brittin Lane
Crazy - Madilyn Bailey, Leroy Sanchez
Linger - Beth
Creep - Daniela Andrade
My Favourite Game - The Cardigans
Private Eyes - Sleeping At Last

Alphabet Boy - Melanie Martinez
They Said That Hell's Not Hot - Marilyn Manson
Like Real People Do - Hozier
Gabriel's Message - Traditional, Advent at Ephesus
Swim - Chase Atlantic
Borderline - Tame Impala
An Unhealthy Obsession - The Blake Robinson Synthetic
Orchestra
Hell is Round the Corner - Tricky
Lover Lover Lover - Leonard Cohen
D'yer Mak'er - Led Zeppelin

"Now is the dramatic moment of fate, Watson, when you hear a step upon the stair which is walking into your life, and you know not whether for good or ill."

— **Arthur Conan Doyle**

# December

# PROLOGUE

**Dayton**

Dayton had been kneeling in the confessional for no more than thirty seconds and a stiffness had overtaken his knees. He wasn't a regular attendee of the place of worship, but he forced himself to pay a visit to St. James every Christmas Eve. Breathing in the cold air, the heavy incense burning in the altar, Dayton was greeted by flashes of his trivial, adolescent confessions. What he would have given to restore that innocence and erase the man he'd become.

The monster.

The consequences of his sins marked his cheek and collarbone. The heart beating in his chest, its absence of feeling, he no longer recognized as his own.

He signed the cross in haste. "Bless me, Father, for I have sinned. My last confession was one year ago on this day."

"Confess your sins, son. I'm afraid you'll have to make it quick. Introductory Rites will begin shortly."

"I ask only for a moment of your time, Father. I've come before you to seek forgiveness for the ones I've used, deceived, and exploited. I believe my deception has brought undue suffering onto others, and I am remorseful for any pain, real or imagined, I have undoubtedly inflicted upon them. I am sorry for these and all my sins."

"Give to someone what you have refused these anonymous others. Deceive them not, for your chance to truly prove your penance, not only to our Father in Heaven but to yourself, lies in your honesty. You may pray."

"Lord Jesus Christ, you are the Lamb of God. You take away the sins of the world. Through the grace of the Holy Spirit restore me to friendship with your Father, cleanse me from every stain of sin in the blood you shed for me, and raise me to new life for the glory of your name."

Dayton was silent as the priest administered his prayer of absolution. He wished their exchange would've gone on the rest of the night, admissions and prayers whispered back and forth through the latticework.

It pained him to think of returning home. Another Christmas alone with the weight of all he had done and the fear of whatever destruction lay ahead.

### Kenna

A chill laced the air in the nave of St. James that had nothing to do with the Oregonian winter storm raging beyond the church's walls.

Kenna stole a seat along the third pew from the entrance, alone, where she hoped to sit through midnight Mass undisturbed. The Christmas Eve service was the closest she came to being home for the holidays.

Rows of votive candles flickered to life as people lit them before finding their seats. Boys and girls clad in flowing gowns swept in to populate the choir, their piercing voices breaking into

Gabriel's Message no sooner than they had assumed their positions. She sang the carol, quietly under her breath, imbued with a deep sense of peace at its familiarity. Watching the children perform tugged at Kenna's heart. She ached for the chance to see her sisters, but a trip to New York was a luxury neither her finances nor psyche could afford.

A slow, horrid creak tore her attention from the choir. Her pulse leveled out upon identifying its source. A towering man in an overcoat emerged from the confessional.

For a fractional moment, their eyes met.

Menacing black orbs burned holes into her skin all the way across the room. A sensation of strangulation overtook Kenna, hand flying to her neck while her chest compressed to the brink of concavity.

The dark-haired man held a match to one of the burning candles and ignited one that was unlit. It did not burn for long before he snuffed it out and hurried up the aisle, hands burrowed in his coat pockets, escaping into the landscape of the snowy Christmas night.

# January

1

# NINTH CIRCLE

**Dayton**

~~Alex~~
~~Bella~~
~~Charlee~~
~~Dakota~~
~~Erin~~
~~Freya~~
~~Giselle~~
~~Harmony~~
~~Ivy~~
~~Jasmine~~

Dayton stared at the creased paper. The seemingly insignificant list that was the center of his perverse universe.

Acquiring his last subject came at the price of an inordinately long recovery period and laying low for more than a year had him thirsting for the chase. Fruitless months without insights or satiation.

January was in its infancy. A new semester with new possibilities. His chest swelled as he regarded the stark white walls of his office. He too had hit a wall.

He couldn't delay his research any longer.

Sliding open a narrow drawer on his desk, he returned the paper to the otherwise empty space where it had taken up residence the last six years. He kept it there, hidden in plain sight, without a lock—waiting until someone, or no one, came to know of its existence. Perhaps a part of him wanted the world to stumble across his dirty little secret.

Waiting for someone to save him from himself.

Drumming his fingers on the cool metal desk, his attention wandered to the trio of windows, fixating with the disquieting earnestness of a marksman on the snow-covered campus below. Students and faculty crossed paths as they navigated the wintry terrain in search of their respective destinations. Dayton had watched the exact scene play out countless times.

Of all the places he could have ended up—a hospital, an outpatient clinic—he'd landed amid the landscape of postsecondary education.

The years he'd spent at Ponderosa University all blurred together, carrying little meaning with them. He deemed the esteemed private liberal arts school as the closest semblance of Hell on Earth. Everything was constant, from the bumbling freshmen to the quarter-life crisis graduate students. The same types of people with the same pitiful range of—what were almost a joke to call—problems milled about the forest-enshrouded campus, no matter the season.

Only, after a finite period of time, the students graduated and moved on with their lives.

Dayton's sentence within the institution was infinite, and he did not dare orchestrate an escape. A particular comfort had grown in the unruly garden of his dissatisfaction; his decaying roots had taken up residence at Ponderosa, and he saw no reason to remove them.

For two hours, Dayton had been locked in his office, failing to do much more than watch the minute hand make the agonizing journey around its dial. That slender black hand mocked him, inanimately making light of his solitary confinement. The first day of a new semester always inched along at an unbearable pace. Drilling a hole in his skull held greater appeal than sitting through another visitless first week of term. He would've been content with a few status checks for his regular patients, anything to get out of his own head, away from the swirling ghosts of faces and memories.

The mental phantoms dispelled as a weak knock echoed against the frosted panel on his door. One backed by the weak essence of timidity; the shy urgency of none other than a female student. The knocker held such profound hesitance in her hands that Dayton swore he smelled her uncertainty pervading below the doorjamb. Like a shark detecting blood in the water, he understood whoever was beyond that door could be his next subject.

An emptiness fluttered low in his stomach as he rose from his desk and stalked toward the shadow in the frosted glass.

## Kenna

The monotonous speech spilling out of Professor Henrick's mouth barely registered with Kenna. He was a walking relic, donned in a faded suit which had seen its heyday decades earlier. Did the garment not beg for mercy each time he slipped it over his wrinkled limbs? His spiel about the parameters for their internship was less than engrossing and many of her classmates had resorted to snickering about his tacky wardrobe.

She maintained perfect posture and concentrated on the

lectern in a feigned display of undivided concentration though she felt weightless, rearing to float out of the class and drift toward her destiny. It was her final semester as an undergraduate.

One semester separating her from graduate school. Kenna's veins hummed with anticipation. She had made it.

The rustling of paper filled the room, mimicking the swoosh of scattering leaves as everyone flipped to the next page of the thick packet that detailed the criteria for the task that lay ahead. She couldn't help but feel triumphant as she stole glances at her fear-stricken peers and sucked in her bottom lip to keep a smile at bay. Giddiness chimed within her like a bell, silent glee ringing throughout her body. She had laid out the course for her internship junior year. Perhaps her triumph was premature. The green light had yet to be lit.

An uncontrolled variable stood in the way.

The approval rested on the shoulders of the university's psychiatrist, Dr. Merino, a man whom she had never met and of whom had heard very little.

Her mouth possessed the aridness of cracked summer soil as the gravity of the situation sank in. Kenna crossed her legs, assaulted by an onslaught of restlessness but bound to her seat. What if Dr. Merino had no interest in working with a student, someone who had zero experience in a clinical environment? Worse, what if someone had taken up the position? It was a possibility she couldn't stomach. Everything was riding on his approval and availability.

There was no alternative.

### Dayton

With each pace toward the door, a vile delight blossomed in Dayton's sternum. To say he was anxious to meet the woman idling in the hall would have been an understatement. As he twisted the lock, the cogs of a machine long out of commission began their slow, reluctant churn, in anticipation that somehow, she was the one. The girl who would resuscitate his madness.

Dayton turned the knob, letting the door creep inward on its hinges.

"Enter," he urged while returning to his desk. With a sidelong glance, he eyed the fire-headed woman hovering in the doorway. "Would you like to have a seat or shall we conduct our business from the hall?"

She mumbled something akin to 'sorry, sir' and rushed to populate the seat across from him. The student hugged an armful of notebooks flush to her torso, as if they were a lifejacket.

Dayton found the sight humorous, clinging to something for comfort in the most uncomfortable place. His office emanated an aura of doom.

The ninth circle of Hell.

But most were unaware of this when setting foot in his office. This woman, however, had something to fear. She shook like a twig in the lightest of storms.

"If you have sensitive matters to discuss, give me some fore-warning so I can shut the door," he advised, looking up from his bullshit heap of paperwork.

"That won't be necessary." She toyed with a strand of her long, straight hair, in grand deliberation of her next move. Dayton marveled at how glorious those glossy locks must feel, waging that they'd glide across his fingertips like the finest silk. "I'm in PSYC4960."

She retrieved a set of papers, which she placed on his desk with one of her milky, glowing hands.

"I came here to inquire about the possibility of carrying out my internship with you. More like a mentorship, really. I'd be required to spend 20 hours with you each week." She continued speaking as she moved to fill the guest chair across the room. "I don't want to come across as desperate, but I'm in a tough spot transportation wise. I need to stay on campus and I hope you take that into consideration as you mull over my proposal. I won't disappoint you." Her feverish green eyes landed on him as she brandished a pained stare, a look that struck him like a luminous spectral—haunting and inviting, all at once. "Please, Dr. Merino. I need this."

He couldn't believe what she was saying. She either had no idea of his reputation at the university, or was well aware of it, in which case she must have been entirely mad.

He thought she looked vaguely familiar but couldn't place it. His focus was split between the woman, reluctant to tear his gaze away from her darling face, and the contract that sat before him. In the most obnoxiously pristine print he'd ever seen read, 'Kenna O'Callaghan,' on the line marked 'name.' The neat capital 'K' stared back at him, begging him to ruin its precision. A calmness settled within Dayton as he drew in a deep breath. He knew exactly how to handle the situation.

"Ponderosa doesn't offer pre-med, so it's safe to assume you aren't on any kind of educational path that will eventually lead to practicing psychiatry. Pray tell, why are you in my office?"

"Please, sir, I'm not incompetent. I understand there are differences between the work of psychiatrists and psychologists. But you see, I plan to go into general therapy upon completing my graduate studies and I need to–"

"No."

"Excuse me?" Her grip tightened on the notebooks, anguish reflecting in her once hopeful irises.

"I'm not interested, kid."

Oh, what a lie. Nothing existed on Earth that could've interested Dayton more in this moment than the red-headed girl, looking every bit like a prized forest nymph.

"And, not that it's any of your concern, but I have an ongoing research project that demands a lot of attention." He stared at her for one calculated second that seemed to span a minute. "Babysitting isn't part of my job description, Miss O'Callaghan."

Body rigid, she rose slowly from the chair, flaunting a supreme elegance unbefitting her young age. Kenna snatched the contract from his desk as she went, as if she couldn't get out of the office fast enough.

And yet, she surprised him by pausing in the doorframe. Her hair whipped around, a tumble of raging flames, as her head snapped in his direction.

"The dean will hear about this," she threatened before disappearing through the hall.

2

# PREDICAMENT

**Kenna**

enna occupied the decrepit rolling chair behind the check-out desk in Ponderosa's library. In her two years working there, she'd grown accustomed to the stubborn metal spring digging in her backside. She no longer winced as she sat in it day after day.

Not a soul lingered on any of the three floors. Had there been at least one person milling about, their footsteps against the wood would've echoed through the cavernous space like delayed musical notes.

The lack of visitors didn't bother Kenna. It left her time to study, though her gaze sometimes strayed from the textbook to admire the library's outdated beauty. The mahogany tables and their army of banker's lamps. The polished floors and tall windows. She delighted on each occasion the late afternoon light streamed in, illuminating dust motes with an impossible ethereality. She imagined a painter, eyes squinted, with a tiny tipped brush poised and dotting those little specks onto a canvas.

But the immense beauty of the space nor the comforting smell of the decaying books quelled her unease as she replayed the visit she had paid Dr. Merino.

She'd immediately recognized him from St. James, the owner of those black eyes that had penetrated her soul in one sweeping glance. She didn't dare bring up the fleeting connection during their hostile meeting.

Their interaction weighed heavily on her mind. How could things have gone so horribly wrong in the short amount of time she occupied his office? He hadn't given the offer a moment of consideration, as if he'd made his decision before she walked through the door. She swallowed hard to dispel the thought but the notion alone had her brain sizzling.

Dr. Merino's refusal was incomprehensible. It was outright rejection. Rejection without cause.

He had been in her company for no more than five minutes and in that span had found a reason to dismiss the idea of spending the next five months with her. The more she thought about it, the more enraged she became. Her fingers itched to tangle in her hair, pulling and pulling until her scalp popped and the uprooted strands lay at her feet.

Kenna did no such thing. Instead, she sat still, fuming in silence like a tea kettle on the cusp of squealing.

"Hello? I'd like to check these out," said a scrawny guy with a bowl cut. He aimed a spindly finger at a short stack of books and raised an eyebrow, insinuating it wasn't his first bid to get her attention.

"Sorry, I'm a little out of it today." She scanned the titles into the system and thrust them toward the puffy jacket-clad student with a tight smile that pained her cheeks. "They're due on the 20th."

Without a passing phrase, he swiped the books and went on his way. She didn't blame him. Students kept their visits strictly in and out save for the rare occasion some nested at the long tables and studied by the yellow light of the glass shaded lamps. The avoidance stemmed from an executive decision the university had made a decade earlier to remove all non-academic offerings from the shelves.

The guy with the bowl cut was her only checkout of the evening. A couple of girls came in to use the computers, but they had gone within ten minutes.

Six o'clock arrived, signaling her release. Slinging her maroon backpack onto her shoulder, she lifted the counter's partition. It was yet another out of style feature that added to the building's nostalgia, making it seem like she worked in a centuries-old research library. That wasn't entirely untrue; the place hadn't been renovated in God knows how long.

Her replacement, Ravi, arrived as Kenna was on her way out. They nodded in passing and she noticed a new patch of dark hair below his lip. She remembered kissing those lips with unimpeachable clarity, the silken feel of his face.

It was a drunken mistake at a bonfire party freshman year, two shy students free of their inhibitions for one night, crumpled cans at their feet and the acrid stench of smoke swirling around them. They'd applied to fill part-time shifts at the library, and Ravi had offered to retract his application because he didn't want to make things weird for Kenna. She'd always smiled a little brighter at him after that.

Her robin's egg Beaumont City was waiting where she'd left it, chained up to the otherwise abandoned bike rack. The juvenile mode of transportation landed her at the center of endless mockery to which she'd built a resistance. She was saving money and getting exercise while they emptied their pockets and polluted the environment.

With no car, distance was the primary factor in pursuing the mentorship with Dr. Merino. If she were to spend the semester at an office off campus, she'd have to bike at least 10 miles each way. An oppressive heat boiled within her despite the 37-degree weather. Kenna mounted her bike and pedaled along the concrete path, slicken from the midday rain. She channeled her frustration into the worn pedals, letting them carry her away from the university, away from the maddening predicament. Turning onto the main road, her agitation quieted. Her grip relaxed on the handlebars as calm wove through her like a sedative.

Her greatest resource had not been exhausted. Kenna had great faith that if she couldn't make Dr. Merino see reason, the dean would.

## Dayton

He killed the lights in his office, their glow fading with reluctance. The orange-tinted lampposts of the campus followed in their wake, providing sufficient illumination for Dayton to finish packing up. His gaze fixed on the narrow desk drawer as he slid on his sherpa-lined coat.

Even in its resting place, the piece of paper taunted him. The representation of delayed research. He was at a standstill with himself, his work, and their distasteful intersection.

Three semesters had passed since his tryst with Jasmine, though it seemed like a decade. Guilt had kept him away and he equated the resulting dormancy to priesthood.

Deprived of what he lusted after.

Though, he was far from saintly. A new subject had fallen into his lap and he refused to let the opportunity pass him by. The dueling hunger and shame within would soon be quieted by the acquisition of the O'Callaghan girl. Did her pale, slender body hold the cure he'd long searched for? Dayton scoffed and slung his briefcase strap onto his shoulder.

It was utter nonsense. He was incurable. A beast without the hope of the rose.

Staring ahead at the crisp white wall shadowed by orange light, he thought of the box resting below his bed at home, the progress and insights he'd collected over the years.

A fire roared to life in his mind. Its flames parted to frame a face whose features came into focus and resembled Kenna O'Callaghan. However unwittingly, she had entered his realm of chaos of her own accord. Etched herself into his thoughts and desires. A raw ache lavished his chest.

They were acquainted. That was all it took.

Dayton locked his office and pocketed the keys. His footsteps echoed in the darkened hallway, obscuring his mumbled, preemptive prayer. "Lord Jesus Christ, you are the Lamb of God ..."

## Kenna

The stench of charred sweet potatoes and broccoli overwhelmed Kenna as she entered her shared apartment. Kicking off her dampened, grass-covered boots, she waved a hand in front of her nose as if to ward off the pungent odor. She had taken to burning candles, but found that the scents competed rather than eliminating the detested one.

Alex, her roommate, pulled the tray of vegetables out of the oven. A monstrous pot of quinoa sat on the stove and an army of identical plastic bowls lined the counter.

Meal prep day. Alex was a graphic design major who ran a branding business on the side; so when she'd discovered the art of meal prepping, it changed her life. She preached about it like it was a religion. Never-ending diatribes about batch cooking aside, Kenna admired her hard-working spirit. Alex served as the big sister she'd never had. At home, Kenna had been the oldest, the role model by default, and she had fled.

Had the others followed her example?

"Hey, hey, Special K. How was your day?" Alex asked while scooping a spatula full of vegetables into each container.

Kenna refrained from rolling her eyes at the despised nickname and climbed onto one of the bar stools at the kitchen island that doubled as their dining table. She questioned whether she could verbalize just how wrong her day went. Dr. Merino had been more terrifying in his office than at Mass, with his scarred skin and cold denial and eyes so empty she wondered if he had ever known joy.

A sour taste spread in her mouth. "Disastrous."

"I know that look. Should I crack open the moscato?"

"No, it's okay. It's my internship. My plans are sort of off the rails."

Alex flipped over her caramel-highlighted mane and gathered it into a messy bun. Once the bun was in place she scraped the last of the quinoa out of the pot, weakly shrugging a shoulder. "It's the first day of term. How bad can it be?"

"I'll figure it out. You're right. It's not a big deal."

It was, but after her demoralizing day she didn't have the stamina to articulate the full scope of the dilemma to Alex.

She pointed to one of the portioned containers. "Buddha bowl?"

"Hard pass." Kenna wrinkled her nose. "Although, I've given more thought to the moscato."

3

# THE MEETING

**Dayton**

The dean's waiting area was empty, with the exception of the weathered secretary, Gloria, who he supplied with a curt nod. Dayton leaned against the wall beside a pair of club chairs meant for visitors. Mentally, he was bound and gagged and refused to confine himself any further so he stood. He zoned out on Gloria's fingers manufacturing laborious keystrokes at her desktop computer. The methodical clicking should've been calming but his forearms tensed beneath his sleeves as he drowned in the tide of his thoughts.

He felt like a criminal undergoing a trial, unsure if he would walk free with the O'Callaghan girl at his side or if he'd be denied light and contact.

The clunking of boots announced Kenna's presence before she swept through the doorway. She greeted Gloria and ignored him without effort, standing on the opposite end of the chairs. It was clear she had chosen the spot to have some distance between them and Dayton reveled in the choice.

With her along the same wall, she was easily observable in his peripheral. Dueling French plaits, not one strand out of place. Flared black jeans and a cream blouse. Full lips, taut.

In that limited view, in the sweeping, incomplete glances, she quickened his pulse.

Determination masked her exterior. She was a good little actress, he'd give her that, but he detected what lay beneath. A certain naivete he found irresistible. Even so, he was inclined to believe that her innocence was merely a facade and that brought him immeasurable delight.

Gloria's whole face broke into a tired smile as she gestured toward the shut door with a trembling hand. "Merino and O'Callaghan, Dean Raza will see you now."

He smoothed his graphite dress shirt while approaching the arched medieval looking door. Kenna followed at his heels like a lapdog and he rejoiced in her closeness, wholly consumed by the notes of her fragrance and melody of her movements.

Little had changed since Dayton's last visit. Outdated rugs fought for attention amid the dark hardwood floors. Drapes in the school's colors adorned each of the many windows in the bizarre hexagonal room. The same man seated behind his cluttered desk, five years past due for retirement.

Dean Raza was a thorn in his side.

The position at Ponderosa had almost slipped through his fingers because of the dean's hesitance toward his negligible criminal past. Perhaps it went beyond that small yet crucifying detail and he sensed that Dayton was hollow, and that it would be unwise to let a lost man treat his students. Unfortunately for Dean Raza, when he had to select a candidate for the job, there was no better choice than Dayton. It would've been ludicrous to sweep him under the rug with his background and credentials.

"Miss O'Callaghan, Dr. Merino, I invite you both to have a seat," Dean Raza said, gesturing to the mid-century armchairs stationed in front of his desk.

Dayton sunk into his chair. Kenna perched on the edge of hers, a caged bird ready to sing.

It was clear she'd never been in such a situation and he found her anxiety delightful. Her posture was poised, calm, yet she pulled at her wooden saint bracelet.

The front fringes of the dean's salt and pepper combover fell out of place as he glanced at the paper he held. "This memo reflects that you were the one who requested the appointment, Miss O'Callaghan. What is the nature of your predicament?"

Her mouth opened but her brain lagged behind and her spiel rolled off her tongue, sparing no room for breath. "I have to find placement with someone relating to my field of study for my undergraduate internship this semester. As a psychology student, I thought Dr. Merino would be a safe choice. I suppose I realize now why my classmates weren't racing me to get their contracts signed. He rejected my offer. Not only that, but without sound reason." Her chin dipped to her chest in tandem with the lowering of her voice. "Sir, I have unique transportational constraints which prohibit me from seeking out an off-campus alternative. I believe if anyone is given the slot in Dr. Merino's office, it should be myself since I was the first to proposition him."

She hadn't come for chitchat. She had come to secure her position in his office for the next five months.

Kenna was persuasive but he could've bested her on his worst of days. For the sake of his unruly lust, it was imperative that she won this particular argument.

"Is this true, doctor?"

"Yes," Dayton said.

Dean Raza's thick eyebrows scrunched together. "And tell me why you rejected the contract?"

"As I'm sure you can appreciate, my line of work can be sensitive. It doesn't seem ethical to let a student eavesdrop on the deeply private matters of her peers. I think it would be in everyone's best interest if Miss O'Callaghan proceeds with her mentorship search off campus. I'm sure, despite her protests, she can work out another mode of transportation."

He felt Kenna's eyes burning holes into his flesh and he relished in her choler. The ball had tumbled into his court, and he had no intention of relinquishing it.

## Kenna

Her nails bit into the armchair's soft, worn leather.

Kenna hardly knew the man seated beside her, yet he made her blood boil. She'd studied herself to the bone for three and a half years at Ponderosa. This degree program, her future career, meant everything to her.

She squeezed her Saint Rose bracelet and prayed the meeting would soon reach its end. Why, she wondered, would Dr. Merino turn away a passionate, capable student?

Her visage grew pale as droplets of cold sweat percolated at the nape of her neck.

"While I admire the consideration for your patients, Dr. Merino, if my memory serves me correctly, you've previously taken on mentees."

"One time, Hasan," Dr. Merino corrected.

The dean gave a tight, unamused smile. "Furthermore, isn't it only logical that under a mentorship Miss O'Callaghan would be expected to abide by the same regulations to which you're bound?"

"I can assure you, if I were to become her mentor I would absolutely enforce the same expectations upon her. But it seems Miss O'Callaghan is a bit of a tattletale, seeing as I'm sitting in your office. How can we be sure she won't breach the sanctity of psychotherapist-patient privilege?"

He asserted the claim as if she were a criminal and his gaze rested on her with finality, as if he'd gotten the last word, as if he'd won. His eyes were hollow. Bottomless black pits that refused to let in the slightest light. The emptiness in those eyes was depthless, incapable of reflecting anything but darkness.

Dr. Merino's penetrative stare had practically reached out and caressed her. Her skin crawled below her billowy blouse. She kept her gaze firmly on the dean and resolved to not let it stray to her left for the remainder of the meeting.

## Dayton

"That comparison is a bit of a stretch, even for you, Dr. Merino," the dean said.

Seconds of silence stretched on as he scribbled across a piece of paper. He flashed the form at Dayton and he accepted it without a trace of hesitation.

"I have it on good authority that you aren't terribly busy these days. I'd advise you to iron out your guidelines for the mentorship so the two of you can get started." Dean Raza jammed a finger into his desk. "Now, I'm warning you, if Miss O'Callaghan has to call for a second appointment it'll be much more than your pride on the line. Is that clear?"

"Crystal."

Dayton rose, straining to decipher fragments of hushed conversation on his way out. The dean adopted a more casual tone once he was alone with Kenna. Gloria offered a quiet goodbye but it was lost on him as he tuned into the dean.

*This isn't the first time I've had him in my office.'*

*'You'll straighten him out for me, won't you?'*

It didn't matter what Dean Raza made of his character. It was over. He held the formal decision in his hands.

Glancing at the paper, his bones turned hollow, buoyant. Everything had played out on par with his speculations. He knew the dean would never rule in his favor over a student, especially one with a 4.0. Handing her the mentorship was out of the question—no, that would've been much too easy. He knew that in denying Kenna's request, she would go straight to Dean Raza, bemoaning the injustice.

That was precisely what he'd wanted.

Dayton wanted her to fight for the position, fool her into thinking she had control of the situation, all the while unaware he had orchestrated the entire thing.

Kenna, that darling marionette, had signed herself over to him, surrendered her body, mind and soul for his taking.

## 4

# GUIDELINES

**Kenna**

*H*er boots scored her ascent to Dr. Merino's third-floor office as she climbed the stairs in Markham Hall. Other students and professors buzzed throughout the stairwell but she was only aware of her steady steps and shaking hand that yearned for the handrail.

Kenna's preparation for the day was overzealous. Ironed clothes. Gel weighing down her hair. Teeth brushed twice. She had done all she could to craft a confident image, praying that seeing the final product in the mirror would silence the voice in her head that insisted the mentorship was a mistake. His dark eyes and refusal were warnings she'd ignored but she had no choice.

She stood on the precipice of everything that she wanted but she had to ace her hours with the dark doctor if she expected to get anywhere. She'd been to Hell and back a few times before.

One more pass wouldn't hurt.

Kenna passed an adjunct on the third floor and the doughy

scent wafting from his crinkled white bag turned her stomach. She had skipped breakfast, far too nervous to conceive of eating.

Dim light shone overhead as she walked along the hallway of private offices. The distance between herself and the door with the frosted glass window shrank but she didn't give her pulse permission to accelerate. She controlled her breathing.

Even if she and Dr. Merino did not get along, she was sure she'd learn a lot from him. They'd have to make the daily mechanics work.

The door was ajar and she let herself inside, finding it empty. Kenna had arrived several minutes earlier than their agreed upon meeting time but doubted her new mentor would reprimand her for enthusiasm.

She took up post in the lone visitor's chair. Three of the walls were a crisp white, contrasting with the black accent wall behind Dr. Merino's desk. Four windows lined one of the white walls, flooding light into the small office.

The black wall showcased his licenses, certifications, and degrees. Framed, pristine. She zeroed in on the one that read, 'State of Oregon Medical Board,' with its bronze seal. It bore his full name and credentials: Dayton Edward Merino, Doctor of Medicine. An oil diffuser crowned a short pile of tattered reference books. Smoke escaped, dancing against the dark wall as it drifted toward evaporation. The fumes smelled of peppermint, but Kenna was certain she detected a vaguely familiar, competing scent.

There were no decorations or plants or any real trace of evidence that the space belonged to anyone besides the briefcase and framed papers. It was clean, sterile, calming; a room which fit its intent.

"Just make yourself at home."

She jumped at the sound of his voice and shame soon overtook her. Blood rushed to her cheeks, warming the skin.

Dr. Merino spared her a fractional glance on the way to his

desk and she caught a glimpse of his austere face and the over-grown, wavy hair framing it like a dark halo. His hand curled around a mug which he retired to an electric coaster. Kenna hoped some of his sternness would dissipate once he'd had his coffee.

"You scared me."

"You are in my office, you realize?" He licked his thumb and sifted through a pile of papers. "The next time you arrive and find this room empty, wait in the hall. My line of work has given me startling accuracy with first impressions and with you, Miss O'Callaghan, I get the impression that you're a nosy young lady."

She offered a small smile. "Accurate, indeed."

"Let's review our rules, for the sake of formality, since the dean made it clear he'll have my head if I mishandle this. I've read the contract your professor put together and I'm sure you're well aware of everything there so I won't waste my breath going over it." With a crook of his finger, Dr. Merino beckoned her to the front of his desk. He pointed to a blank line at the bottom of the page. "Sign there."

Kenna picked up the pen but faltered as it hovered over the paper. "Shouldn't we go over the rules before I sign? What if I find something objectionable?"

"You made it quite clear you have no other choice."

He indulged in a sip of his coffee while she signed the contract and she noticed it wasn't coffee at all. A cotton string hung over the side, a red rose printed on its tag.

"I retrieved a copy of your schedule from the registrar, and filled out a semester-long calendar with dates and times I've reserved for your mentorship hours. They are not flexible. If I instruct you to arrive at 7 a.m., 1 p.m., whatever the case may be, I expect to see you in my office on the dot. Tardiness will factor into my final calculation of your performance. Are there any other obligations of yours, outside of your course schedule, that I should be aware of?"

His expectant gaze locked on hers. Her eyes followed the scar cutting along his cheek. The first two buttons of his dress shirt were undone, providing an incomplete glimpse of a thicker scar that swooped across his collarbone. Pink outlined its rippled white center. It required enormous strength to redirect her attention to his face and respond.

"I work part-time at Nicholson."

"You'll need to speak with the librarian or whoever's in charge over there and get them to rearrange your shifts to suit our schedule." The critical note in his voice shot down Kenna's instinct to argue. "I do ask that you refrain from listening to music, podcasts, and the like. Headphones are not a loophole to this rule. Refrain from using your cell phone. Pretty self-explanatory. Most of this is common sense, which I pray you have at your age."

She'd expected Dr. Merino to have harsher, borderline ridiculous rules. Though, she had a feeling he wasn't finished.

"I don't think we'll encounter any problems."

An unsettling intensity ruled his stare. "I would hope not."

Something brightened in his eyes. A slathering of honey glistened against their foreboding umber. There it was, the elusive light she had thought him incapable of producing.

**Dayton**

Her nose twitched like a rabbit's.

If she were that small and helpless, adding her to his backlog of subjects would've been an easier feat.

Dayton knew he stared longer than was permissible but found it hard to look away. Her face, its delicacy, was enough to inspire insanity. The fine tip of her nose, the permanent pout of her bottom lip and seductive set of her cheeks.

Kenna O'Callaghan was ordinary, plain by all accounts, but within her there lived an otherness that clawed to the surface and bathed her features in irrefutable beauty.

Finally, he averted his gaze.

"If I assign you an errand, I expect you to do it without question. Should I ever be out, we will devise a time for you to recover the missed hours. In the event of your absence, you're SOL, I'm afraid. I also expect your presence at any related events off-campus upon my request. There's a run for self-harm awareness in March, so we'll be participating together. I'd like us to exchange numbers should we need to send communications relating to the event or my unexpected absence."

He pulled out his phone and copied her number into the contacts as she recited it. Dayton liked the way it looked on the screen, the way it sounded spoken aloud.

Pretty and to the point.

"I sent you a message. Check it later and save the number."

"Is that all?" Kenna asked.

"That's it."

She returned to her seat, swinging one leg over the other. He envied the denim that clung to her porcelain skin. Skin that was so close but just out of reach, not yet his to touch, and he found their entire partnership cruel, that he should be kept from what he desired by layers of fabric and rules and the flimsy trappings of sexual politics.

She wore the same wooden saint bracelet from their meeting with the dean. Dayton had gotten a closer look at it when she signed their mentorship contract.

"Family trouble?" he dared.

"Pardon me?"

"Your bracelet. Saint Rose."

Lips parting, Kenna looked at him as though disoriented. "You've just finished laying out firm guidelines for me and now you're asking me about my personal life?"

Cautious. Already worried about jeopardizing her academic future on day one. She'd be tough to crack.

"You're right. It's none of my business, so let's stick to what could be construed as my business. May I ask why you're so intent on going into therapy?"

"I want to help people."

She gave a slight shrug as if it were the most obvious thing in the world and he was filled with grim amusement.

Dayton crossed his arms atop the desk, his smile one of condescension. "You think you can save people? I'll tell you what it's like on the other side. You will expend all of your energy trying to help someone, and they'll still put a bullet in their head. Refuse to eat until some judge has to order the insertion of a feeding tube. Whatever the case may be. And you'll feel like you've failed. You failed yourself. You failed them. Their family. This is a dark business, Miss O'Callaghan, and during these five months I'd like you to consider whether this is where you should be. Where you're heading, therapy? You get the privilege of hiding behind the curtain. I'm responsible for what they do on the stage, and that's precisely what you'll see during our time together."

"I assure you I can handle whatever goes on in this office day to day." Her pale pink mouth pursed in defiance as she tucked a thick section of hair behind her ear. "How do we begin?"

He found himself staring at her lips again, those lush fixtures. One kiss and he'd sink into that soft skin. Disappear.

"Observation."

## Kenna

Dr. Merino expected her observation phase to last an entire month but she gathered throughout the day that, as the dean had said, he wasn't terribly busy.

She had to stop herself on several occasions from asking what exactly she was supposed to observe if there was no one around.

Two students visited during the five hours Kenna spent in his office. While she wasn't anticipating a slammed morning of appointments, she was shocked at the pitiful sampling of patients.

Both walk-ins opted out of having her in the room while they spoke to Dr. Merino. Each time he kicked her into the hall, he issued her a dismissive nod and closed the gates to an interaction she would've died to be a part of.

Though the sound filtering through the door was muffled, she thought she overheard the distinct, deep roll of Spanish passing between him and a patient.

Conditions were no better within the office than in the hallway. The room was cold and cramped, and the company was dreadful. Dr. Merino didn't utter a syllable to her unless he responded to an occasional question, but even in those instances she gleaned he was in no mood for conversation.

Kenna resorted to reading her social psychology textbook but once the diffuser cut off, eliminating the precious white noise, her concentration waned. She felt his eyes on her as she read, lingering longer than was appropriate.

It was this way they worked in a somewhat comfortable silence; as comfortable as two semi-strangers could've been in close proximity.

She watched as he drained the tea over the course of their session, consuming it slowly as if it were an elixir.

"Are you sick?"

His black eyebrows shot up but his expression neutralized as she pointed to the mug.

"Plenty of men who aren't on their deathbed drink tea. It seems I overlooked sexism in my first impression of you." The severity of his features betrayed the warmth radiated by his beige skin. He glanced at the clock stationed above the door. "We have 56 minutes to go, kid. Can we forego the interruptions? And here." He tossed her a canister of raw almonds. "Eat something or go sit in the hall for the rest of the hour. Your stomach is rearing to give me a migraine."

She ate the almonds in resigned silence and they ignored each other for the rest of the hour.

At noon she was, mercifully, free to go.

Once she was out of Markham and crossing campus, she checked her phone. The only notification was the text from Dr. Merino. No 'hello' or self-identification.

It read simply, 'test.' Kenna wondered if that was the reason behind his rules. He was testing her, seeing if she would buckle into submission.

Molars sinking into her tongue, she shook her head and put her phone away. His first impression of her had been accurate but not thorough.

She was unbreakable.

5

# PENROSE

**Dayton**

Flaxen streaks of light hit the juniper walls of Dayton's bedroom. The sun clocking out for the day.

He was slumped on the floor, back to the dresser, eyeing the shoebox beneath his bed, that graveyard of sin. Sins in the name of progress. Understanding.

Months had passed since he'd peered inside. The mess with Jasmine almost prompted him to give up his disciplined lifestyle. He feared he had hit a point where the risk far outweighed the reward and that fear kept him quiet for a while. Until Kenna waltzed into his office. She opened her pretty little mouth and he felt the pressure, a belt tying off his arm. She was a necessary tool in acquiring his high. It had been too long since Dayton last felt the rush, the frenzied excitement of an addict as they held a lighter to a spoon and watched with delight as their euphoria bubbled.

For him, it was the promise of a warm body.

Adrenaline enveloped him like an embrace. He slid the box

34

across the floorboard with care and placed it in his lap. Hands trembling, he lifted the lid and set it aside.

A cacophony of steady ringing filled his ears as he took in what was on full display.

Trophies of his research.

He never kept shoes, underwear. A lady might go looking for her wares but never a picture she didn't know existed.

Plucking one of the Polaroids, he admired his photography skills against the moonlit backdrop. His chest hollowed out at the sight before him. A young woman in her underwear, body half-covered by Dayton's black bedsheets, bronze flesh glowing brighter than the dim light.

*Jasmine. May 23 '18.*

His last victory. The sight of her face tore at his insides and conjured flashes of memories he'd fought to bury. The scars had faded but they would never heal. Lifelong reminders of his lustful gluttony.

He moved on. *Ivy. Dec. 1 '17.* She lay on her back. Deep brown blunt bangs and flowing straight hair framed the soft features of her slumbering face. A delicate death's head hawkmoth tattoo rested below the right side of her collarbone. Their mutual interest in Thomas Harris had been an early bonding point. She had openly confessed her love near the end of their affair. Love, that silent weapon most of them possessed but dared not brandish.

"Enough." Dayton discarded the Polaroid amid the rest and returned the box to its home, pushing himself off the floor.

He tugged at his hair while pacing the room. Disgust crawled over his skin and frustration closed off his throat. One ugly emotion scaffolding off the next. Regret was absent from the swarm.

Being in the space where he'd slept with all of the women hidden away in the box did nothing to quell his unrest. He needed to immerse himself in the natural beauty that lay beyond his four walls. Fresh air. Pines. The biting chill of the constant January rain.

Dayton traded his office clothes for a pair of athletic pants and a faded David Geffen School of Medicine sweatshirt, somehow still intact from his days at UCLA. He slipped into his sneakers and grabbed his reflective belt on the way out.

A slither of sunlight persisted among the clouds as he sprinted off through the freezing winter mist, building speed with each footfall.

He had not always been a runner; he picked it up midway through college when he'd finished grieving a high school lacrosse career cut short. It was freeing, an escape from the pressures of performing well in medical school. But he was older, jaded, and his mind had become a prison, the confines of which had steadily extended to every corner of his life.

It required every ounce of restraint to successfully lead his new research-oriented life. Running was a temporary haven from an existence dominated by self-control and calculation.

Coming upon the intersection of a major road, he bent and caught his breath, waiting for traffic to disperse. Once it was clear of headlights, Dayton crossed to the other side, continuing his path through the sleepy streets of Branch Spring. He breezed past the brick storefronts, blurring the lights and neon signs in their windows. The city center was hip yet historic. Century-old buildings that had been preserved but renovated. A small group of students made fun of his reflective belt as they all waited for the pedestrian crossing to flash white.

Assholes.

An amplified guitar poured out into the street and threatened to deafen any passersby. Couples and groups of friends emerged from bars and restaurants, laughing, cursing. Some jaywalked to feed their parking meter. It didn't matter that it was the middle of the week; people were out in full force. The party never stopped in a university town.

Bursts of icy wind chipped at his face and burned his cheeks. Just past the historic district, he slowed to a leisurely jog as he reached Pacific Heights, an apartment complex with mostly college residents. One such resident?

Kenna O'Callaghan. 2102 Apt. E.

Maybe he'd lifted more than her schedule from the registrar, but where lay the danger in that? He wasn't prowling Penrose Lane to pay her a visit. Not directly.

Sticking to the edge of the parking lot, close to the trees, he searched for building F. She was on the second floor but Dayton wasn't sure of the exact unit. Fleetingly, he considered scaling the stairs and lingering on the landing long enough to find a door marked 'E.'

It was too risky. Senseless.

He tucked himself amid the trees and split his attention between the windows of the second floor's front-facing units.

The sun had faded, giving way to the deep blue twilight. Night would be settled above the trees long before he returned home.

6

# HIGH-STRUNG

**Kenna**

*B*aby snow flurries descended upon Ponderosa's campus, livening its seasonally decimated scenery. Flakes landed on Kenna and dissolved as she crossed the lawn toward Duniway Hall. Her biological psychology class started a few minutes earlier. She channeled all of her energy into her legs and willed them to move faster but she found herself traveling at the same pace. Her feet smacked against the pavement and that force shot into her calves. Biking between buildings would've been a better solution.

Alas, her bike was chained up by Markham Hall, where she had spent an excruciating morning with Dr. Merino.

Observing his daily routine sans the exposure to patients had grown stale. Kenna had shot her mouth off and demanded something to do and he'd tasked her with cleaning his office, top to bottom.

He was the reason she was running late.

"Kenna," someone called.

Audible footsteps quickened as the caller jogged to close the distance between them. She kept her movement brisk but the chaser materialized beside her, falling in step.

He was easily identifiable out of the corner of her eye by the signature short thatch of curls that he combed upward and hair sprayed until it was stiff and he'd inhaled enough xylene to knock him unconscious. Will Morris, fellow psych major and annoying leech.

"You ignoring me, Red?"

She despised nicknames in reference to her heritage, and 'Red' was the worst of all.

It was almost enough to make her halt dead in her tracks and unleash years of pent-up torture caused by the many jokes she'd been the butt of growing up. She was American, a third-generation immigrant, but no one cared about the details of her lineage. They saw her hair and transparent skin and made their own assumptions.

She didn't have the luxury of stopping to berate Will, even though she would have loved nothing more.

"You're giving me the cold shoulder, is that it? C'mon, lighten up. It's cold enough out here."

Much to Kenna's dismay, they were heading for the same place. She would have to suffer through the conversation until they reached their class. Redistributing the weight of her bag, she pressed forward, determined not to speak to him.

"It's because I called you 'Red,' isn't it? I didn't mean to offend you. It honestly just slipped out," Will pseudo-apologized. He threw up his hands as they went. "You don't have to talk to me, I get it, that was pretty rude, but at the very least hear me out."

Kenna was confident he didn't have anything of interest to discuss, but listening wasn't a choice.

"Me and some other seniors—Brandi, Liam and Rebecca—all get together for trivia on Thursdays at The Rusted Monkey. 8 o'clock. You know the place?"

He casually omitted the last names as if there weren't 1,400 students at their university.

"Brandi Wright?" she asked.

"That's the one."

Brandi had been part of her study group for elementary statistics during sophomore year. She had brought some much-needed cheer to the abysmal cloud that hung over them as they toiled over regression analysis, possessing a smile that lit up whatever room she entered. Kenna could hardly fathom how someone like Brandi could stand to be in the company of Will, let alone voluntarily hang out with him on a weekly basis.

"You realize *today* is Thursday? If that was an invitation then sure, I'll go. I've had a few classes with Brandi. It'd be nice to catch up."

"Awesome. We need all the help we can get beating Rorschach's Sheets." He exhaled in a whistle while consulting his smartwatch. "Coleman is going to give it to us for being late. I had to drive over from my mentor's office downtown. You took the only spot on-campus, didn't you? With Dr. Asshole? What's that like?"

Will held the door open for her when they reached Duniway Hall. Had they not been in danger of missing their class, she would've rejected the kind gesture.

"He's," she struggled to find the right word, "unconventional."

"Right, well, I don't envy you."

## Dayton

With the exception of the two men, Markham's faculty lounge was empty. A faint note of cigarette smoke, that banned indulgence, hung in the air, mixing with the hodgepodge of uneaten leftovers lurking in the garbage. Dayton had considered, on more than one occasion, donating his diffuser to the lounge so that he and his colleagues wouldn't be subjected to the stench of smoke and rancidity. He sat at a round table, rolling a clementine beneath his palm.

Professor Nathan Scott, his colleague turned friend, idled by the communal microwave. He was the natural accompaniment to Dayton's tall and broad. Shorter, rounder.

It was in the same lounge they had met six years prior. Nathan had approached and asked if he was the new psychiatrist but Dayton had been so distracted by the electric green glasses washing out his deep copper complexion that he'd had to ask him to repeat himself.

He was much the same though he'd traded the tacky eyewear for a pair of black, square frames.

"This batch of 1101 students are giving me hell and we're only two weeks in. Right hand to God, I've never met a group of kids this thick-headed." Nathan let loose his weird, stilted laughter. "You should come and check it out if you have some downtime. It's one of those things you have to see to believe."

Kenna had given him hell, too. She tested his restraint every day but when she'd parted her sweet lips and demanded that he give her something to do he had lost himself in the possibility of the request before his sanity resurfaced. No doubt they had different tasks in mind.

The microwave's shrill dinging disrupted the memory. Steaming tupperware in tow, Nathan joined him at the table. Dayton lacked an appetite but he peeled the flesh of the clementine anyway. He always felt off when he smoked his afternoon blunt on an empty stomach.

"Why do you get all of the entertainment? Here I am, living out one of the most anti-climactic careers in psychiatric history. Maybe I can stop by one day. My schedule is a little out of whack since Raza dumped that high-strung senior on me."

"Oh yeah, how is that going?"

"It's an experience, alright. I don't want to talk about it now. I was with the bloodsucker all morning."

"Charlaine's been driving me nuts about the wedding cake." Nathan spoke between bites of his alfredo. Flecks of sauce dotted his chin. "She thinks the world is going to spontaneously combust if we don't pick the right flavor. What the hell does that even mean, the *right* flavor?"

"Just nod and go along with whatever she says."

Superficiality ruled their bubble of male bonding. They didn't know anything deeply personal about one another and stuck to core topics. Women. College football. Academia.

Nathan did most of the talking, but Dayton didn't mind. They'd settled into their friendship like one of those rare marriages that lasts an eternity, carrying with it an aura of mystique. It just worked.

"By the way, I got the invite in the mail. Why'd you waste a stamp when you could've hand-delivered it?"

"I wanted to bring it to you, but Charlaine insisted that we send all of our invitations by mail. She did the same for her co-workers. Waste of time and postage, if you ask me—of course, she didn't."

"I'd have to agree with you but, hey, what do we know about weddings?"

Dayton often felt like an impostor during these interactions. In the beginning, he thought it might have been too complicated to pursue their friendship. He had much to hide. Protect. Moreover, socialization didn't exactly align with his regimented way of life. But Nathan had weaseled in through the cracks and he'd grown too fond of him to kick him to the curb.

They rose from the table and headed for the door, lingering in the hallway outside of the lounge. That final, cordial hesitance before parting ways.

"Pick you up at 7:30?" Dayton asked.

"I'm glad it's your turn to drive. I could stand to knock back a few after the week I've had, you know what I mean?"

"Trust me, I know the feeling."

## Kenna

Kenna stared at her open closet for what felt like an entire day as the distorted sound of Led Zeppelin filled her bedroom. It was a casual trivia outing with classmates. She knew she was over-thinking it but she couldn't help herself. A hidden, foolish part of her brain was hung up over the possibility of meeting a guy at the bar. Things had been stagnant in the romance department since she'd been a student at Ponderosa.

She didn't necessarily mind the absence.

Without a romantic attachment, she was free to study herself into the ground, to play guitar until the early hours of the morning. But sometimes she ached for another's touch.

A familiar tension spread in Kenna's chest as her fingers absentmindedly swiped across the rack of fabric. Reid Emerson. His name flowed through her mind like poison.

He'd torn everything within her asunder and she remained convinced that, even after all this time, she hadn't fully stitched herself back together.

Alex abstained from dating and the longer Kenna was exposed to the preachy philosophy, the more she adopted it as her own. Alex was right. College was a place where one should get to know and learn how to take care of oneself.

"If you aren't a complete person, you can't handle being in a relationship." The clothes in the closet were her only audience as she stated the mantra.

Robert Plant's suggestive vocals competed with her mantra and insisted that he still loved her so, couldn't let her go. It was a voice that encouraged sin. She refused to be seduced by his innuendo or anything else.

Besides, she didn't have time to pursue a dating life now that she'd chained herself to Dr. Merino.

Combing through the scarce selection of clothes a final time, she yanked a chunky-knit olive sweater from its hanger and grabbed a pair of black leggings from the shelf above. Sitting on the edge of the bed, she wiggled her feet into a pair of brown ankle boots. She flipped her head over and shook her hair out of the bun it had been prisoner to all afternoon. Kenna had manufactured it in haste that morning when Dr. Merino, dissatisfied with her janitorial performance, had asked her to scrub his baseboards. She brought her nails to her nose and recoiled. They reeked of cleaning supplies, a sharp malodor that persisted despite countless rounds of hand washing.

She observed her reflection in the not quite full-length mirror that hung against the closet door.

The leggings were a Christmas gift from Alex, tags still attached. She felt naked in the form-fitting cotton and spandex. Her usual flared jeans maintained some degree of modesty. Kenna reached for a pair on the shelf but stopped. She studied herself in the mirror, without scrutinizing the strange pants, and was in awe over the woman she saw.

Loose waves had transformed her straight hair, courtesy of the bun. The oversized sweater draped appealingly. Though she had skipped cosmetics while getting ready for class, her skin flushed with a rosy glow. Kenna saw someone who was beautiful, young, and capable.

Someone who didn't need anyone else.

7

# RORSCHACH'S SHEETS

**Kenna**

*A* row of oversized wooden booths occupied the left wall of The Rusted Monkey and an event space occupied the right. It was a galley-style bar. Narrow but not small.

Fairy lights weaved through the network of exposed pipes gracing the ceiling, casting a minimal yellow glow on the bar's interior. Kenna had passed the storefront hundreds of times, but had never set foot in the establishment. Music blared through the speakers and a dull headache graced her skull as she brushed shoulders with patrons.

The sounds, the people, the lights. It was overwhelming. Unfamiliar.

She rarely found herself downtown after dark. Her visits downtown were limited to cramming in extra study time at Bigleaf Coffee Company, but her avoidance of social situations was unrelated to her 4.0. Reid had left her with more than a broken heart. Fear. Mistrust. Though her heart had healed, his other parting gifts remained. She was done with that flickering apprehension.

Tonight, she played by a new set of rules.

Will's stiff hair peeked over a chestnut booth and gave away the team's location. She shook off her nerves and fashioned a faint wave as she closed in on them.

Brandi sprang to her feet, drawing her in for a hug. Her mass of tight onyx curls tickled Kenna's cheek and her raspy voice squealed, "I'm so glad you came. It's been forever."

Part of her wondered if Brandi was genuinely excited to see her, or if she was thankful to have one extra person around to detract from the horror that was Will Morris.

"How's photography going?"

She cupped her ear. "What?"

The music had grown so loud, the bass vibrated through her chest.

"Photography."

"Ah, I switched majors." One gold-shadowed lid shut and she scrunched up her face before a thousand-watt smile broke out. "Poli-Sci. I kept photography as my minor, though. I figure if nothing else pans out, I could shoot someone's campaign. You're still in psych, right?"

"Yeah, I—"

"We're here, too." Will gestured with his beer bottle.

Brandi and Kenna exchanged knowing looks but uttered no complaint as they joined Rebecca on the ladies' side of the booth.

The guy seated next to Will extended his hand over the table toward Kenna and they shook. "Liam."

He seemed more tolerable than Will. At the very least, he was polite, which was a huge step up.

"You know what, I think we've met."

She studied his face, waiting for any shred of recognition. "Freshman lit, right?" But I thought your name was—"

"Sung-min? Yeah. Liam's my middle name. I've gone by it since high school and it sort of stuck."

As a psychology major, Kenna often caught herself analyzing people's speech and behavior. She couldn't help but feel stifling his identity was an effort to fit in.

"I like Sung-min, but Liam's fine, too." She smiled.

Liam returned the smile without looking at her.

The girl she presumed to be Rebecca gave a half-wave fitting of a debutante. Kenna leaned across Brandi to greet her. She sported a messy fishtail braid and her timid grin revealed a mouthful of braces. "I'm Rebecca, Brandi's roommate."

Will held up a hand to silence them.

Something grim came over his boyish face. "Rorschach's Sheets are in the building."

The students adopted their sharpest glares, aiming the theatrical hostility in the direction of their rivals. Kenna's gaze gravitated to the walkway. The place teemed with patrons but it was easy to identify the two men in question among the predominantly younger crowd. Her headache magnified as Dr. Merino and Professor Scott sauntered toward her group, an audacious edge in their step.

### Dayton

"I'm surprised they let you sit in here among humanity. If I was the owner, I'd make you guys play by the dumpsters out back," Nathan said.

The remark echoed faintly through Dayton's ears as he registered Kenna seated amid the Barenaked Philosophers and he was too overwhelmed to supply a slight of his own. He was suspended in a haze of infatuation. They were no longer in the bar but lost in the Ponderosa pines. He and his forest queen. Her sweater hung freely, swallowing her lithe form. Her modesty made his heart twitch. Dayton yearned to demolish the purity that diffused from her body with the strength of an expensive perfume.

Their eyes met for a brief moment, her blazing jade burning into his lifeless black, until Kenna tore hers away.

"Nice one, Prof, but we'll be wiping the floor with you guys tonight." Liam's tongue flicked against his silver lip ring before his mouth contorted in a smirk. "Again."

"Let's not get ahead of ourselves," Dayton said.

He dared one last look at Kenna and caught her peeking at him through her lashes.

Satisfaction lightened his chest. As the emptiness faded, it grew heavier and heavier, and the chatter coming from the Barenaked Philosophers' table was lost to the pounding music as he and Nathan padded off to the end of the bar. The bartender, Sasha, slid their drinks toward them and some spilled over the rim of the tumbler, pooling on the counter. A pale lager and a vodka lime. Their order never changed. They nodded at her as a silent show of thanks.

Nathan drained half of his bottle in one pull.

"Those kids are always on their A-game. We have 22 years of college between us, and they still keep us on our toes."

"They're not kids," Dayton corrected.

He savored the inaugural sip of vodka, shutting his eyes as it singed his throat. Alcohol was a coveted indulgence, forbidden by his cardiologist and reserved for trivia outings.

"To me, they are." His nose wrinkled in displeasure. "They really will be sweeping the floor with us tonight and every Thursday after this if O'Callaghan is a permanent addition to their team."

Dayton's ears perked up beneath his thicket of hair like a curious canine. O'Callaghan. The name rolled from his friend's tongue with utter casualness.

He set aside the drink and ran a thumb along his soft jawline. "You know her?"

"She was in my cognitive class last semester. Why?" Nathan arched a brow but he soon connected the dots. "That's who you're mentoring?"

"Yep. Anything I should be wary of?"

"She didn't give me any problems. But you seem to have trouble with everybody so I can't wait to see how this unravels." Nathan slapped Dayton on the back.

Feedback screeched through the sound system, replaced by the trivia host's voice. "Alright folks. It's that time of the night. Send one person from your team to the back to get signed up and we'll kick things off shortly."

"I'll sign us up. I have to piss, anyway," Dayton offered.

Michael's collapsible table was in the back corner, sandwiched between the end of the bar and the restrooms and conveniently located behind their seats.

He resented that Michael made them sign in every week, even though their team name had stuck for the last five years. He'd scribbled the name on the list and was about to dismiss the pen when Kenna appeared in his peripheral.

The out-of-focus glimpse of her green sweater and red hair set his body ablaze. He held his breath so as not to inhale her sinful redolence. Surrendering the pen to her required the utmost concentration. The meaningless action was a test without a curve and he had nearly failed.

Dayton thought she'd say something. A 'thank you' would have sufficed. Instead, she searched his eyes. He didn't know what she was looking for but he knew she wouldn't find it. They held opposite ends of the pen through their silent shakedown and the rest of the bar was oblivious to her turmoil and his intent, this quiet war that had all but begun.

The music flooded his eardrums as if it'd been on mute. He was still gripping the pen.

"Good luck," he ground out, yanking his hand away and brushing past Kenna toward the men's room.

## Kenna

"What were UFOs called during World War II? Again, the answer was foo fighters."

Collective groans sounded throughout the bar.

"I guess flying saucers didn't cut it," Rebecca joked.

"Well, guess what, Becca? They don't give points for wrong answers." Will had drunk one too many but he showed no sign of slowing down.

Half-eaten plates of nachos, grease-coated fry baskets, empty glass bottles, and aluminum cans littered the table. It would have been a miracle if they escaped the bar with a trip to the gastroenterologist instead of the morgue.

Kenna had polished off one wildflower honey cider and was nursing a second. On several occasions, she'd caught Dr. Merino staring at her, expression unreadable.

Their silent exchange during trivia sign-up had rattled her. She had looked into his eyes and in a matter of seconds they claimed her. She thrashed in those black pools, kicking and fighting to remain at their surface where her lungs burned but she was fortunate enough to breathe.

And then he'd yanked his hand away and it was over. She was dry, no longer drowning.

Just a girl standing alone in a crowded bar.

The alcohol, the interaction, and his unapologetic stares came together to form a dangerous trinity that goaded Kenna into sharing. "Dr. Merino's actually my mentor for the semester. Imagine my surprise when I found out he's half of your rival team."

Will's face tightened, features puckering as if a sour taste lingered in his mouth. Brandi's eyes widened to such an extent that they eclipsed her iridescent shadow.

"Oh, God. Why?" she shrieked.

Almost simultaneously, Rebecca asked, "By choice?"

Kenna yielded to a lengthy swig of the cider before aiming the bottleneck at them. "Spill."

"He has an attitude, that's for sure," Will muttered.

"Halftime bonus. I'm going to ask a question and you can put up to 10 answers. Your team will be awarded two points for each correct response. The question is as follows: name 10 films written by John Hughes."

Liam, a film major, snatched the paper from the center of the table and listed the movies like it was a no-brainer.

"Listen, I had an appointment with Merino when my parents were getting divorced, and he basically told me there was no reason to be upset about it because—and I quote—'divorce has become a part of our culture.' How's that for insensitive?" Will slammed back the last of his chocolate stout like a vindicated schoolboy.

Her first instinct was to shrug at his comment but levelheadedness won out and she refrained. While the response wasn't the most apropos way of dealing with a patient, she held steadfast to the idea that all clinicians operated differently. Whatever works. If Dr. Merino took a harsh, grounded in reality approach, so be it. The office was his jurisdiction.

Nothing out of the ordinary here.

"Someone told me they overheard him call Professor Addington a dusty old cunt, but that's just a rumor." Red splotches covered Rebecca's cheeks, skin resembling the sangria shade of her velvet dress. "Who knows if he actually said it."

"Professor Addington *is* a dusty old cunt," Liam said.

Will pinched the bridge of his nose. "Can everyone please stop saying cunt?"

"Why'd you want to study under that guy anyway? He must be a pretty shitty shrink since that girl killed herself. Jumped off the roof of her dorm complex." Liam smacked a hand on the tabletop. "Splat. What a fucking waste, huh?"

Though Kenna was disoriented, she managed to muster a defense for the man she barely knew.

"Not all mental illnesses are curable. When a patient chooses to end their own life, the provider really has no control over—"

"Died by suicide, Liam, would it kill *you* to be politically correct, for once?" Rebecca narrowed her eyes but they neutralized as they fell upon Kenna. "It's true. They still hold a vigil every fall on the anniversary of her death. I can't think of her name. Bella, something."

"Swan?"

"Liam Park, I swear to God."

Grabbing an armful of empty beer bottles, Will said, "The direction this conversation's heading, I'm gonna need another one. Anyone else?"

The girls shook their heads and Liam followed Will to the bar, muttering not so quietly that he'd need another, too, if he had to put up with Rebecca for another second. Kenna didn't know if she had overheard the comment but she excused herself to the restroom. As soon as everyone else had gone, Brandi turned toward Kenna with a conspiratorial smile.

"Hey, I wasn't up for sharing in front of everyone else, but I have something juicy on your doctor."

The seconds-long pause was tortuous. She was in the electric chair and Brandi was a sadistic executioner, finding pleasure in delaying her death.

"He slept with my sister."

"Were they dating?"

"From what she gathered, he doesn't date. He just has 'encounters.'" Brandi signed air quotes.

Encounters? Dr. Merino was shaping up to be a first-rate asshole. Saliva pooled in her mouth like a stoppered sink. Her knees pressed together, a subconscious guarding of her femininity. As Kenna tried and failed to shake off the disgust, a sickening realization donned in the face of Brandi's statement.

"If your sister was his patient, or even his former patient, he should've been fired, bare minimum. We met with Dean Raza last week and I got the feeling he'd do anything to send Dr. Merino packing."

"I guess she didn't view it as being taken advantage of. She liked him. Hell, I think she loved him. I mean, she didn't talk about him much, but when she did?" A dreamy gleam sparkled in Brandi's deep amber irises. "Erin told me he had this way of making her feel otherworldly, like they were the only two people who existed."

She could have gone without hearing about Dr. Merino's exceptional talents in the bedroom but the fact that he'd slept with a patient had her rapt. The night at St. James, Kenna had recognized the darkness in his eyes and now she had proof that his malevolence was real rather than imagined. She signed the cross and mumbled a prayer of thanks and when she opened her eyes, Brandi stared at her as if she were possessed.

"You okay?"

Kenna's lips parted to pose another question but she was dissuaded from speaking as the guys returned to the table, heady foam spilling over the rims of their drafts. Will praised Liam for his performance on the halftime bonus.

"I can't believe you got all 10."

"It wasn't hard. It's not like John Hughes is an obscure director. Everyone knows him."

Rebecca came back from the bathroom and the conversation around Kenna became background noise. Her tipsy gaze hovered to Dr. Merino, sizing up his features through her lens of inebriety. His lustrous, tousled waves were just shy of sweeping his khaki sweater. His social posture was a curiosity in itself: head angled back to accentuate his Adam's apple, broad shoulders sagging. She loathed the way her throat grew thick as she stole glances at his occasional toothy grins.

Was he always this attractive or was the seductive incandescence of the fairy lights aiding his cause?

That'd be the alcohol talking, she thought.

He caught her looking. Kenna froze, muscles stiff like a vulnerable deer in a clearing faced with the threat of a hunter. Dr. Merino surveyed his surroundings, as if to confirm that he was the object of her blatant staring, and his eyes landed on her once again. Jabbing a finger into his chest, he mouthed 'me?' The finger transitioned to his entire hand, at which point he raised his glass and she did the same.

She didn't fully know what to expect from her semester with Dr. Merino but in that shared, drunken moment she knew one thing. Their time together would not be free of complications.

## Dayton

"This doesn't happen often, folks, but we have a tie for first place. Can I please have one member from Rorschach's Sheets and the Barenaked Philosophers report to the back. The category for the final question is Catholic Saints."

"That'd be your department." Nathan's lips captured the mouth of the bottle and emptied his fourth beer. "Pull through for us. We can't let them win two weeks in a row."

Dayton made the two-step journey to the host's table and waited to face off with the other team's sacrificial lamb.

He didn't expect to see Kenna stumbling along the narrow walkway that led to the back of the bar. She echoed the graceless determination of a child in their mother's heels as she struggled to keep steady in her flat boots. She was sauced.

An opportune moment at a most inopportune time.

Kenna greeted him with a reserved ghost of a smile. Even amid her drunkenness, she had a noticeable air of reservation toward him. Shouldn't he have appeared more approachable in light of her lowered inhibitions?

There was the issue of her teammates. Who knew what nonsense they had filled her head with.

"You two ready?" Michael asked, snuffing out the mic. When they didn't object, he continued, "Okay, guys, for the win. Who was the first American woman to be canonized by the Catholic church?"

"Elizabeth Ann Seton," they answered in unison.

Kenna's eyes sobered, electrifying with wildness, either baffled by his knowledge or his quickness. He was just as baffled but he kept his expression neutral. With a few blinks, she settled, sucking in a fragmented breath.

The hair raised on Dayton's forearms, beneath his sweater sleeves. Enamored with her breathing?

His celibacy was showing.

"For the first time in Rusted Monkey history, we have a tie on the tiebreaker. Unbelievable." Michael's hand flew to his forehead as if he'd been handed a Publishers Clearing House check and Dayton noticed Kenna's chest heaving as she did a poor job at staving off laughter. "I've written down a number between 1 and 3,000. Both of you will give me a number and whoever's closest will take the $50 bar tab grand prize."

"416."

No sooner than the number sailed over his tongue, he understood the gravity of the mistake.

He watched Kenna's mouth form around a number but he heard only the thrumming of his heart as Michael slipped him the second-place prize and he turned on his heel, retreating to the bar. Everything happened in slow motion. Kenna waving the bar tab voucher at her teammates. Nathan's lips as he spoke words Dayton was too far gone to comprehend. He got Sasha's attention and gestured for the check and his hand felt leaden as it swiped through the air.

His mind floundered as he involuntarily braced his hands on the counter. It was too early for mistakes.

Nathan's voice punctured his spell.

"Did I just witness some sexual tension back there?"

"There's something different about her, Nate. You look into her eyes and it feels like the Last Judgment."

"Then you better stop looking into them before you land yourself in Raza's office again. You can't chase tail on campus. Don't shit where you eat."

He leaned into Nathan, veins straining against his neck, and deepened his tone. "Don't talk to me like I'm some kind of addict who needs guidance. I have my life under control."

"I love you, man, but respectfully? Fuck getting in a car with you right now."

Dayton walked away before any more damage was done. Between the vodka and the slipup, he wasn't thinking clearly. The Barenaked Philosophers hurled antagonistic remarks at him as he passed their table on his way out of the bar. He couldn't afford to expend any energy on the petty rivalry, not when he had a mentee who was guaranteed to have a damning question the next morning.

# 8
# PEOPLE TALK

**Kenna**

*S*he waited outside Dr. Merino's office at 6:45 the following morning. Fifteen minutes early.

So early, in fact, that he wasn't there.

Brandi's words had planted seeds of suspicion in her mind and Kenna was all too eager to tend to them. Who knew what dwelled in the drawers and cabinets of that office.

Upon twisting the knob and discovering the door was locked, she mourned the loss of the few minutes of sleep she'd sacrificed in order to execute the futile mission.

Tired and defeated, she sank to the polished concrete floor, popped in earbuds, and shuffled her favorite playlist. The familiar tunes vanquished her troubling thoughts. She was temporarily at ease, chugging water and feeling grateful that she'd avoided a hangover. And though alcohol had coursed through her bloodstream hours earlier, it had not clouded her memory. She recalled with bone-chilling accuracy the way Dr. Merino had stared her dead in the eye and said 416.

Her birthdate.

She might have thought it was a coincidence if the answer hadn't been so immediate, as if it was fresh in his mind.

Kenna scrubbed a hand across her face. There it was again. The paranoia. Reid's influence. She had sworn she was done being a prisoner to that feeling yet she was succumbing to it over what, something as innocuous as a number?

Her stomach rolled as she spotted a tall, shadowy figure approaching from the end of the poorly lit hallway. Kenna force closed the music streaming app and shoved the phone inside her bag, shooting to her feet modeling the urgency of a frightened private in the company of a higher-ranking soldier. Dr. Merino didn't spare her a glance as he assumed the position of unlocking the door.

She kept her back against the opposing wall while he fumbled in his coat pocket for the keys, cursing under his breath. He held a Bigleaf Coffee Company cup in his other hand.

It was comical that her intimidating mentor's lateness was borne out of a coffee shop run when it was an excuse more typical for a student.

Once he finally remembered how to operate a lock, the door eased open and Kenna trailed behind him inside the office. He flicked the light switch and a sterile, fluorescent white brilliance flooded the room. Dr. Merino winced at the light's intensity, stifling a groan.

He was the one with a hangover.

Great, he'd probably make her day miserable—or it could be amusing. She would have to gauge his mood.

"How is it that you get to show up three minutes late?"

His bag dropped on the desk with a loud *thunk* that sent his hand shooting to his forehead. "The rules don't apply to me, kid."

The statement struck her in a much different way given what she knew about Brandi's sister. Were she loose with her morals, she might have used the information to blackmail her way through the mentorship.

A hollow bang made her jump. The filing cabinet.

"I have three appointments scheduled this morning, the first of which is at 7:30. Walk-ins are from 10:30 to noon."

Three folders were tucked under his arm. He'd be meeting with established patients. Kenna scrawled the schedule in her notebook, if for no other reason than to humor herself. He hadn't given her a single thing of substance to do all week.

Dr. Merino thumbed through the folders, penning notes on a pocket-sized pad as he flipped through their contents. His sleeve receded through the motion and revealed a gunmetal bracelet on his right wrist.

He must have felt like garbage, judging from his bloodshot eyes and his mismatched socks, but it didn't diminish his intense focus. His obsidian hair hung around his face, invoking a curtain-like effect. Kenna watched in reverence as he labored over the documents, each stroke of the pen disturbing his bracelet. She relaxed at the sight of his pensive face, the sound of rustling paper and fluidity of his wrist. Too relaxed, it seemed, for confrontation welled on her tongue.

"Interesting number you picked last night."

The paper quieted. The pen stilled. His eyes landed on her, cold and sharp.

## Dayton

The number had slipped out.

A micro accident that could've cost him everything.

Dayton had pored over Kenna's file in the days leading up to trivia. He was unrelenting in his review of the single page—so little to know about the bewitching girl—scanning the lines until his vision turned bleary and the information was ingrained in his memory.

*Kenna Aisling O'Callaghan, born April 16, 1998.*
*Lives at 2102 Apt. E, Penrose Lane*
*Attended Jamesville-DeWitt High School*
*Most recent semester's GPA: 4.0*
*Emergency contact: Declan O'Callaghan*
*Relationship: father*

Chills prickled his skin as her expectant stare locked onto him, a piercing look as sharp as a weapon. Extinguishing her distrust was vital. It was for the best if she thought he was bending to her investigative nature.

"How did you know?" she asked in a whisper.

"The truth?"

Kenna's eyes widened before returning to their disconcertingly large though natural resting state. Her appearance resembled that of a cartoon character. Extreme features clashing with the more fragile ones.

"I looked at your file. Clean as a whistle. I wanted to see if I'd be dealing with a miscreant all semester." He ironed on a smile and omitted the part about photocopying her information.

Why scare his darling lamb away?

### Kenna

Kenna said nothing in response to his admission.

Her heart beat with the steady uncertainty of an ignited grenade, oblivious to which pulsation would lead to its unavoidable explosion. Beads of sweat percolated on her lower back.

He had looked at her file.

Dr. Merino had collected more data about her than, if given the choice, she would've cared to share. She wasn't worried about him showing up at her apartment in the middle of the night but she didn't like that he knew where she lived.

His unnatural smile lingered as he extended a folder in her direction. "Would you file this?"

Rising without protest, Kenna attempted to grab the folder from the edge of the desk but Dr. Merino tugged on the opposite end, mirroring their transference of the pen at the bar.

"Question my intentions again and you'll find yourself without a mentor. Understand?"

A noise resounded in her throat that must have sounded like assent for he relinquished it and she migrated to the filing cabinet, skin on fire beneath her sweater.

One hand plucked at her collar for relief as the other combed through the meticulously alphabetized files until she came upon the slot for Mathers, Dustin.

Though Dr. Merino was silent and hard at work, she felt safer with her back to him. She had more or less grown used to his company in the office but now his presence felt threatening, like she was being mentored by a violent ex-convict rather than a licensed clinician.

Just as Kenna started closing the drawer, she stopped, fixating on one of the names. McAnders, Bella.

She wasn't sure it was the same girl that Liam had spoken of but chills began to prick her arms the longer she stared at the printed label. Her fingers itched to reach out and glimpse its contents.

"My tone was harsh, wasn't it? I'm not in optimal condition today. Can I be frank with you?"

Dr. Merino's speech startled her into action. She shut the drawer and reminded herself to walk to her seat at a normal pace though her mind urged her to make haste.

"Of course."

"Your accusation, I know it wasn't direct but it was there, in your tone. It struck a nerve. I'm here to help you sluice out whether this is the type of work you'd like to carry on with once you leave this institution. And despite whatever your trivia teammates undoubtedly had to say about me, I have no intention of harming you or anything else you've dreamed up."

"How did—"

"This is a small town. People talk."

Knocking reverberated on the glass panel. His 7:30 had arrived. This time Dr. Merino's faint smile was genuine, one of amusement.

"In the hall, Miss O'Callaghan."


Kenna didn't leave her apartment the entire weekend.

In the 12 days she'd known Dr. Merino, she'd deemed it appropriate to dedicate an entire notebook to him in which she recounted their meetings, paying close attention to anything peculiar she had encountered.

*-tea drinker*

*-staring problem*

*-slept w/ a patient (maybe?)*

Okay, when the list materialized on paper, it was far less compelling. She left off the bit about Bella because she didn't deem it suspicious but the third item alone was sufficient cause to shift the amateur investigation to the internet.

She'd had only four years of public school to master using computers before hopping on a Greyhound and heading for Oregon—18 with her life savings rubber-banded in a shoe.

So much had changed since then. She had changed.

The search engine lit up her screen.

Her trembling fingers typed 'Dr. Merino' into the query bar. Under normal circumstances, she would have never considered googling university staff but he had an agenda.

Of that, she was certain.

Within seconds of clicking the icon, Google delivered a concerning number of results. Scrolling along the page, she noticed all of the entries were people named 'Dr. Merino' from other states. An illogical part of her insisted that the inconclusive results were a sign, warning her not to meddle in the personal dealings of this man.

A burning pain spread in her chest; the palms of God, pushing her away from the laptop.

"Father, forgive me," she mumbled.

She tried again, tacking 'Ponderosa University' onto the end of the search phrase. The first listing was for the faculty page on the university's website which provided a direct link to his page. Kenna instantly gauged that the photo was out of date due to minor changes in his appearance.

Shorter hair, cut even with his rounded ears. Skin free of scars. Face ornamented by a mustache and goatee.

It was a stark contrast from the shaggy-haired, clean-shaven man she saw five times a week.

There was a short bio next to the photo and Kenna absorbed those sentences with the ardency of a detective without a lead, jotting down the relevant pieces.

*-has been w/ the university since 2012*

*-graduated from UCLA*

Returning to the search page, she selected the next entry, a *Branch Spring Herald* feature from 2015 headlined, 'Ponderosa Psychiatrist Founds *Race to Remember*.'

Kenna skimmed the article detailing the creation and first-year kickoff of the 5K dedicated to raising awareness for Alzheimer's. While it offered next to no useful information, she gleaned that he was 'a native of Oregon' and that he was 'passionate about giving back to the community.'

Except that was bullshit. A front for something ugly, something he didn't want anyone to know about—and she had a feeling it tied back to Brandi's sister.

She was well-acquainted with the sort. Giving back had always been the central philosophy of her church-going, orchard-tending family.

Where safe was synonymous with control.

Halfway down the page there was a photo from the event, captioned, 'Dr. Merino and Charlee Pender, a psychology student at Ponderosa, pass out t-shirts to the run's participants.' She recorded the student's name in her notebook as a potential future contact.

If Charlee had a similar experience to Brandi's sister, Kenna may have been onto something.

### Dayton

A cool breeze stirred the night air as Dayton snapped a picture of Kenna's bike leaning against the building's black exterior. The idea of slashing her tires appealed to him.

She would approach him with the awful news, and he'd offer her rides to campus in a completely organic way. But as soon as he had tiptoed out of the trees, pocket knife in hand, his phone buzzed in his pocket. Nathan wanted to know about getting drinks, to which he responded with a polite no.

He didn't dare leave the trees again.

The bike was sitting outside her apartment each time he stopped by that weekend.

Warm light flooded through the semi-sheer curtain guarding her bedroom, not extinguishing until one or two in the morning. What 21-year-old stayed cooped up in their apartment the entire weekend?

Either she was more of a brainiac than he had anticipated, or she was up to no good. He suspected the latter.

Though his hunting skills had been forced into dormancy during his two-year dry spell, the keenness of his intuition had not faded. Her preparations swirled through the air and enveloped his neck, choked by the imagined ribbon of her mistrust.

Three runs in two days barely qualified as out of the ordinary, but it was a sign—however small—of his building desperation. He was out of his element.

Even gathering intel on Kenna had been exhausting. Her file was chaste, leaving much to be desired.

Social media presence? Nonexistent.

She didn't have a car to bug. What was he to do, place a GPS tracker on her bicycle?

Dayton's late-night visits were often fruitless but he sometimes caught a glimpse of her, hair raising as her shadow drifted across the curtain.

It was satiating. For the moment.

This was how he'd confined himself to exist, chasing and being a part of something from a distance, hoping to gain an understanding of himself in the process. The spark of joy that came with the eventual physical contact was designed to be ephemeral and he held onto them like treasure.

Memories that lived on once the girls had gone.

# February

9

# JUST AN ASSUMPTION

**Kenna**

*S*tudents filled the library's long oak tables, all finishing presentations or delegating responsibilities for group projects.

Kenna didn't mind the din of quiet conversation and she had minimal interruptions at the checkout desk as she buried her nose in the spine of her social psychology textbook. The aged smell of the weathered pages riddled the space with the potency of an incense stick. Their first test was fast approaching and she had to ace it.

She was relying exclusively on scholarships and grants to fund her impending graduate studies. Repaying student loans for the rest of her life was not an option.

The only reason she was at the private, prestigious Ponderosa was because she'd studied with every spare minute she had in high school, not to mention the help of an exceptionally kind career counselor, who sent her application off when her parents refused.

Her eyes scanned each line of text with precision, pausing only to highlight key terms and phrases.

*Social behavior is goal-oriented.*

That phrase sent Kenna down a rabbit hole. Her spiraling thoughts claimed center stage, making her forget where she was and what she was doing. On the tail end of her digression clung an undeniable thought about Dr. Merino. Though he'd been forced into this social situation with her, he most certainly had a goal.

Alright, she wasn't sure, but there was no denying something was off with him and she prayed whatever transpired would be less nefarious than the avenues her mind had explored over the last couple of weeks.

"Hey, Kenna."

She jumped in her seat at the sound, frightened to near cardiac arrest as her adrenaline spiked like a seismograph during an earthquake. How was Kenna able to share a room with Dr. Merino five days a week if the mere thought of him had such an effect on her?

Closing the book, she regarded the visitor, any residual anxiety tamed upon seeing Liam's face.

"Hey. Got anything for me to scan?" She waved the black scanner she'd hardly touched all morning.

"Sadly, no, so I guess you have to retire your magic wand for now." He held up a leather jacket shrouded forearm to shield his eyes, at which point she realized she'd been aiming the blinding red strip at him. Biting the inside of her lip, she returned the scanner to its holster.

He stood there, as if unsure how to proceed, and jerked his head to swish the razor-cut black hair out of his eyes, gaze falling to the floor.

His bad boy exterior contradicted his shy nature, which Kenna found amusing—perhaps a tad alluring.

"Do you need something?" She hated when people, guys especially, played coy.

"There's this student film festival, not this weekend but the next," he began, shoving his hands inside the pockets of his dark-wash jeans. "I was wondering if you wanted to go … with me. If you want, but it's no pressure. I was going to ask you at trivia but then I thought it might be weird with everyone around and—" he sighed. "I'm making a complete ass of myself, aren't I?"

"Yeah, you are." Kenna laughed as Liam trailed off in the direction of the exit. "If your film is even half as entertaining as that performance you just gave, I'm sure we'll have a great time."

He spun around with a wide grin, pointing at her as he backed toward the double doors. "Wagner Theatre, 7 o'clock on the 15th."

"Can't wait."

She tapped her fingers against her textbook, joy radiating all the way to their tips. She needed to get out of her apartment more often. It remained to be seen if Liam was trustworthy but Kenna took comfort in the fact that they'd be in a theater full of people rather than one-on-one.

No more than twenty seconds after she resumed her study session, a more troublesome voice echoed in passing.

"See you at one, kid."

A chill ran up her spine, so bitterly cold it may as well have been accompanied by the formation of ice on her bones.

Dr. Merino's face twisted up, attempting but failing to form a smile. It was like his muscles denied him of the expression, or perhaps he was altogether incapable of it.

Her eyes did not stray from his back until he passed through the exit and the doors shut behind him.

### Dayton

Dayton's thumb struck his lighter and a flame bloomed from its tip. He inhaled, igniting his blunt, and a plume of smoke escaped his lips. Lurking among the towering shelves of the library had been worth inhaling the stench of rotting books for an hour. Someone else had their eyes set on *his* lamb.

What he found even more infuriating was Kenna's lack of protest upon Liam's proposal. She seemed—dare he say—a bit eager in her acceptance. Her interest in other men simply wouldn't do. He had to lure her back in and sink his hook, before that boy sailed off with her into the sunset.

He blew a final puff of smoke out the window and with it came clarity as he snuffed out the blunt and discarded it on the brick ledge outside. Dayton knew better than to leave things to chance where his subjects were concerned.

Liam Park had to be dealt with.

As he locked the window, a knock sent his hands into a tingling fit. Kenna.

"It's open," he said, flipping on the humidifier.

She said nothing as she entered, ignoring him while carrying out her routine of settling in. Kenna retrieved the two notebooks she'd dedicated to their sessions. Her ghostly fingers clutched the journals, pale skin creating a jarring juxtaposition even against the lighter, pastel bound book. He'd noticed she wrote in the indigo one with growing frequency, not often reaching for its lavender companion.

Cracking the indigo notebook open, she scrawled on its lined pages with urgency. Her grip on the writing utensil was frightening. Aggression ruled her pen strokes and Dayton sat watching, wondering what had her so fired up.

He propped his feet up on the corner of his desk. "Most people keep those under lock and key."

She didn't acknowledge his comment as her pen continued sailing across the pages. His pulse picked up its synthetic pace. He delighted in Kenna's emotiveness, savoring the pinch of her brow and flush of her cheeks. If only they could've spent the afternoon together, free from patients, with him sitting in silent reverence as she filled those lines.

"Aren't you too old for a diary?"

## Kenna

One corner of Dr. Merino's mouth tightened and Kenna forced herself to look away for she knew that if she stared, her heart would overshadow her purpose.

To find out if he'd slept with a patient.

His smirk would have vanished in an instant if he saw what lurked inside her notebook. Notes detailing his behavior. It wasn't much to look at in its current state but Kenna had faith that she'd pick up bits of information over the course of the semester. As things stood, she had no reason to contact Charlee Pender though she burned to learn what connection she had to Dr. Merino. What would she have said?

*Hey Charlee, I stalked my mentor online and noticed that you two have some kind of history. Also, I think he slept with an acquaintance of mine's sister. Know anything about that?*

She had resolved not to message Charlee unless a situation arose that warranted doing so.

"It's not a diary. It's a journal."

He was having one of his mellow days, feet on his desk and head resting casually on the back of his chair. Conversations with Dr. Merino were not as unnerving on these occasions—a welcome change from his no-nonsense persona. Since she started notating his behavior, she'd figured out that his moods were unfiltered in the afternoon.

The exact cause for this evaded her, but medication was high on her list of possibilities.

His gaze stayed glued to the ceiling, dazed and confused. "Is there a difference?"

"Yes, I'd say so." She curled up in her chair, mimicking his vibe of comfort. "Diaries are for egocentric little girls who put so much stock in their secrets, they feel compelled to 'keep them under lock and key,' as you said. Journals, at least in my case, are curated with academic intent. But yes, feelings sometimes play a part in my research process."

"I have a diary, of sorts. Does that make me an egocentric little girl?"

"You do?"

Dr. Merino nodded, folding his arms over his stomach and shooting her a sidelong glance. "You talk like a textbook that came to life. I bet you don't set foot outside of your apartment on the weekends."

Kenna's shoulders tightened. "Apartment?"

"Just an assumption," he amended, but the way he converted to his a.m. desk posture belied this forged assurance. "Houses aren't exactly cheap to rent around here."

Had intimidating young women been Dr. Merino's profession, he was due for a promotion.

He wasn't trying to scare her—he was succeeding—but it was rage rather than fear that consumed her. Her teeth clenched as her insides boiled.

Kenna refused to sit idly by as he employed his intimidation tactics. Blood-curdling screeches erupted from her chair as she dragged it across the floor toward Dr. Merino.

She plopped into it, planting her forearms on the desk. "What were you doing in the library this morning?"

He hunched over the desk on his side.

"Is it a crime to wander the aisles of the library?"

Unsafe was an underestimation of how she was coming to feel in his presence. He'd looked at her file and shown up at her workplace. And though there was some degree of plausible deniability since she worked on campus, she came up empty for a reason as to why a psychiatrist might need to visit the library.

"No, it isn't. But you know what is?" Kenna asked, stoic posture inflexible. "Stalking."

**Dayton**

Though his high had started to take effect, Dayton didn't flinch at the allegation. Deflecting such comments had become second nature. An evolutionary adaptation he'd acquired in his role of ruthless researcher.

"I'd be careful slinging around false accusations, Miss O'Callaghan. Dean Raza doesn't take lightly to liars."

"Because you and the dean have such a chummy relationship." Kenna's nose twitched, as it often did when she made a smart remark.

She was a spitfire, emotions shifting with the unexpectancy of light rainfall transforming into a torrential downpour. Without warning.

"Listen to me, you red-headed bitch. I'm growing tired of your mouth." Lies. It aroused Dayton beyond measure, but he ran his tongue along his bottom row of teeth and composed himself. "If you think you're going to spend the rest of the semester disrespecting me in *my* office, you're sorely mistaken. Need I remind you, I decide 90% of your grade."

"As if I need another reminder. You threaten me with that every day I'm in this godforsaken office." She sprung from the chair and bolted toward the windows, staring out at the campus. "I have a right mind to take this conversation to the dean. I'm sure he'd love to hear that you called your mentee a 'red-headed bitch.' Fortunately for you, I believe in second chances." She pivoted to face him, slouching to a half-stance like a wilted flower. "So, I'm going to ask you again: What were you doing in the library?"

Her beautiful face, earnest and open, almost tricked him into revealing the truth.

"Don't ask a question if you can't handle the answer."

## 1 O

## REHEARSED



*K*enna didn't speak to him the rest of the week.

She accepted the errands he'd assign, never uttering a word, and her silence drove Dayton mad. It didn't help that she seemed to know he was following her around. She was pulling back and time was slipping away.

February would soon be halfway over.

All of this ran through Dayton's head Saturday morning as he wandered the condiment aisle in Roth's, shopping basket in hand. He didn't need anything from that section of the store but Liam Park penetrated the fortress of his mind and he zoned out, gaze boring into the rows of glass and plastic bottles lining the shelves. He'd eliminated potential suitors and boyfriends in the past, and, so far, he had lived on without consequence.

Memories came crawling back to him. Rain. Trees. Sirens. Blue and red lights. Hot blood flowing down his face.

Things couldn't get out of hand again.

He'd see to it that Liam remained alive.

"Excuse me," a stocky man interjected.

The man grabbed two bottles of barbeque sauce and went on his way and, though Dayton was alone again, his train of thought had been disturbed and he felt compelled to move to another aisle.

He wandered to the expansive produce area and chucked a variety of vegetables into his basket. He always enjoyed the solace of an early-morning grocery run. The store was mostly empty, quiet. The perfect place to clear his head.

As he reached for a bag of spinach, a familiar shopper inspecting a pile of apples caught his attention and he forgot where he was, what he'd been doing.

There was only her.

## Kenna

Most of the time, Kenna and Alex did their shopping together. Today, she wasn't so lucky. Alex was attending an on-campus seminar about generative typography, and she had reiterated its importance no less than a thousand times.

And so, Kenna had biked to Roth's, pledging to get only what would fit inside her backpack.

She arrived not long after the store opened. It was uncommon for her to be out of bed this early on the weekend, but sleep had proved impossible the previous night, prompting the unusual outing.

Dr. Merino had gotten under her skin.

The week of silence between them had permitted her plenty of space to think. She'd convinced herself that most of her evidence against his alleged stalking was purely coincidental. After all, he'd admitted to raiding her file. An admission of wrongdoing didn't fit the bill of stalker behavior. The fact remained that Dr. Merino was a huge prick. Maybe that's all there was to the story, and Kenna had let paranoia creep in and get the best of her.

Sifting through a mountain of gala apples, she assessed each one for bruises or other flaws, chucking the ones that passed the examination inside her bag. An apple tumbled from her hand as a man materialized on the other side of the fruit display and panic welled in her throat. Dr. Merino stood before her in a thin athletic jacket and jogger fit sweatpants. It was strange to see him in such casual clothing.

That paranoia came crawling back, begging for validation. She refused to let it control her.

Kenna knelt to retrieve the apple. "You can't sneak up on people like that."

"I didn't mean to scare you." Dr. Merino cracked an amused half-smile. Perhaps she hadn't given his range of emotion enough credit. "I guess your stint of silence against me has been lifted. Or was your admission of shock purely accidental?"

She moved down the produce stand, eyeing the lemons and limes, willing to look everywhere but his smug face. He moved along with her on the opposite side.

"You called me a bitch. What did you expect?"

This gave him pause. It looked as though he was having an internal deliberation, and doing a poor job of disguising it.

"I've given that some thought. That was out of line, uncalled for. Can you forgive my unprofessional behavior?" He almost became charming while apologizing, gaze softening with brows raised.

Maybe he wasn't a huge prick, just a prick.

"I suppose I owe you an apology, too. That was a pretty strong accusation. I had a bad experience with a guy sophomore year. Not exactly stalking, but it left me rattled."

She owed Dr. Merino an apology, nothing more, and yet the explanation fled her mouth. Just because he showed a sliver of humanity with a partial smile did *not* justify opening up to him, she scolded herself.

Especially not about Reid Emerson.

"If I've made you uncomfortable, I'm sorry. Truly." A second apology. The softness in his eyes vanished, expression as blank as an untouched canvas. "I'm passionate about my work, and having you in the office has been an adjustment. I know I come off kind of intense."

The apology was different from the first. This one had been tuned and strummed, like her battered acoustic guitar before a performance. It felt rehearsed. Kenna's skin prickled as the dissection of his speech washed over her.

She had to get rid of him. End the conversation.

"I'm sure I'll get used to it," Kenna joked, struggling to keep her tone light as she backed away. "I'll see you on Monday."

**Dayton**

But it wasn't Monday when he saw her next.

It was a mere fifteen minutes later as Dayton headed out to his Caprice and noticed Kenna unchaining her bike from an otherwise empty rack. A backpack full of groceries rested near her feet as she fiddled with the combination lock. The universe was offering her on a silver platter, and he wasn't one to decline this sort of egregious enticement.

No, he would graciously accept what the cosmos had proffered on this fateful Saturday morning.

It was the perfect opportunity to earn her trust.

"Need a ride?"

He maintained a respectable distance. He'd already spooked her with his heedless demeanor; the last thing he needed was to give her a reason to refuse the ride, one he desperately wanted her to accept.

"I don't know." Kenna glanced at the heavy bag of groceries, probably thinking about how her back might have felt later. "What about my bike? I can't leave it here."

"I have plenty of room for it."

"Okay, sure, thanks."

Her speech was rushed and Dayton felt transcendent as she guided her bike, all nerves and nearness, alongside him toward the ancient station wagon. He unlocked the trunk and laid her bike inside with unexpected gentleness.

"This thing is a relic."

"I drove a BMW, once upon a time. This tin wagon is my self-imposed punishment for wrecking it." A palpable tension hung in the air as they climbed into their respective seats. Kenna's light eyelashes fluttered at an alarming pace, her swallows audible in the dead silence of the vehicle. "Where to?"

"Pacific Heights. Do you know it?" She dared a glance at him.

"I do."

She was so close that he could decipher all of the scents that encompassed her being, the delicate notes he associated with his resuscitated lunacy: the faded mint of her toothpaste, the tea tree oil on her face, the warm, vanilla perfume that lingered on her neck and mixed in with her freshly washed hair.

Pure bliss.

### Kenna

She bit her tongue before a question about knowing the apartment complex slipped. From now on, she would keep her suspicions to herself until they were debunked or a substantiated conclusion was reached.

Bringing Dr. Merino's attention to the stalking theory had been unwise and she would have to be more guarded if she expected to get anywhere with her investigation.

She'd accepted the ride in the name of research. Sure, not having to bike home with a load of groceries was an enticing bonus. Kenna was anxious to see how Dr. Merino behaved with her in such an intimate, confined space. It could be insightful to his character.

Or, he could smother her with a chloroform rag and the rest would be history.

For the sake of discovery, she took the risk.

While the view of the pines along 99W had been scenic as she biked to Roth's, Dr. Merino's presence tainted the beautiful scene with something ominous. The trees towered above and promised death to anyone who veered from the road.

Much to her surprise, he was silent during the drive, though his not so inconspicuous gaze drifted to her with unsettling frequency. She pretended not to notice. All the while, her stomach quivered at the lack of distance between them. He had one hand on the steering wheel, and the other a few inches from her leg on the gear shift. Several veins protruded on the one that gripped the shifter, presenting a faint blue against his tanned skin. Her eyes began to trail up his arm but stopped short at his wrist. The gunmetal bracelet. In the center of its black plate, there was an engraving of the Rod of Asclepius.

"You seem tired," she said.

"Completely bushed. I was at Owens-Adair all night."

"Are you sick?"

"No, no. Moonlighting. I work in the emergency room Friday nights, anyone who's there for psychiatric reasons. I consult with them and determine if it's safe to release them or if they need to be held."

"Do you enjoy that?"

"It's night and day from the university, but yes. I do it mostly because it reminds me of residency. The adrenaline and exhaustion."

Kenna felt confident they had a good dialogue going and it gave her the courage to inquire about his strange jewelry. "Is your bracelet some kind of swanky doctor thing or am I missing the mark?"

"More like a shackle. Should something happen to me, it contains all of the relevant information."

Her brows knit together as she stared at the symbol. There were no other markings.

"The engravings are on the back. To keep people like you from nosing around in my personal life."

She kept quiet the remainder of the ride and covertly studied her surroundings. The interior of the station wagon was clean, too clean, not a speck of dust in sight. The random assortment of items lurking in most people's cars was absent. No CDs, books, sports equipment, junk mail. There was nary a dead body in the vehicle, and Kenna supposed the absence of such horror qualified as a silver lining in the potentially perilous situation.

"Which building?" Dr. Merino asked when they neared the complex.

"F."

## Dayton

The engine cut off and with it his erratic heartbeat settled. Every nerve ending in Dayton's body screamed for him to escape the small space. He had done well during the brief ride but he could only resist temptation for so long.

He tore out of the driver's seat, racing to retrieve her bike from the trunk. Kenna wasn't far behind, slinging the bag of groceries on her shoulder and joining him at the rear of the station wagon.

Reaching for the handlebars, she insisted, "I can get it."

"Like you can lift this." He emitted a single, derogatory laugh. Dayton's fingertips brushed against the tops of her hands as she surrendered control of the bike. The warmth Kenna transferred to him in that split second was inconceivable. It was as if a fire burned within her at all times.

Liam Park was unworthy of such euphoria.

"Thanks for the lift." Kenna's appreciation was forced, like she had to remind herself to acknowledge his generosity.

It was something he'd noticed not long after they met, a quality they shared. Her mind was often elsewhere.

He shut the trunk in one fluid push.

"It's no trouble."

"Dr. Merino?" someone called from a few parking spots away. A voice he instantly recognized. The woman in question hit the automatic lock on her keys and her Kia's headlights flashed as she approached them.

"What are you doing home so early?" Kenna asked.

"We get an hour for lunch." Alex directed the comment at Kenna, but her eyes were locked on Dayton.

Just five feet away from him stood Alex Guerrero. His original sin of Branch Spring. Her naivety and gullibility had made her an easy point of entry for his research six years ago.

But something in the way she looked at him now was different. She was older, wiser. The sunny smile that Dayton had loved was missing, hidden by her inexpressive taupe lips.

"Ha pasado mucho tiempo, Señorita Guerrero."

Kenna did a double take upon hearing the polished Spanish rolling off his tongue.

Crossing her arms, Alex clipped, "No es lo suficientemente largo." She gestured to Kenna. "¿Qué es esto? No pudiste arruinar mi vida la primera vez, ¿ahora vas tras mi compañero de cuarto? Ella es una buena niña. Estás pidiendo problemas."

His head spun at her unmistakable words: they were roommates. How had he missed this? How had he not spotted Alex a single time in his frequent stakeouts of the complex?

Perhaps she had passed by, but his focus was so hardwired on Kenna, he had overlooked Alex entirely.

Either way, he was fucked.

11

# CAUGHT

**Kenna**

'*P*roblemas.'

The word stuck with Kenna as if it had been branded in her memory. She didn't need to know Spanish to understand what had been said. Nothing spoke louder than body language. Alex's mood had changed on a dime, confusion whipping into volatile fury within a nanosecond.

They had bad blood.

This is where her frenetic mind drifted during a Friday morning patient meeting. For the first time, someone had been kind enough to let Kenna observe their session. Sydney Chambers, a junior music theory major, was prattling on about a series of intense nightmares she'd had for months.

Her first observation. She should have been over the moon about what was transpiring in the office.

Instead, she found it near impossible to focus on the plight of the Chambers woman amid her own internal disarray.

"Every dream is the same setup," Sydney said. "I've been practicing for months. Something crucial to the progression of my studies or career is coming up."

She occupied Kenna's usual seat, relegating her to a borrowed fold-up chair next to Dr. Merino. An unbearable cold radiated from its metal, seeping through the material of her pants and further freezing her in the frigid room. The sparse distance separating them reminded Kenna of that bizarre car ride, which she had somehow survived sans chloroform. She chided herself. The chances of Dr. Merino being a murderer were slim, and she fought to dismiss the idea altogether.

Fear made her mind sink to the darkest places.

He scribbled notes on his 6x9 yellow pad. Kenna tried to catch a glimpse of the writing, but it was illegible. A graphologist would've had a field day with Dr. Merino's amalgam of print and cursive. She regarded her own blank pad.

How could either one of them have reached any conclusion when the patient had uttered three sentences?

"The day of the showcase, audition, musical, whatever it is, arrives." Sydney's features tensed as she exhausted her recall. "I take the stage but when it's my turn to sing, I can't. I open my mouth and strain to make any kind of sound. Nothing comes out. I can't even hear myself breathing. Not a sound. And then I wake up."

He deposited the pen atop the pad, folding his hands on the desk. "And what happens when you wake up?"

Kenna was bored with the issue being presented but she knew it was an unrealistic expectation to hope for something beyond a basic, guided question scenario for her first sit-in. A girl could dream.

"I'm covered in cold sweat. My heart's beating out of my chest and I don't calm down until I hear my breathing, until I feel the vibration of my vocal chords."

Dr. Merino didn't seem much more enthusiastic about the session. Kenna supposed after so many years of working for the university, he could deduce when a student was pining for medication, bearing no interest in any other avenue of treatment. He tugged the top right-hand drawer of the desk, retrieved a prescription pad and addressed Sydney as he filled out the sheet.

"I'm going to prescribe you a low, low dosage of sertraline. As low as you can go, 25 milligrams. I'd recommend taking it 30 to 45 minutes before you go to bed. It should help you sleep through the night, but no guarantee."

Ripping the paper from its binding, he handed it off to Kenna who delivered it to Sydney.

"This medication sometimes prevents people from sleeping, but that's pretty uncommon. Just know it's a possibility. If that happens to be the case for you, come back to see me and we'll find an alternative."

Sydney thanked Dr. Merino and ducked out of the office. As soon as she left, Kenna's need to return to her seat amplified. That plan fell to pieces when her mentor rotated his entire body toward her, as if he were settling in for a cozy chat with a colleague.

"Well, that was riveting," he said.

"All part of the job."

She wanted to abandon the rickety fold-up chair but her lower half was glued to the hard metal seat and she forced a smile that sent a sharp pain shooting through her cheeks.

Dr. Merino's legs were spread in a display of ultimate comfort. His left arm lay across the desk, while his right elbow dug into the chair's armrest, forearm dangling over his lap. The sheer size of his person made him tree-like. Frame wide yet lean.

That disturbing, honeyed glow flickered in his eyes.

He'd caught her staring. Kenna's chin made a quick dive to focus on the tiled floor beneath them.

The sip he took from the now cold Darjeeling tea was much too ginger for a man of imposing malice. "Any plans for this horribly commercial holiday?"

Was he seriously asking if she had Valentine's Day plans? Kenna couldn't believe it. He watched her through his long, dark lashes, awaiting her response.

She wagered his idea of a romantic evening started with a date-rape drug and ended with a semi-conscious romp in the hay. Maybe he was a touch classier than that.

She'd rather not find out.

"No plans." Dr. Merino gave a slow, singular nod, as if he'd been hoping for a different answer. Kenna took the bait. "I have a date on Saturday."

A wide, closed-mouth smile spread across his face, accentuating sets of refined lines at either corner of his lips that resembled parentheticals.

"That's a relief. I was starting to worry you were planning to study yourself to death."

## Dayton

Of course he knew about Kenna's upcoming date. After all, he'd been plotting its demise since he overheard the arrangement in the library. But Dayton was curious to see if she trusted him enough to volunteer such delicate information and his darling lamb did not disappoint.

Everything was on track for his satiation and her predestined heartbreak.

"Lift your arms, sir," the seamstress instructed. The woman with the graying bun circled him, wrapping her measuring tape around his chest. She wrote the number on a post-it note and continued the tedious procedure. "Relax. Show me your usual posture so I can get your shoulder measurements."

Dayton obeyed her direction—anything to speed up the process. He was raring to drive across town and slash Liam Park's tires. Though it was a childish attack, it was a nonviolent means to cut down the boy's chances. But he had planned something vile that guaranteed Kenna would never look at Liam again. His insides vibrated with premature excitement.

Alas, his best man duties beckoned.

"You look sharp. You better not make me look bad on my big day," Nathan joked.

He'd endured the entirety of his fitting, relishing in poking fun at his friend's displeasure.

"I look like I'm in mourning. If you ever see me this dressed up, there's a good chance somebody's dropped dead."

He stared ahead at the mirrored wall, taking in his suited appearance. The jacket was itchy and the wedding was in May. Outdoors. The second the ceremony and photos were over, it would have to go.

"How's the babysitting going?"

At first, he didn't realize it was in reference to Kenna.

"She sat in on a patient today. It wasn't too exciting, but I think she got a kick out of it."

The seamstress sunk to her knees, measuring the inseam of the dress pants. His mind replayed the memory of Kenna's eyes wandering all over his body that morning. What he loved most of all was the shame plastered on her face after the fact. It gave him a rush, knowing he was capable of stirring such conflicting emotions within her.

With Liam out of the picture, the bewitching Kenna Aisling O'Callaghan would be his to love—if only on a temporary basis.

# 12

# X-RATED

Dayton

It was a quarter to seven when Dayton turned up at the 12th Annual Student Short Film Festival. Waiting outside for the arrival of the young couple was tempting, but he didn't allow his eagerness to get the best of him.

He couldn't afford to make any more mistakes. Kenna was already suspicious. Restraint would be a critical factor in the success of the evening.

He kept a low profile in the rear of the theater, blending in among the film department faculty. Several of the professors must have recognized him because he found himself at the receiving end of a few absentminded handshakes.

Wagner Theatre roared with conversation as students, staff, dates, family, and members of the community gathered in the 2,000-seat space. The room filled with a steady buzz that multiplied as more people poured through the entrance; it was the kind of environment where it became impossible to hear your own thoughts. Dayton found it exasperating. His mind lacked a silent moment.

Internal monologue lost to the uproarious attendees, he felt like a cymbal-clashing monkey figurine. He was vigilant in his surveying of the crowd, searching for the red-headed woman, reasoning that only she could silence the noise.

And then, as he looked to the entryway, he saw them.

Liam dug in the back pocket of his tight-fitting jeans, fishing for his student ID to present to the ever-patient ticket attendant. Kenna had walked in with her ID ready to go; Dayton could see it clutched in her hand from where he stood.

The sight of her that evening was a true marvel.

She wore a thin black turtleneck and a fitted rust skirt. Her legs glowed against the brown boots she wore.

The longer Dayton focused on her bare legs, the more he fantasized about their texture beneath his fingertips. His knees almost buckled at the simplicity of the erotic imagery but the tassels of jealousy flogged his imprisoned heart and kept him on his feet.

Why hadn't she ever dressed like that for him?

They descended the aisle together in search of their seats. Liam seized her hand, guiding them through the venue. He'd had enough of this Ingmar Bergman wannabe competing for the affections of his girl, and the night had just begun.

A hush fell over the audience as the lights dimmed and Dayton stood against the back wall of the venue, vowing to remain there until the doomed lovers made their exit.

## Kenna

"Sorry I couldn't pick you up," Liam apologized. They were seated in the middle of the theater, waiting for the screenings to begin. "Kinda spoils the charm of the first date."

"Don't worry about it. I promise I'm not as traditional as I seem." Not leaving room for her last phrase to be misconstrued, Kenna continued, "I can't believe someone slashed all of your tires. You must've really pissed them off. Maybe it's one of the film-makers you're up against."

Liam scrunched his mouth off to one side.

"Nah, I don't think so. They're all chill. Whoever did this has serious issues. Maybe they thought it was someone else's car and I'm the unfortunate victim of their delinquency."

She knew he was more upset than he was letting on. If she had a car and a stranger took it upon themselves to damage it, she would've been in hysterics. Kenna couldn't exactly empathize since she had never driven a car, much less owned one, but she showed her support by offering her hand. He squeezed it in a silent show of appreciation.

The seats were packed together so closely that whenever they turned to talk to each other, their faces were inches apart under the dim lights of the cavernous room.

"So, what's your film about?"

He gave a moment's hesitation, searching for something in her subtly made-up features. Permission?

She would not grant it. It was too soon.

"You'll just have to wait and see. They're all shorts, obviously. Sorry to let you down if you were on board for 15 features, but that would run much later than 7-9, wouldn't it?"

"You're a regular comedian," Kenna teased. She waved her program around. "I suppose you didn't anticipate my literacy."

Liam glanced at her in his peripherals, forming a smug smile while his knee bounced up and down.

A spotlight beamed on center stage. The audience applauded as the geriatric head of the film department, Professor Marlowe, situated himself behind the podium.

As he spoke, the lights dimmed further to compensate for the glaring spotlight. Liam's hand grazed her thigh and Kenna's whole body was rendered immobile. She shot him a questioning look and he immediately retracted it but his touch lingered as bumps pebbled her skin. The professor's voice distorted into static as she inhaled deep breaths through her nose.

It wasn't that she was opposed to being touched. The last man who'd laid a hand on her had broken her heart.


Liam turned to her and whispered, "Mine's up next."

While it wasn't Kenna's idea of a good time, some of the films had been of admirable quality considering they were produced by students. The climate of their date had improved, too. He kept his hands to himself after she basically threatened to murder him with a singular glower.

She wouldn't be going home with him and she hoped her vehement dismissal of his wandering fingers had illustrated that point.

A smattering of applause disrupted the stillness of the room as brief credits soared across the screen. Giddiness persisted within Kenna knowing that Liam's film was to follow. He could've chosen anywhere for their premier date, but he chose to share this night with her and she understood he must have liked her a great deal to endure something so vulnerable during their first outing.

He was willing to share his art with her.

The announcer came on in her smooth, ASMR voice. "*Gray October* directed by Sung-Min Park."

Alluring jazz music crescendoed as the film faded into focus. It was shot in black and white, a distinct choice that set it apart from the rest of the showcase. A woman with a blonde bob, which looked to be a cheaply made wig, entered a private office, slamming the door once inside.

"I've been waiting for you," said a man sporting a ponytail. A fat cigar was lodged between his lips, mangling his dialogue.

Liam tapped Kenna's forearm, glancing at her in horror. "This isn't my film."

"What do you mean?"

"What do you mean what do I mean? I'm telling you, I've never seen this in my life."

Before she had time to process Liam's concern, shrieks broke out in the audience, diverting Kenna's attention to the film. The blonde woman bent over the desk, the absence of underwear made obvious by her hiked-up skirt. The man snatched the cigar from his lips, extinguishing it on the blonde's backside. Instead of screaming, she moaned at the sensation. Kenna averted her gaze before the villainous voice of curiosity persuaded her to further ogle the bizarre film.

A booming baritone rang out through the PA system as the screen went black.

"It seems someone has taken it upon themself to hijack the evening with this distasteful piece. Ladies and gentlemen, I apologize for the unscheduled breach in tonight's program. Let us continue to the next film."

Kenna's eyes flitted to Liam. He maneuvered the lip ring with his tongue, appearing to be on the verge of tears.

She knew he was telling the truth, that it wasn't his work, and his string of misfortune was shaping up to be anything but coincidental.

Someone had it out for Liam.

### Dayton

The two hours Dayton stood in the packed, darkened venue were torturous. Sure, the reactions from the first few minutes of the X-rated flick filled him with a sickening delight, but beyond that, the affair was mind-numbing. He could hardly make out the tops of Liam and Kenna's heads from such a distance, let alone monitor where their hormone-driven hands were undoubtedly wandering. The thought of Liam touching her had him seething.

His lamb. His skin.

Bursting out of the main doors, he barreled down the first set of stairs, and then the second. He crouched on the bottom step and gazed up at the clear night sky. Dayton planted his legs apart, cradling his head in his hands. Weakness devoured him. Had he become softer since scoring Jasmine? Or had it been the misery that followed?

Either way, the thought made him ill. He was getting too attached to the woman who was solely sought out for his passionate harvest. Once he'd ravaged Kenna, she'd be gone.

As if on cue, her distinct feathery voice resonated in the foreground of Dayton's pity party. Heels and sneakers clacked and clomped against the cement steps, the hideous symphony of a mass exodus.

"That sucks they couldn't find your film," he heard her say. The sound was not so distant.

"Guess I'm having a string of bad luck," Liam said.

Dayton spied through a ridge on his coat sleeve as they passed, admiring Kenna's straight strands dancing in the breeze. A glossy pumpkin shade coated her lips and complemented her natural hair color. He'd spent so much time staring at her magnificent mouth since they started working together, he knew its every crease, curve, and crack.

Liam scuffed his shoe on the sidewalk. "Do you wanna grab a slice at Vinny's?"

Pathetic. Surely Kenna would never be interested in someone who bathed in the waters of such cowardice.

"I ate earlier, actually. But I'll see you at trivia next week."

Her declination rang in Dayton's ears like a victory bell.

"Maybe you can come over sometime to see my film." He backpedaled from where she stood in the middle of the deserted walkway.

Over my dead body, Dayton thought.

He reached inside the breast pocket of his coat, feeling the

DVD he'd lifted from the projection area. The chances of reclaiming his filthy tape were unlikely. It wasn't a considerable loss; an expansive collection lived beneath the floorboards of his home, some of which were personally directed.

"Maybe."

Judging by her tone, she wouldn't give the offer a second of consideration and it made his heart soar.

Even though Liam had gone, Kenna lingered.

Her arms were wrapped around her body as if shielding herself from the biting cold and she stared out into the dark expanse of the campus. The blue bike was anchored on a nearby rack—but she was in no hurry to retrieve it. Kenna remained on the path, mute and unmoving, studying the sinister landscape of the university under the ominous lens of the starless night.

Dayton couldn't let her stand there a second longer, angelic and abandoned in the moonlight.

## Kenna

Kenna fixated on Markham Hall, which appeared less stately under the shadowy veil of nightfall. A couple of lights illuminated windows throughout the building.

None on the third floor.

This eased her worry for all of five seconds, but an unrelenting doubt persisted. She didn't know what kind of company Liam kept, and perhaps someone in his social circle—or an enemy—was responsible for the car, the film. But the day he asked her on this date blared in her mind like a siren.

It was the day in the library, the day Dr. Merino had been there. As she considered this, Kenna reflected on their Valentine's Day conversation, when she had volunteered information about the date. The reexamination gutted her, leaving her insides hollow.

"Didn't anyone ever tell you it's dangerous to go somewhere alone at night?"

Speak of the devil.

A cocoon of chills coiled around Kenna's spine at his menacing intonation of the comment. She spun around to face Dr. Merino. "What are you doing here?"

He shoved his hands into his pockets, emitting a throaty laugh. The low, manufactured rumble was terrifying.

"Why do you always question my whereabouts? This campus is mine as much as it is yours."

"For the record, I wasn't alone until a few minutes ago." A tightness settled over Kenna's features as her guard went up. Like a unified mental front would protect her in this situation. "Why are you here?"

"Oh right, your date."

The condescending overtone of the remark implied that he had not forgotten. Not for a second.

"If you must know, I was working late."

Kenna glanced around them, revealing not a soul in sight. He could've thrown her in the trunk of his station wagon and no one would bear witness.

An intense shiver radiated from her core but she regained enough strength to offer a jab. "Funny, I didn't think you had enough work to keep you here this late."

"Are you freezing or are you just happy to see me?"

The tip of his statuesque nose was pink, implying he had been outside for a prolonged period of time and it led her to believe his presence outside of the theater wasn't entirely coincidental.

He ventured closer. Kenna fought the urge to create more distance. She couldn't come off as outwardly frightened by him. He was undeserving of that satisfaction.

She had to forge bravery.

"You're the one with the doctorate, why don't you figure it out?"

Dr. Merino bent down, his cracked lips brushing against her hair. The moment that passed before he spoke seemed like an eternity. Fear had her in its chokehold and the suffocation was real, not a figment of her imagination, and her blood ran cold as he hovered in her personal space.

His breath blazed across her cheek.

"Good evening, Miss O'Callaghan."

13

# MEDICINAL

Dayton

Kenna had stoked a ferocious fire within him—one which required herculean might to contain until he returned home.

Dayton battled with the clasp and zipper of his slacks, pinching a bit of skin in his haste and muttering a curse at the sharp pain. The front door sealed as he collapsed against it; he slipped a hand under the band of his boxers no sooner than it clicked shut. The coolness of his fingers curled around his heated sex made for a pleasurable contrast.

A faint hint of Kenna's perfume played off of his coat. Those hardly detectable notes of sweetness gave him a livelier rush than the purest methamphetamine.

He had never felt more alive, more present.

Closing his eyes, he released a ragged breath, lifting his chin to expose his neck. His back remained flush with the door, stance unfaltering. Lightheadedness overtook him and his wrist ached from its forceful mechanics.

His full lips parted, permitting a tortured moan to escape as his climax neared. The image of Kenna spinning to face him in front of Wagner Theatre looped and swelled in his mind, as if it were refracting off a piece of broken glass. Dayton focused on the memory of her lush mouth, wondering how that sticky gloss might taste, how it might stain his skin if he were to claim those divine lips.

His orgasm raged through him, paralyzing every nerve ending in his quaking body, the hot fluid dampening his underwear and seeping onto his dress pants.

Steadying himself, Dayton opened his eyes.

Catching his breath proved more strenuous than usual and concern rose within him as it took a concerted effort to regain a healthy rhythm.

A tightness resonated in his chest, one that was all at once familiar and frightening.

## Kenna

Heartbeat thrashing in her ears, Kenna checked the lock on the apartment door three times before bolting through the hall. She tripped over her guitar case in the pitch black bedroom, mumbling a grunt of annoyance when she shoved herself off the carpet. A yank of her lamp's cord flooded brightness into the space.

She grabbed her laptop and sank to the floor at the foot of the unmade bed. Fingers fidgeting on the keyboard, she typed the password incorrectly—twice. As the homepage of Facebook loaded, Kenna pulled up a separate window which contained bits from her internet sleuthing and zeroed in on a single line of text in the sparse document: Charlee Pender.

Did her madness have any merit?

Waiting around for the answer was no longer an option. Dr. Merino's sudden appearance after Liam had gone felt like a personal threat. A threat she refused to ignore.

Kenna typed the name into the site's search box. Three results. She clicked through the first two profiles, weeding out the impostors. Faintness threatened to claim her when she stumbled across the correct page.

This woman lived in Missouri, but the 'Ponderosa University Class of 2016' in her bio section did not go overlooked. She was *the* Charlee Pender.

The cursor hovered over the 'add friend' button momentarily before she had the nerve to go through with it. Her stomach churned like a cement mixer, willing her to succumb to a permanent state of anxiety.

She caught her breath. There was no turning back.

*Charlee,*

*We don't know each other, but I'm reaching out with the hope that you'll shed some light on something I'm going through.*

*What can you tell me about Dr. Merino?*

No relief came from pressing 'send.' Kenna was stuck with Dr. Merino the rest of the semester, regardless of what Charlee had to say about him.

But she'd already opened this can of worms. It was no use coaxing them back in their vessel.

## Dayton

Thursday afternoon, Dayton perched in the windowsill of his office. The fumes from his blunt danced through the cracked window and dissolved into February's fog. On occasion, students pointed or shot him dirty looks, but he never paid them any mind. It's not like he owed them an explanation; they weren't his employer.

He drew in a deep drag, resulting in a fit of coughing that stung his chest, followed by a fragmented exhalation.

"Fuck," he mumbled.

Phoning his cardiologist wasn't on the day's to-do list. The idea nauseated him.

A quick consultation of his wristwatch revealed that Kenna's arrival was still an agonizing nine minutes away. He brought the blunt to his lips once again, inhaling with less vigor. Dayton's hand braced his forehead then migrated into his thicket of charcoal hair. When he looked up, his green-eyed seductress stood shell-shocked near the entryway.

Kenna's appearance was God's way of insisting, 'Don't say I never gave you anything.'

Dayton carried on smoking, ever nonchalant.

"You're early."

Her eyes communicated her embarrassment more than any expression or speech; the way they twitched at the tear ducts, struggling to maintain the width to which they were stretched.

"I didn't mean to intrude. I ran out of things to fill the time and thought you'd be free. I can step out if—" she rambled, turning to leave.

"Settle in. I'll be done in a few minutes."

There was something about her Dayton was coming to adore. Her shy apologies and pure aura made Kenna more addicting than her predecessors and he had no doubt she'd be a harder habit to kick by the end of it.

She watched him as she unpacked. He could feel her eyes boring into him from across the room. It was not an unwelcome sensation. "Sorry, is that …?"

"It's medicinal." He blew a concentrated line of smoke out the window. "Okay, it's not. Actually, my doctor is begging me to give it up." He shrugged. "Old habits die hard."

A calculative stare crossed her face. What was circulating through her pretty little head? What Dayton wouldn't give to have known.

He extended the blunt in her direction, "Want some? Midterms are coming up."

Dayton was the snake proffering the apple, but Kenna made for a reluctant Eve. She smiled like he was a madman.

If only she knew.

"I don't do drugs."

"This grows in the ground. I'd hardly call it a drug." Dayton extinguished the embers and left it on the outer ledge as per standard operating procedure. He started the diffuser on the way to his desk. "I'm relieved this is out in the open, but I guess you would have found out eventually."

Kenna stifled a laugh by clasping a hand on her mouth. What a glorious sight, innocence abounding. She began writing in her journal, as she called it.

"What's so funny?"

Setting her pen down with a degree of gingerness, she said, "Your afternoon pleasantness isn't such a mystery anymore."

Half of his facial muscles flexed to produce a shrug of a smile. "You're entertaining, kid."

## Kenna

High on the list of things Kenna couldn't stand was Dr. Merino's insistence on calling her 'kid.'

It was always 'kid,' or 'Miss O'Callaghan.' 'Red-headed bitch' was preferable to *kid*. She'd walked in on him smoking pot. Surely they'd entered a new circle of honesty.

"Dr. Merino?" He glanced up from his paperwork, glassy gaze acknowledging her for half a second. Even in that brief window, Kenna felt like a live sample squirming under the lens of a microscope. "I don't enjoy being referred to as a kid. I'm 21."

He leaned back in his chair, chest heaving. Was he tired? Annoyed, maybe? She didn't care. Still, her mind wandered to these corners.

"I didn't realize it upset you. You're a lot younger than me, is all. I'll stick to Miss O'Callaghan."

She noted his sharper style. Dr. Merino wore a white dress shirt, a navy sweater over top. Why the sudden shift? It wasn't the weather. In fact, it was starting to warm up. If it was a bid for attention, it had worked, as much as it pained her to admit. Handsome as the Devil had never rung truer.

"You look nice."

God, what had she done?

Forearms planted on the desk, he disregarded the haphazard stacks of documents completely. She became Dr. Merino's sole focus. This would've been a show of respect with anyone else, but with him it felt like a punishment, as if she were shoveling coal in the fiery pits of Hell.

"Are you flirting with your mentor while he's under the influence?"

"No." Kenna cast her eyes away.

They both knew it was a lie.

14

# CHARLEE

**Kenna**

*S*he'd scheduled a video call with Charlee for 7 p.m. and the clock read 7:08. Eight minutes was enough to warrant panic. Charlee had second thoughts. That was it.

If the Pender woman flaked on her, Kenna would have entered an undefined degree of psychological distress.

A walking, not yet recognized DSM entry.

The apartment was empty. Quiet. Alex was at a concert in Portland and wouldn't return home until late.

She poured a generous amount of red moscato. The rose-tinted liquid sloshed around in the glass until she retracted the bottle. The scene presented itself as a pair of girlfriends gearing up for a casual conversation though it was destined to be anything but. A pen and notebook stood by for their deployment. She was armed and ready. Still, an air of unease simmered in her gut.

The call would either quell her fears or worsen them. She'd spent the bulk of the afternoon praying for the former.

But if there was nothing to tell, Charlee wouldn't have been calling.

Kenna nearly spilled her wine as a loud, cheery ringtone blared. She accepted the incoming call and her adrenaline descended from its astronomical peak as Charlee materialized on the screen.

"Sorry for the delay. I'm notoriously awful with wine corks."

Her golden blonde hair was identical in length to Dr. Merino's, stopping short at her shoulders. It bobbed while she scooted her chair in at what Kenna assumed was a dining table.

She raised her own bottle. "Twist top."

"I need to make that switch." Charlee sipped from a petite stemmed glass. A faint smile played at her raspberry glossed lips, like the forced joviality was an effort to cheer herself up. She looked like the poster girl for some off-brand antidepressant. "I almost canceled."

"I'm glad you didn't."

"How did you find me? He didn't say anything, did he?"

Her defensive, paranoid edge made Kenna's scalp prickle. With those two questions, Charlee had set the tone for the conversation that lay ahead; the one that she had awaited with raging anxiety. Now, that anxiety morphed into a more menacing feeling. One of terror, uncertainty.

Despite the obvious threat of danger, she proceeded.

"I saw a picture of you two on the *Herald*'s website, taken at the Alzheimer's 5K." Realizing the information may have sounded creepy, she added, "I googled him."

Charlee redirected her gaze to the keyboard. "So, is Dr. M your shrink or your mentor?"

"Mentor."

"Just like me." The murmur almost went unregistered by the laptop's microphone. Her mouth twisted in a grim manner, resembling neither a frown nor a smile but rather something that was altogether unpleasant. She deadpanned, "Is he still calling you 'miss?'"

Kenna didn't like the aura of discomfort that accompanied the woman's foul expression, nor did she like the pointed question. Whatever answer she provided, she'd be met with an unfavorable response. There was something in Charlee's face that hinted toward horror, the way her damp eyes pleaded through the poor resolution of the display.

"Miss O'Callaghan."

"Try to keep it that way. When he starts calling you by your first name, you're fucked."

She skimmed the list of questions she'd jotted down. Charlee had communicated her pain before the verbalization of a single one.

A formal approach would've been inappropriate, especially since she had skin in the game. Script be damned.

"What happened with the two of you?"

"Fall of senior year, he was my mentor. When we started working together, I thought he was an asshole—but in a sexy way, you know? Later, I found out he was just really lonely; but there was something enticing about that."

Kenna knew precisely what Charlee meant. Dr. Merino was mysterious—there was no denying that—but it was tinged with malevolence and that was decidedly not sexy.

Not by her standards.

"Our dynamic shifted over the months. It was so subtle, I didn't realize it was happening, but thinking back on it now, it's clear as ever. Like he'd had everything planned from the start, from our first meeting." Charlee tugged at one of her teardrop-shaped earrings and her mouth pulled into something reminiscent of a smile as her eyes brightened. "That picture you saw, from the 5K? He kissed me that day. Really kissed me. Toe-curling, heart-pounding, magic. But I was in a committed relationship at the time, and I didn't know how to handle Dr. M's advances."

Kenna's throat went dry.

She should've taken notes, but she was so engrossed in the

story that picking up the pen became an impossible task. The comment about Dr. Merino's planning called to mind the snafu with her file.

She feared that his methodical hunt for information went beyond vetting her for their partnership and, as she pondered this, her lungs bordered on collapse, crushed beneath the weight of possibility.

"Not long after that, my boyfriend broke it off with me. No explanation. I was crushed. I mean, things between us were never great. We had our fair share of problems, maybe more than most, but the way he ended it, it was out of nowhere. Three years of our lives thrown away." Her speech yielded to the fist pressed to her trembling lips. "I knew Dr. M had a thing for me, and I know this sounds awful, but I used him as a distraction."

"Then we started sleeping together and he became clingy, the closer we got. I didn't see it as a cause for alarm." Charlee's arms drew close to her torso, protecting herself from the resurfaced memories. "But the clinginess turned into jealousy. Fast. He always wanted to know where I was, who I was with, and I guess my answers weren't enough because at one point, I found a GPS tracker on my car. And he'd yell," her soft voice cracked. "He'd yell at me, make me feel worthless, like I didn't mean anything when I wasn't loving him."

Kenna felt a pang of regret at making her revisit the trauma. Then she reminded herself that Charlee had volunteered to disclose the information and that's what she was after, wasn't she? Research.

If she could use this experience to keep herself, and other women, safe, then the result of the evening would far outweigh resurrecting Charlee's hurt for 45 minutes.

"I'd planned to stay at Ponderosa for grad school, but I was ready to get away from Dr. M. I ended it with him, told him I was going back to Missouri for my master's. He seemed relieved, almost, that I was leaving. I thought it was really weird, you know?

One minute, he was obsessing over me and the next he was scrambling to get rid of me. He even offered to write me a letter of rec for my application to Missouri State. So I packed up and here I am. Haven't spoken a word to him since."

Kenna teetered on the edge of her wooden desk chair.

"And the letter?"

"He wrote it and mailed it to the school. As promised."

Charlee sunk into her own seat. The portrait of a defeated woman. Years had passed, and yet she still reeled at her fling with Dr. Merino, still trying to make sense of it.

Eyes shining, she whispered, "He broke my heart."

Kenna's own heart ached for her. She understood perfectly well what it was like to fall for someone and then to have it all ripped away. She gripped her knees and let loose what she'd wanted to say since the call began.

"I think he's stalking me."

Laughing through tears, Charlee swept her pointer finger beneath each eye and when she caught her breath, she poured a third glass of wine. "Dayton can be intense, but seriously?"

"You said he put a GPS tracker on your *car*."

"Sure, it was a little creepy that he kept tabs on me, but we were in a relationship. It was different."

She and Charlee had differing definitions of stalking.

There was something else she was dying to ask, and with Alex out of the apartment, she couldn't pass up the opportunity. "Can I ask you one last thing?"

"Shoot."

"My roommate hates him. The problem is, she won't say anything. I guess I was wondering if, maybe, you knew her. She would've been a sophomore when you were a senior. Her name's Alexandria Guerrero."

Charlee froze, repeating, "Guerrero?"

A knot twisted itself in Kenna's stomach. "Yeah."

"Dr. M kept this book on his coffee table. I don't remember

what it looked like or the name or anything, but it had an inscription. *Love, Miss Guerrero.* The rest of it was in cursive. Hard to read. I never bothered asking him about it. I just figured he had a habit of dating his mentors. He's not the most agreeable person, in case you haven't noticed."

Miss Guerrero, 'Señorita Guerrero' as he'd called her in the parking lot. Kenna bit the inside of her cheek until she tasted blood. The bombshell left her dizzied by manic curiosity.

Alex was indisputably tangled in Dr. Merino's mess.

# March

# 15

# PONDEROSA PINES

**Kenna**

She smoothed out the numbered sticker on the hip of her yoga pants, identifying her as runner 326 among the crowd of 512. Getting up at 6 a.m. to run a 5K with Dr. Merino wasn't how Kenna pictured spending her midterm break.

It was part of their contract and he'd made it clear she was in no position to refuse.

Orange ribbons and rubber bracelets were being passed around to bring awareness to self-harm awareness month. Small groups gathered and took pictures of their 'float on' and semicolon tattoos. Some paraded their scars, wearing muscle shirts and shorts in defiance of the low temperature. It was a beautiful thing to witness people rallying around each other.

Survivors and their beloved.

The sun greeted the sky, golden rays of morning light shining through the gaps in the army of pines.

Even in the midst of the serene, Oregonian daybreak, Kenna likened the scenario to a nightmare. Being with Dr. Merino outside of campus had her anxious, especially in light of the call with Charlee.

At least if something went wrong, there were 510 people around to rescue her.

"You're going to be sore later if you don't stretch." Dr. Merino bent and twisted his body, resembling an origami crane while gripping an ankle to prime his hamstrings. The muscular tone of his calves didn't escape her notice.

She hated herself for staring.

"It's a chance I'm willing to take." Kenna tugged on the cuffs of her snug-fitting athletic pullover and rotated her upper half from side to side in an effort to humor him.

He wore a similar jacket, with an identical high neck and a quarter zip. She wondered if it made them look like a couple to passersby. The idea sickened her. He kneeled to sit on the damp grass, grabbing his toes while lowering his torso to the ground and she got a good look at his sullied tennis shoes.

"Is this something you do often?"

"What, running?" His unruly locks fell over his face. "All the time. It keeps me somewhat sane."

"I had a boyfriend who ran cross country. I never understood the fascination."

She never saw the so-called boyfriend beyond the walls of her high school but she didn't consider that a relevant detail.

Dr. Merino adopted a pinched expression, as if the mention of past lovers had upset him. "It's freeing. It makes your problems seem insignificant, if only for a short while."

Charlee had said he was jealous. Hearing about his behavior and experiencing it firsthand were two different beasts. In researching him, he'd posed little threat to Kenna.

Standing there with him at the mouth of the dense woods, she felt like a nervous zookeeper on their first day in the lion's den.

A crowd formed at the edge of the forest as the start time drew nearer. Kenna recognized a few faces from school, professors and a handful of students.

The event coordinator prattled on about the course and where it ended up, but she couldn't focus on what was being said as everyone advanced toward the speaker. The resulting arrangement of bodies was packed so tightly it would've weeded out any claustrophobes.

Dr. Merino towered beside her, pressed as close as possible without making physical contact. Kenna swore she felt his body heat. It was unimaginable that such warmth could radiate from someone with a chilling demeanor.

He seemed unbothered by their proximity, tucking his hair behind his ears while listening to the man's speech and she was troubled that the lack of distance between them did not bother her, either.

No matter how uneasy he made her, she was drawn to him like a moth to a flame—all at once helpless and sucked in by the sliver of light he seldom spared.

The lines of academic interest and repulsive sexual attraction blurred in the context of this new environment.

Kenna considered the absurdity of the situation.

Any minute, she'd be swallowed by the forest with her possibly deranged mentor for a running companion. They'd both left their cell phones in his station wagon.

A sigh dismissed her overactive imagination. Though he may have had some villainous leanings, she was pretty sure he didn't plan on dismembering her and leaving the body parts to rot at the base of a red alder.

Hacking women to bits didn't quite seem like his modus operandi. Maybe it was foolish to put that blind faith in him but Kenna reckoned it was best to forge a brave front.

The speaker raised a starter pistol in the air.

Dr. Merino whispered, "Try to keep up, kid."

*Bang!*

## Dayton

The scaly, russet trunks of ponderosa pines whirred by in his peripherals as he sprinted off into the thick woods, blending in with the herd of runners and leaving Kenna in the dust. Dayton planned to slow down for her, but not yet. She had to earn it. The course was marked. It wouldn't be difficult to find her if they got too separated.

"Dr. Merino!" came Kenna's distant call.

Rather than wait for her to catch up, Dayton hustled to create more distance between them. He wanted to know how far he could push her. How long would she chase him before throwing in the towel?

The sensation of the wet earth beneath his pummeling feet felt like home. Everything here was beautiful: the tarrish black bark of youthful trees, the decaying moss-covered logs, the way the budding sun and cotton clouds hung overhead like an outdoor Sistine Chapel. The familiar scent of recent rain and the saccharine vanilla fragrance of the pines intensified as he progressed on the trail. Kenna's pleas had become so distant, they were no longer audible.

When it seemed unlikely that she'd reappear, Dayton turned on his heel and retraced the winding course in search of her. Several participants gawked at him, as if to question, 'Do you know you're running the wrong way?' A quarter of a mile back, he found her, trotting along at a beginner's pace.

"You're a jerk."

Wrath guided Kenna's footfalls. She made the most contemptible emotions appealing.

He jogged backward in front of her. "Lighten up. It's going to take us a month to finish at the rate you're going."

"Slow and steady."

"Don't throw that Aesop shit at me. This isn't a race. It's for a good cause."

Kenna bolted past him, exuding a sudden surge of energy. "Oh, yeah? Then why did you leave me in the middle of the woods?"

Dayton closed the gap with minimal effort.

"I came back for you, didn't I?"

"You're infuriating," she spat.

He risked a glance at her form, enthralled by the tight fit of her track jacket. Her figure was revealed to him in a new way, no longer disguised by the loose tops and flared jeans she wore to campus. The jacket's material clung to her fragile wrists, her narrow shoulders, her subtle suggestion of an hourglass waist. For someone who had such delicate features, Kenna was the furthest departure from the word.

Their pace had quickened to the point where conversation became challenging.

He didn't mind the silence, at first, satisfied with stealing glimpses of the ethereal being trotting alongside him. But Dayton's frustration grew as they advanced on the trail. Kenna was a tough nut to crack and she showed little sign of easing up. She'd surprised him when she complimented his appearance in the office.

Beyond that, it was hard to tell if she was interested.

When they hit the two-mile marker, their speed reduced to a jog. Her pin-straight ponytail bobbed in time with her feet hitting the ground.

He yearned to grab a fistful of that glamorous hair, to hear what breathy sighs might accompany such an action.

"I'm sorry I blew up on you. But you have to admit, that was a shitty thing to do." Kenna expelled the apology while rubbing her nose with the back of her hand.

"I deserved it."

A splintering ache spread through his chest. Lightheadedness enshrouded him with the haziness of a fog, hindering his ability to focus on the path ahead. Dayton knew he needed to stop and take a breather, but he refused to appear weak in Kenna's presence. He ignored his body's warning and pressed on against his better judgment.

"You're adorable when you're angry."

She shook her head and let a faint smile slip. If Dayton's heart didn't give out first, that demure expression would be the death of him.

"You can't talk to me like that. We have a conflict of interest. But I don't suppose that means much to you."

"Careful, you're treading hypocrisy."

Irritation bubbled at his core, spiking his body temperature. Her mixed signals were vexing. She had gone from ogling him in his office to rejecting his innocent romantic advancements. Their cat and mouse game had grown stale.

How apropos it would be to claim his forest queen against the backdrop of these picturesque woods. Dayton yearned to rip Kenna from the course and kiss her senseless against a white oak. He knew she wasn't ready for that.

She wasn't convinced; she didn't trust him.

There was more work to be done.

"You smoke recreational pot in your office. Rules mean nothing to you," Kenna ventured.

"Could be worse. Sigmund Freud had a nasty coke addiction."

She laughed through her broken breaths and it sent a jolt of electricity through his spine.

Something akin to butterflies spasmed in his sternum—or maybe it was the cursed heart palpitations. The deceleration of Dayton's breathing begged him to stop. He continued to sprint but fell behind her on the muddied path.

"What's the matter, Rocky? I thought you were in it for the long haul," Kenna teased over her shoulder.

Her look of soft flirtation broke him and he was incapable of a witty retort, incapable of producing any sound. A wildfire blazed his insides as the pain in his chest spread. One that was all too familiar.

This couldn't be happening. Not now.

Dizziness consumed him, blurring his vision, as his knees buckled and he dropped to the ground.

## Kenna

Aside from the bit where he had called her adorable, their light-hearted conversation had put Kenna at ease. Who would've known she was capable of feeling relaxed in the presence of one Dayton Merino.

He had fallen behind her on the trail but she continued to push ahead, reasoning that he would catch up. When he didn't respond to her Rocky remark, that unease crept back as if it had never abandoned her.

Her movement slowed until she came to a stop and she turned around to find Dr. Merino crumpled in the dirt.

Did he really think she'd fall for that?

Faking an injury to get a rise out of her seemed awfully juvenile. Then again, she never thought she'd hear him cracking jokes about illegal substances. Grinning and shaking her head, she sprinted to examine his static body.

"Very funny. C'mon, get up." Kenna folded her arms, eyeing the motionless man.

No response.

She knelt beside him, hesitantly reaching out to grab his shoulder. The action shifted him onto his back. His lids were closed, black lashes glued to his cheeks like a million spider legs. His jaw had slackened, mouth slightly agape. Panic elevated in Kenna.

It didn't seem like he was faking it.

Lightly, she shook him. "Dr. Merino? Can you hear me? Dr. Merino?" She yelled, "Dayton!"

That would've gotten his attention had he been messing around.

His medical bracelet was absent from his right wrist.

*Should something happen to me, it contains all of the relevant infor-mation.* Why did he own the life-saving jewelry if he didn't bother wearing it at all times?

Kenna placed her pointer and middle finger on his left wrist, measuring his pulse. The beating was sluggish, like it would stop without a moment's notice. "Shit."

He needed help. Now.

Her gaze darted around the woods. Not a soul in sight.

She swallowed the lump in her throat and screamed at the top of her lungs. "Help! If anybody can hear me, please help! There's an emergency! Please help us!"

By the time Kenna's lungs burned from the incessant shouting, fellow runners finally materialized at the scene. More and more people emerged in the clearing. One man removed his backpack and placed it under Dr. Merino's head, mumbling something about elevation. The frantic chain of events unfolded faster than she was able to comprehend.

An elderly runner donned in shorts that were much too short waved his phone in the air. "I called an ambulance. They're on the way but we've got to get him to the main road."

"We'll have to carry him," the man with the backpack conjectured.

Her head twirled like a spinning top. The dizzying curtain of reality clouded the questions filtering through her mind. Kenna clung to the small group of people trekking through the woods, never straying from the trio of men carrying Dr. Merino's limp body. Vomit simmered at the base of her throat. Her uncertainty toward his character faded from her subconscious in the midst of the chaos.

Leaving his side wouldn't be permissible.

The ambulance arrived, its blaring siren disrupting the peaceful morning. EMTs sprung into action, transferring Dr. Merino to a stretcher with disconcerting efficiency. Kenna could hardly believe what was happening. And yet, a faint degree of logic persisted. She couldn't let him wake up in the hospital alone, provided that he did wake up.

Approaching the rear of the ambulance with haste, her toes curled as she watched the techs lift her unconscious mentor inside the vehicle. One of the EMTs took note of her sudden appearance.

"Ma'am, are you family?"

"No. I'm his girlfriend."

Kenna lied without effort but felt no guilt.

"Come on up," the EMT motioned, helping her climb through the open doors. The tech gestured to a seat which had been folded down from the vehicle's wall. "You can sit there, miss."

A wave of dread threatened to drown her upon realizing that the EMTs would likely expect her to supply them with a ton of information. She found it funny that the basic facts of Dr. Merino's existence evaded her, but she knew more intimate details of his life. Perhaps if the techs were privy to Charlee Pender's tale, they'd feel less inclined to help the man strapped to their stretcher.

Kenna banished the thought.

The negative headspace achieved nothing. He had treated Charlee poorly but that didn't mean he deserved to die.

She gripped Dr. Merino's hand as the ambulance sped off toward the hospital. Their callousness came as a shock, palms boasting the dull roughness of weathered sandpaper.

Her thumb stroked the smooth topside of his hand. She'd probably look back on this instance and shudder once her panic sobered.

Relief flushed through Kenna when his fingers writhed beneath her grasp.

16

# WARNING

**Kenna**

*D*ouble doors shielded the relative calm of the waiting room from the raging maelstrom inside the emergency room. The people who occupied the lobby pretended to watch the news or scanned magazines, patiently standing by to be called back.

Kenna hadn't an ounce of patience to spare.

She'd paced every inch of the floor and the soles of her feet bordered on raw. An earthy scent clung to her clothing and hair, made more noticeable with each stride. A hot shower and a glass of wine would've worked wonders for her stench and stress.

Three hours had passed since they'd taken Dr. Merino back for diagnostics and a slew of other tests.

For all she knew, he could be dead.

She didn't have her phone, wallet, or a ride home, but none of that mattered. He was an ass most of the time, yet here she was in the E.R. anticipating an update. She couldn't help but think God was punishing her for harboring such opinions.

Heaven shone its divine light in the depressing waiting room when the woman at the check-in desk spoke.

"Is anyone here with a Dayton Merino?"

Kenna's feet were reluctant to propel her in the direction of the desk, her steps unsteady from the ceaseless pacing. Her stomach turned sensitive, either a result of not having eaten since dinner the previous night or her bewildering concern for Dr. Merino's well-being.

In a low voice, she asked, "Is he okay?"

"He's stable. They're moving him to the C.C.U., third floor, Room 319," the woman informed, attention glued to a computer monitor.

"Thank you so much."

It required effort to make her break for the elevator seem not too desperate. As much as Kenna wanted to know what had happened to Dr. Merino on the trail, the knowledge of his stability was satisfactory—for the moment.

Metal doors guarded the wing labeled 'Cardiac Care Unit.' Coldness struck her core upon being faced with the bold black letters. Had it been a heart attack? If it had been a simple fainting spell, Kenna was certain his placement in this area of the hospital would be entirely unnecessary. She scoped out the location of Room 319. When she neared the command desk full of nurses, something piqued her interest.

"Merino's cardiologist cancelled the rest of his appointments for the day. 30 minute ETA," a nurse said while covering the landline's receiver.

Cardiologist? Perhaps his spell wasn't an isolated incident. Her natural inclination was to pity him, but it felt wrong to pity a menace. Sympathy persisted through her recognition of this wrongness.

Good or bad, Dr. Merino was a human being; and since no one else rushed to be by his side during this critical time, Kenna stepped up to the plate. She continued to creep along the hallway until one of the nurses stopped her.

"Hey doll, if you're here visiting I need you to sign in on this sheet." The nurse pointed to a clipboard on the counter. She obliged and filled out the required information. "He might be asleep. They put a mild sedative in his IV."

### Dayton

Dayton blinked several times, adjusting to the dim glow of the hospital room. The bright light filtering in stung his tired eyes. His sluggish movement made it difficult to push himself to a sitting position. The pain in his chest was minimal, no doubt a result from whatever swirled through the IV drip.

He regarded the medical gown he wore and groaned. So much for impressing Kenna with his athleticism. He was sure he'd looked real stoic when he collapsed in front of her.

Worse yet, the weakness he'd fought so hard to keep hidden since starting anew in Branch Spring had been exposed.

"Dr. Merino?"

The lucid voice made him straighten in the bed.

Kenna occupied a chair off to his right, still clad in her running attire. The jacket had been shed and tied around her waist to reveal a gray t-shirt.

"What the hell are you doing here?"

She leaned forward, hands on her knees. "Do you remember what happened?"

"When I hit the ground, I thought you'd rejoice that your midterm break had resumed."

She readjusted her position in the chair, compacting her entire person atop the vinyl cushion. Dirt stained her yoga pants. A lightness settled over his limbs, like he'd been filled with hot air. Had Kenna knelt down to help him? Had she put her delicate hands on him? Whispered soft words of assurance?

"You're a horrible judge of character, you know that? I lied to the EMTs so I could ride in the ambulance with you and I've been at this hospital going on four hours."

Her level of concern was surprising, yet amusing.

The corners of Dayton's mouth twitched, restraining a smirk. "The ambulance. How did you swing that, tell the EMTs that you were my girlfriend?"

"Yeah, not my finest moment." A nervous laugh escaped her lips. He'd been joking. Oh, why wasn't he conscious for this heavenly white lie? "I hope I haven't overstepped, it's just that I was caught up in the urgency of everything. I know we really don't *know* each other, but I see you practically every day and I guess I kept thinking about how weird it would be if you weren't around, all of a sudden."

Kenna's strained expression reignited his madness. Her red-rimmed eyes bore into him, begging Dayton to accept her words. This was what he'd waited for. Despite their disagreements and rocky partnership, there she was.

He had her.

A loud knock startled them both. It swung open without permission, exposing the presumptuous visitor: Dr. Stein, his cardiologist. A white patch of hair hugged his mostly bald head, which was littered with emerging liver spots.

The doctor jerked a thumb at Kenna. "Do you want the lady present for this discussion?"

Were she ever to know of his health problems, she'd hear it from him directly.

Now wasn't the time for such complications.

"Could you step out for a few minutes?"

"Of course." She practically jumped from the chair, shutting the door behind her.

Dr. Stein served him a stern look as he roosted at the end of the bed. "You didn't get my calls?"

"I was on a 5K. I didn't have my phone."

Dayton acted like the mishap was no big deal but the severity of the situation wasn't lost on him.

He had put himself at risk.

"You knew your device was on its last leg. I made that clear at your previous appointment. Do you think tackling a 5K is taking it easy? Though, I'm pleased to see you've heeded my advice about running with a partner. You'd be dead had that young lady not accompanied you."

"It was irresponsible." Pointing to the door, he said, "She's not clued in on any of this. I didn't want her to think something was up if I pulled out of the run."

"Well, the next time you have a burst of macho male energy, you'd do well to recognize when your life's on the line," Dr. Stein warned as he filled out a packet of paperwork, signing things left and right. "We need to replace your batteries and your right atrial lead. I scheduled the procedure for the earliest slot tomorrow. You should be out of here by Monday afternoon."

The doctor stood to leave, pausing when he reached the door. "Try to get some rest."

Kenna reentered the room in Dr. Stein's wake. She hovered by the doorway, as she often did in his office, pinching the skin at her throat.

"Is everything okay?"

He patted the foot of the bed and she couldn't have worn her hesitation more plainly, pulling in a deep breath.

In spite of her downturned lips, the crease between her brows, she was utterly stunning. Who knew being somber could look so lovely. Kenna settled into the designated spot though she looked unsure of the arrangement and Dayton repositioned his legs to grant her more space.

"I'm having minor surgery in the morning. I'll miss the first day back. Do you think you could put up a sign outside the office, letting everyone know I'll be back on Tuesday? I'm going to give the dean a call in a little while."

"It's the least I can do." Kenna kicked off the muddy running shoes, folding her legs beneath her.

He found it difficult to discern whether she was expressing romantic interest or if her kindness simply knew no bounds.

"So, surgery? That's pretty serious." She went mute for a beat. "Do you want me to stay?"

She'd spent all day with him as a result of the unexpected hospitalization yet she was offering more of herself.

Kenna was a saint. An angel he didn't deserve.

"I've burdened you enough today. Don't waste what little energy you have left worrying about me. I'll be alright."

### Kenna

"Really, you should go home."

She'd spent the entire day fretting over his condition and he was kicking her out. Even though he'd insisted that she leave, she saw that he was torn, in deep deliberation with himself. Dark rings clung to his eyes. He looked as though he hadn't slept in days. His collapse had taken a toll on him.

Why was he being so stubborn? Dr. Merino would benefit from the comfort of a familiar face.

He needed emotional support and that's what she intended to provide whether he wanted it or not.

"Dr. Merino, with all due respect, I want to stay. You shouldn't be alone for this."

"I think we're past formal titles. You saw me faint, for God's sake." He crossed his legs beneath the tangled sheets, insisting, "Call me Dayton."

First-name basis.

The muscles in her legs tightened and Kenna questioned her brash decision to stay.

She remembered Charlee's warning. But Dr. Merino hadn't

insisted on calling *Kenna* by her first name. If she personally extended the invitation, would she gain the upper hand? It was all or nothing. Her insides trembled, but her game face was impenetrable.

"In that case, I'd prefer you call me Kenna."

17

# LADY OF SHALOTT

**Kenna**

"I can't believe you're staying in the hospital with that creep," Alex complained no less than two seconds after Kenna climbed into the passenger seat of her Kia.

Her expression and tone aligned with that of a disappointed mother. Alex was particularly adept at making those around her feel guilty, a maternal knack that was equally irritating and endearing. Kenna was in no mood to be judged.

Last night had been pure hell.

She'd hardly slept between worrying about Dr. Merino and panicking at his nearness. How had she stumbled into this precarious position, caring for someone she feared?

She buckled her seatbelt as they pulled away from Owens-Adair Hospital and entered the main road. It pained her to leave the C.C.U., but she was in dire need of a shower and change of clothes. With Dr. Merino out of his mysterious surgery, she felt confident stepping out for a while.

"He's not all that bad."

"That's the thing about Dayton." The car rolled to a stop at the traffic light, and Alex stared Kenna dead in the eye. "He's charming, until he isn't."

"You're like that annoying person in a horror movie who warns someone about going into a haunted house. Except you won't say why it's haunted."

Her grip tightened on the steering wheel. "Maybe it's not something I want to discuss."

"And that's fine, but stop dropping hints if you aren't willing to open up about it. You've made it clear you hate him. I get it."

Kenna buried a hand in her greasy hair. Seeds of regret burrowed into her migraine-enveloped skull but exhaustion precluded her from forming an apology.

Had Alex been ready to share whatever happened between herself and Dr. Merino, she was convinced it wasn't the most apt time to stomach the news—not when she'd be stationed at his bedside another night.

## Dayton

Dayton refused the medication the nurse had offered as Kenna swept into the room. Something that might help him sleep. He eyed the pills. "What, is it your first day? I could get you fired for this."

"Sir, I just got here. I'm just following orders."

Hadn't they read his file? The hospital was a lawsuit waiting to happen.

Kenna's company was a painkiller in its own right, making the soreness in his chest subside. Damp tendrils of hair framed her makeupless face. She didn't wear much to begin with, but the bare-faced look suited her. The vibrancy of her tresses against her ashen skin likened her to a painting, something beautiful and layered and textured, too perfect to exist alongside all that was flawed in the world.

His Lady of Shalott.

He'd die to awaken to such magnificence.

"Just press the call button if you need anything." On her way out, the nurse disposed of the mini paper cup of pills but held steadfast to her attitude. "Man thinks he's invincible."

Dayton watched as Kenna set her backpack beside the chair and squatted to peer inside one of its compartments, ultimately retrieving nothing. Fists on her hips, she turned to him. "How are you feeling?"

"Fine," he shrugged. The minor movement triggered a sting below his collarbone.

The truth? He was worn to a frazzle. But this time with her was valuable. Rest was not an option.

Kenna plopped on the end of the bed, her new spot. Nimble fingers threaded her wet hair into a loose, thick braid, tying it off with an elastic that had been on her wrist. Her vacant stare fixed on the window, but he could tell she wasn't concerned with what lay outside. Returning to the present, she released a weighted sigh.

"Is something wrong?" Dayton asked.

She brought her knees to her chest, as if to protect herself from the question. He'd injected the right amount of sincerity in his tone to make her feel safe.

But it wasn't that easy with Kenna. She tested him, made him rethink his strategies, and that was the main contributor to his ever-growing adulation of her.

That, and the glaring issue of trust may have dissuaded her from letting a stream of honesty flow.

"I am a psychiatrist, in case you've forgotten."

"Just because we're on a first-name basis doesn't mean you get to rummage around my head." Something unfamiliar edged her tone.

A subtle note of flirtation?

"And who, dare I ask, gets that privilege? Your boyfriend?"

She stared at him with an unexpected intensity, which he found thrilling, but her response diminished some of that excitement. "If I had one, you'd know."

A friendly animosity hung between them. Kenna was the Clarice to his Hannibal. They needed each other, even if it was for wildly opposing reasons.

"I take it your date didn't go well?"

"Unfiltered response?" Kenna transitioned to her trademark criss-cross pose. A coy smile graced her lips. "A hand on my thigh 10 minutes into a first date is a huge red flag."

"Young men are like animals. Truthfully, aging doesn't save all of us." He laughed, wincing at the pain from the incision. His hand flew to the spot in reflex.

What followed was unexpected in the most delightful way. She placed her hand over the one that was limp at his side.

He marveled at the sight of her delicate hand atop his own, admiring the glow she radiated on the backdrop of his tanned flesh. Dayton studied the creases of her knuckles, the length of her nails, the chipped navy polish.

The pain in his chest worsened as she retracted her perfect hand. Grimacing, she quietly asked, "Does it hurt?"

"It's not that bad."

"Why do guys always do that?"

"Do what?"

"Pretend something's not a big deal when, clearly, it is." She accentuated the arches of her thin, pale brows. The faintness of their flex still proved intimidating.

"Miss O'Ca—Kenna, this is the second occasion I've had this surgery. The minor aches and pains that accompany it aren't unfamiliar."

## Kenna

She didn't think hearing Dr. Merino say her name would have an effect on her. To call it profound would've underplayed what she felt. The fact that he was her mentor became easier to ignore when 'Kenna' tumbled from his lips.

The lines were no longer blurred, but entirely absent. The vulnerability that shone through on his face was inescapable, piercing her like a dagger.

Therein lay the danger.

Kenna glanced between him and her backpack before crossing the room and retrieving a plastic bag from the main compartment.

"I ran across the street to the drugstore earlier, when Alex dropped me off." Her breathing accelerated as she surrendered it to him. "It's not much, but maybe it'll help you feel a little more human while you're trapped in this place."

She tugged at the hem of her shirt while awaiting his reaction. As he undid the knot, she noticed the relevant details of his hospital band: Dayton Edward Merino, birthdate 11/13/81.

He untied the bag containing deodorant, shampoo, bodywash, toothpaste, and a toothbrush. His eyes settled on her, gaze unfocused. "You're an angel."

Heat crept over her neck and shame encased her with the intention to drown. Foaming white water rapids.

He swung his legs over the side of the bed.

"Do you need help?"

"Didn't have leg surgery," Dr. Merino deadpanned as he padded to the bathroom with his new commodities.

She shook her head, smiling like a lunatic, but the second he left the room her cheeriness subsided and she grabbed her laptop from the backpack.

With any luck, he'd be in the bathroom long enough for Kenna to do some recon. The water creaked on, and she felt it was safe to pull up Facebook.

Clicking on the message tab, she scrolled through her conversation threads until she found Brandi. Her confidence faltered when the message box queued up. She rubbed her ears, releasing a fractured breath.

A few days ago she wouldn't have had any qualms sending this message. As she sat shifting in that chair, it felt like a betrayal. It would have been rotten continuing to go behind Dr. Merino's back after everything that had happened that weekend. Yet, a dogged persistence broke through Kenna's wall of guilt and that determination triumphed over the heaviness in her body. No matter what condition plagued him, he remained a danger to society—at least to the female population.

*Hey,*

*Do you think your sister would be willing to meet up with me? I can't shake what you said about Dr. M.*

Right as she pressed send, Dr. Merino partially ducked out of the bathroom. Kenna dared a glance at the bandaged left side of his bare chest. The bandage was much smaller than she'd expected, and it was in a peculiar place.

"I don't want to seem needier than I am, but could you track down a few towels?"

"Yeah, no problem."

She nearly stammered the response, fighting hard to tear her eyes away from his smooth skin. She prayed he hadn't noticed the staring and internally bemoaned what that discovery might have brought about.

A tingling sensation coasted across Kenna's cheeks as she made the short trek down the hall to the command desk. An older nurse with curly, graying hair offered a tight smile that was poised to crack her wrinkled face.

"Could I get a couple of towels for 319?"

"Sure, hun. Wait here," she said before disappearing around the corner.

Her heart lunged into her throat and her stomach bottomed out when she spotted Professor Scott approaching from the wing's entrance.

This was bound to be awkward. She could have sprinted to Dr. Merino's room and hidden in the cramped closet, could've run around the opposite side of the command desk and crouched until the unexpected visitor had left.

She did neither. Worry consumed her like an infectious disease, feasting on every cell in her body.

He beheld her with an air of suspicion as he approached, tone brimming with inquisition. "Kenna?"

"Hey, Professor Scott."

Conjuring an illusion of casualness required all of her energy. She knew this run-in wouldn't be great for her mentor's reputation. Maybe he'd ruined that on his own.

"Are you here to see Dr. Merino?"

"Yeah. How long have you been here?"

She came up empty with a reply that wouldn't result in the theorization of a scandal. The truth would have to suffice.

To hell with the consequences.

"I haven't left. Well, I went to my apartment to take a shower once he came out of post-op. Other than that, I've been here the whole time."

The candid explanation absolved her fear. If Professor Scott thought something was going on between Dr. Merino and herself, that was his problem.

"Here you are." The nurse returned with a neatly folded stack of towels, handing them to Kenna, and Professor Scott rubbed his eyelids at the exchange.

"He's uh, in the shower. It's a few rooms down."

Had Dr. Merino known he was on the way? Assigning her this errand that was perfectly primed for embarrassment. The shower was still running as they approached Room 319.

"You know what? I'll give these to him." Professor Scott seized the towels. "Why don't you give us a minute?"

"Sure thing."

Kenna had never felt a greater flush of relief as she walked away from her former professor, her mentor, and the messy predicament in which she'd found herself.

## Dayton

The hot and cold valves screeched as Dayton terminated the waterflow. Before cleansing himself, he had smelled of forest rot mingled with a malodor that was unmistakably male; and yet Kenna stayed by his side like a thirst-stricken doe who'd at last come across a stream.

A jerk of the shower curtain revealed Nathan, head cocked and a perturbed look ironed onto his face.

"Jesus," he breathed.

Dayton yanked a towel from the lopsided stack on the sink's ledge and wrapped it around his bottom half. Had Kenna been the one lurking on the other side of the curtain, he wouldn't have been in such a hurry to cover up.

"What the fuck ever happened to knocking?"

"Do you mind telling me what the hell is going on with you and Kerrygold?" Nathan snapped.

A tightness guarded his eyes, restraint working overtime. He always thought Dayton was up to no good. Usually, he was right.

And, oh, how he wished the accusation had any merit.

"Absolutely nothing. Nothing is going on between us." His hand sailed through his waterlogged hair, affording him all of two seconds to strategize a response. "We were on that 5K for self-harm awareness; I put the event in her contract. The doctor said I'd be dead if she hadn't been there."

"A convenient explanation. Too convenient. When I asked you about this at the start of the semester, you told me you had it under control and now she's bringing you *towels*?"

He exited the narrow shower stall, stepping onto the bacteria-laden hospital floor with his bare feet. "Why are you giving me such a hard time?"

Nathan threw his hands up.

"Look, I know you like to womanize, that's all. This isn't the time or place. You're mentoring this girl. Do yourself a favor and don't give her any ideas."

He wouldn't necessarily call himself a womanizer, but he'd embellished his romantic life to skew Nathan's suspicions. Dayton had slept with 10 students from their university under his colleague's nose, and those encounters had gone off without a hitch. But this was different.

Nathan knew Kenna. He'd taught her. Though, unbeknownst to Nathan, the indulgence of his fiery enchantress was not up for debate.

Dayton slipped on the crinkled hospital gown, letting the towel fall to the ground. He stepped a little too close to Nathan. "And what advice would you give me if I thought something might happen?"

"I would suggest you wait until the semester is over."

18

# ERIN

**Kenna**

The Pink Cadillac was a '60s style diner off of I-5, halfway between Branch Spring and Portland. The joint screamed Americana to the nines: a refurbished jukebox, checkerboard floor, red vinyl booths.

Though, the owners had missed a tap on the nail of nostalgia in letting the staff frolic around in jeans and t-shirts.

Brandi had been kind enough to give Kenna a ride; an opportunity to see her sister was all the incentive she needed. She left her journal in the car, planning to take notes after the discussion. This is what she'd done with Charlee and she felt it was the polite thing to do.

The last thing she wanted was to make these women feel like test subjects.

Their waitress delivered three mugs of coffee to the table. Brandi shook out two pink packets, ripped away the edges and poured the contents into her coffee. It vanished within the obsidian lake of caffeine. Kenna glanced outside, scanning for Erin's possible arrival.

Dark clouds framed the gray sky. Steady rainfall pelted the gravel in the parking lot, droplets clinging to the diner's windows. Had they been anywhere other than Oregon, the overcast weather would've been perceived as a bad omen.

"Does your sister know you're here?"

"No. If she knew I was, she'd probably turn around and go home."

"Why's that?" Kenna's fingers wrapped around her mug, taking comfort in the heat it provided.

"There's some stuff that went on between her and your kooky doctor that even I don't know about. She's made it a point to keep it from me." Softly, she added, "You're not the only one who's here to uncover the truth."

The scene was ripped straight from a movie: three women meeting at a rest stop diner by the woods to exchange valuable information. But these weren't Hollywood level stakes. This was real life.

Kenna bounced a foot as Erin's ETA drew nearer. Would she be able to face Dr. Merino once she'd unearthed another woman's truths about him?

A woman in her mid to late 20s with copper box braids and a stylish violet raincoat strode through the front door. Coming up to their table, she slipped Brandi a grim smile. "I should've known you'd be tagging along."

"She needed a ride."

They were sisters. Kenna knew what that was like. There was no hope of pulling the wool over each other's eyes.

Erin slid into the unoccupied side of the booth and shimmied out of her coat. Her attention fell to the stranger. "You must be Kenna."

"Thanks for agreeing to meet."

While Charlee had been a mess with emotion, Erin had a calmness about her which carried a hint of severity. She was poised, collected, and ready to get down to business, but some of that calm was diminished as she regarded her younger sister.

"You don't have to sit through this, Brandi."

Eyes set to kill, Brandi leaned on the table. "I want answers just as much as she does."

"I started seeing Dayton my junior year. Nothing serious, I was dealing with some mild anxiety; questioning my major and my career choices. Pretty standard." Erin conjured a knowing smile but it departed in a flash, here and gone with the awe-inspiring beauty and quickness of a lightning bolt. "He was easy to talk to, so I kept going back."

"Were you still his patient when you two became romantically involved?" Kenna interjected, pouring more coffee from the carafe. The waitress had long since surrendered her serving duties.

Brandi's form was rigid beside her, unflinching as her sister opened up about what she'd kept hidden for years.

"No, I'd stopped attending sessions with him at that point. I knew I liked him, but it didn't feel right to pursue that interest under the circumstances." Erin's hand trembled on the handle of her mug, a crack in her carefully built armor.

Was Kenna a sadist for making these women recount their haunting memories? The simple answer was no. She didn't take any joy from seeing the anguish plastered on their faces. But her motivation to engage in these discussions tied back to settling her own paranoia, and that made her selfish at the very least.

"I started seeing a psychiatrist off-campus. I'd planned on going to Dayton's office and confessing my feelings, but he approached me before I had the chance. It was like he already knew I had a thing for him."

"He *is* a psychiatrist," Kenna said, mirroring his joke in the hospital. The remark resulted in a gentle elbow jab from Brandi. "All I meant is, he's more observant than most people."

"The sex was unreal, and the way he treated me outside of the bedroom? Even better." Her rich voice lost its power. "I should've known it was too good to be true; we were doomed to fail."

"How so?"

She felt like she was in Dr. Merino's office, conducting a patient session without his interference.

"We were together for two months. In that time, Dayton learned everything about me, but he never breathed a word about his past—college, his family, his childhood. He'd always talk about work, mostly his shifts at the emergency room. Things were always very physical with us. Opportunities to talk weren't exactly in abundance. I felt like maybe he was hiding something, but I didn't have time to mull that over." Her gaze flitted between the two younger women, eyes misting. "I found out I was pregnant."

Brandi stared at her sister with fierce incredulity while disorientation swallowed Kenna whole.

The room spun, a maddening pirouette of color, before coming into focus once more. A sour taste spread in her mouth that had nothing to do with the acidity of the subpar diner coffee. Had she heard Erin correctly?

"Once I told him about the pregnancy, the Dayton I knew morphed into this cold-hearted bastard. He told me I had to get an abortion, that it was the only logical way to deal with the situation. I told him I was keeping it, and he basically said not to expect any support from him." A single tear escaped, rolling down her cheek. "I went to the dean. I wanted to see him punished, but nothing came of it. Raza told me that he couldn't interfere with the relationship since it didn't happen while Dayton was my psychiatrist."

"That's bullshit," Kenna and Brandi uttered in unison.

She knew for a fact that wasn't true.

Psychiatrists were ethically bound to not involve themselves with either current or former patients. Maybe the dean had been worried about what light it would've painted the university in had word of the scandal gotten out.

"Nine weeks into the pregnancy, I had a miscarriage. Call it divine intervention. Dayton and I weren't on speaking terms, obviously, but I gave him a courtesy call." Erin paused, appearing to consider whether she wanted to push forward. She looked out the window and lost herself in the rainy scenery. "He said something ... bizarre. It was enough to make me never speak to him again."

In what universe was a miscarriage considered divine intervention? Kenna's pulse picked up speed. Its erratic beating nearly dissuaded her from asking the next question.

"What did he say?"

"He was talking about why the pregnancy failed." Erin's voice cracked and gave way to a raspiness. Her mouth fell open but the words were in no hurry to follow. "He said, 'There's too much light inside you to give life to such darkness.' I'll never forget those words."

"Sounds like the devil to me," Brandi mumbled.

She planted her palms on the sticky underside of the table. It may have been disgusting, but she had to make sure she was rooted in reality, that the three of them hadn't entered some alternate dimension. Because in this dimension, Kenna spent five days a week with this monstrosity.

Her stomach went rock hard. If someone were to punch her, she'd feel nothing.

Erin slid on her raincoat, signaling the end of their discussion. She rose from the booth and fanned her hair from the coat's collar. "So, I never asked, what's your connection to Satan in-the-flesh?"

"He's my mentor. It's my final semester of undergrad."

A stiffness settled over Erin, resembling someone who had been asked to identify the body of a family member amid a brutal crime scene—and her face was a haunting portrait of that moment of recognition.

Nostalgia. Quietly mourning and so obviously immersed in something that was once hers.

"If our cozy little chat wasn't warning enough, I'll give you some parting advice." Kenna's skeleton burst through her skin as Erin's hand clamped down on her shoulder. She whispered, "Don't let him get too close. He'll destroy you."

"Well, that was delightful. I'm glad I sacrificed binge-watching Riverdale for the umpteenth time to watch my sister cry in a crappy diner," Brandi said once they were en route to Branch Spring. She rubbed the back of her neck, hand lingering. Her mouth fell in a flat line. "I can't believe she never told me about the baby, never breathed a word about it. I could've helped her."

"Everyone deals with grief in their own way. Maybe your sister needed to turn inward to heal. Don't blame yourself. You had no idea what was going on. I'm sorry you had to sit through that."

Kenna scrawled away in her journal, notating the most useful pieces from the conversation. She fixated on the haunting, parting phrase Dr. Merino had delivered unto Erin.

Did he consider himself evil, or was it all an act?

She got the sense she had barely cracked the surface of the enigma that was Dayton Merino and she'd fallen into some sort of fatal attraction scenario in which she was intrigued by and frightened of him.

"So," Brandi hesitated, drawing out the vowel while flipping through the static-laced radio channels before finding an in-tune throwback station. "This guy sounds like a sociopath. Why are you so fascinated with him?"

The timing of the commentary was uncanny, as if she'd read Kenna's thoughts. She slid her pen in the notebook's spine. "Because at his core, he's still one of us."

19

# FIND THE ANSWER

Dayton

Kenna was distant that week.

His hospitalization had, without a doubt, brought them closer. He had at last scratched and peeled a corner of the mask she wore on university grounds but Dayton quickly found out that whatever degree of closeness they had shared in the C.C.U. did not extend to his office.

The repetitive, clunking echo of metal scored the room as his pen rapped atop his desk. He'd miscalculated something.

Identifying that error consumed him; he became a seven-day dry heroin addict, needle poised to penetrate a vein.

By now, he should have held some sort of sway over Kenna. Hooks anchored far too deep in her flesh to break free. She had seen through his enigmatic bait and swam away.

She sensed something rotten. Rancid.

It couldn't have been him alone that deterred her. Outside factors warranted concern. Alex was in her ear, for one, and who knew if Nathan had dared to counsel Kenna on student-faculty relations in the hospital.

Dayton's submergence in his sea of potential missteps made for a welcome distraction from his 10:30 walk-in, a melodramatic, eyeliner-wearing junior.

"I've been late to my 8 a.m. class the last few weeks. I haven't missed any classes yet but it looks like things are heading that way and that's not really an option for me, you know?" Juan shoved his hands inside the pockets of his hoodie and slouched in the chair.

Judging off appearance alone, Juan didn't fit the bill of someone who might have worried about missing classes, and Dayton had to stop himself from snorting over the concern. Beneath that Pete Wentz wannabe exterior lay a scholarship student, and those kids were held to fantastical standards at Ponderosa.

His surgical scar itched below the veil of his dress shirt. It felt as though a toothpick were dragging along the incision from the inside out. Dayton tried to be covert when his anxious fingers succumbed to the scratching, but earned a sidelong glance from Kenna. A fluttering sensation swarmed his stomach. She worried about him.

That had not changed.

"Do you think masturbation is a distraction from a more pressing issue?" she inquired, jotting notes in time with her question.

Kenna screamed self-assurance in her tight ballerina bun, spine ramrod straight and legs crossed.

She looked like a pro—if one overlooked the fact that she dressed like a long lost member of Fleetwood Mac. Dayton thought her inquisitional skills could use some finessing, though he was confident she was miles ahead of the other undergrads.

"My girlfriend broke up with me over winter break." Rubbing the back of his neck, Juan asked, "Do you think that's relevant?"

"I think it's the most relevant thing you've said," Kenna replied, oblivious to the cruelty of her words. Dayton buried his amusement and slipped into his mentor role. Head cocked, he shot her a pointed look that had her clearing her throat in an instant. "Sorry. It could be the root of your problem is all I meant. Excuse us for a second, Mr. Romero."

She bent forward in her chair, whispering, "My opinion is OCD."

Having Kenna this close and forbidden from acting was grade-A torture. Intellectual curiosity alit her face, her own brand of aphrodisiac.

He studied her jade eyes, for the first time noticing the ring of rust that clung to the edges of her pupils. "That's an apt guess with what you have to go on."

"It can be triggered, even in adults, after a traumatic event, right?"

She was right, but he wouldn't grant her instant gratification. Doing so would have been a disservice to her studies. That, and seeing Kenna sweat always left him buzzing with want, a rare occasion upon which a humanizing vulnerability shone through the academic queen's veneer.

Dayton dared to lean in a bit closer despite his supersonic pulse. "You're the student. Find the answer."

She flipped through her beat-up copy of the DSM-5, flying through its endless highlighted and sticky note-flagged pages. Running a finger along a passage, she reviewed and verified the claim before presenting it.

"Based on what you've presented us, it seems like you have adult onset obsessive compulsive disorder."

Dayton found her use of extraneous words in the diagnosis charming. Phrases like 'adult onset' bore meaning to them, but not to this patient.

"OCD?" Juan righted himself in the chair. "I don't clean my apartment seven times a day."

Biting his cheek, Dayton suppressed a smile. "Perfectionism is not the sole factor that's indicative of OCD, Mr. Romero. That's actually a harmful stereotype of the disorder. OCD is marked by a compulsion, a strong, repetitive desire to perform a certain task. In your case, it's masturbation, but yes, in someone else it might manifest as reorganizing a sock drawer or disinfecting a toilet."

## Kenna

Listening to Dr. Merino discussing their work delighted her more than she cared to admit. A flush of pink graced Kenna's cheeks as she pretended to read over some notes while he wrapped up the session, but she found herself stuck, rereading the first half of the same sentence on a loop.

The thought alone of what she had resolved to do once they were rid of Juan had a faint headache infringing on her temples. Though it was foolish, reckless, Kenna had a plan.

She'd prayed all week for the bravery to execute it.

The second the door clicked shut, Dr. Merino turned to her, chin resting on his fist. "What's going on with you lately?"

Being alone with him felt different after the handful of days they had spent together in the hospital. Muscles, more relaxed. Stomach, riddled with fewer knots. Pulse, less erratic.

But fear still sailed through her bloodstream as if it had attached itself to the elements of which it was composed.

"I'm zapped from my coursework."

He squinted. "You have three classes this semester, and I'm sure you know the subject matter well enough to do the homework in your sleep. Cut the bullshit."

Moments like this left chills pricking her skin; his convenient segues to topics she had yet to vocalize.

Kenna tucked a section of hair behind her ear and sucked in her bottom lip. She grabbed Dr. Merino's hand, resulting in a wild stare on his part.

"It's been strange readjusting to office hours given what's happened. Your … incident. Are we supposed to overlook the fact that, now, every time we step into this room, there's something thawing this space that was once so cold? Each day, this office feels less clinical and more familiar. We don't exchange niceties. We get straight to work. And while you're quizzing me on clonazepam or escitalopram, sometimes I want to stop you, because I remember you lying on the ground in the Ponderosa pines. I want to ask how you're doing, how you're feeling." Her voice begged to crack but she forbade it. The aim was to appear sympathetic, not weak. "I can't help but care after that, Dr. Merino. It's only human."

Eyebrows knitting together, his hand escaped her grip.

"I can understand how awkward this must be, and I'm sorry to have put you in that position but while we work alongside each other, we should remain professional."

Kenna gathered her belongings with great deliberation. Her body and mind required the recovery period to stabilize from what had been said. What *she* had said.

There was one thing left to do.

She hovered in the doorway and honed perfected embarrassment, fiddling with a sweater sleeve as her gaze refused to focus on Dr. Merino for more than a few seconds at a time. "I'm performing at an open mic night. 8 o'clock on Saturday, same place we do trivia. I was wondering if maybe you wanted to come out and see me play. Unless, of course, you think it would violate our professionalism."

In the unending silence that slipped by, Kenna imagined all of the cruel things he might say. She waited for rejection, to be reprimanded, for revocation of the mentorship.

None of it came.

He gave an impartial nod. "I'll consider it."

2 0

# PURGATORY

**Dayton**

Eschewing all common sense, he decided to attend—if only to keep their puzzling relationship from careening off its track. Dayton was eating out of her hand when it should have been the other way around and his acceptance of Kenna's invitation painted him an unbecoming shade of desperate, one which he intended to neutralize with his usual steely resolve and one too many vodka limes.

As he stole the last spot at the bar, he recalled her nervous little act in his office. Kenna performed about as well as someone who had taken a couple of acting classes under a second-rate instructor, someone who had starred in a singular commercial and had the gall to label it an acting career.

Yet there he was, proof of her salesmanship. Though, Dayton had only turned up because she seemed keen on skirting this professional line he had drawn between them.

Damn, if he didn't want her to cross it.

He had to constantly remind himself that Kenna wasn't a

regular hit. He was responsible for 90% of her grade, a gatekeeper to her shot at grad school.

He was approaching Charlee Pender territory.

But every time he peered into Kenna's eyes, his judgment turned cloudier. Gossip at Ponderosa spread like an air pollutant; once it made it into the airwaves, its potential for contamination was infinite. Dayton's presence in The Rusted Monkey felt like kindling for whispered accusations.

Many students socialized within the bar, along with other members of the community. A cold rush of relief flowed through him upon not recognizing any university faculty.

The performance area occupied the space where the trivia table usually stood. Its current tenant was a gaunt man who had been cursed with an unfortunate balding pattern. He clung to the microphone for support as he delivered an angsty poem in a near whisper. His father didn't love him, woe is me, every word drowning in existentialism while co-mingling with some skewed sense of self-importance.

Headache inducing.

Sasha slid a vodka lime his way without a passing glance, rushing to the other end of the bar to tend to the higher than average volume of patrons. Dayton consumed the drink within 45 seconds. He needed all the liquid courage he could get, for his eventual drunken state would make his actions later that night more believable.

"Jesus, Merino. One of those days?" Sasha asked as she poured a line of tequila shots.

"Hardly."

A sprinkling of half-hearted applause coaxed the failing to be edgy poet out of the backlit corner.

The emcee's voice broke through the sound system, "Our next guest is Portland-based author Shawn Flowers. He'll be reading the first chapter of his latest publication, *Wailing in the Wind.*"

Shawn, poorly dressed in a sweater vest and orthopedic sneakers, took the microphone and replaced it on the stand.

Jane Austen level prose wouldn't have warranted his attention once he spotted Kenna off to the left of the stage, standing in the narrow hallway by the bathrooms. Shawn's reading dialed down to near silence as Dayton studied his forest queen, undisturbed. Unaware.

Perfection ruled her tightly wound curls, hinting at synthetic creation. She tossed a bundle of them over her shoulder with a flick of her wrist. It was wondrous how Kenna's most minute movements captivated him. He often wondered if it was a result of his two years of celibacy or if a uniqueness lurked within her, a special magic she possessed that the previous women lacked.

Dayton knew better than to give in to fantasies. He could see through the pheromones and see the bitter truth.

Their tryst would end no differently.

The author was met with greater applause upon the completion of his reading when he exited the makeshift corner stage. Dayton nursed the remnants of his second drink as Kenna approached the microphone, acoustic guitar in hand. Between his earnest vodka consumption and her lethal combination of a dress and tights, it would be a miracle if he made it out of the bar alive.

He would've had no complaints had that been his final glimpse of the world.

She whispered something to the emcee and he returned with a folding chair. Lowering the mic to accommodate her seated position, she situated the instrument atop her lap and made adjustments to the tuning pegs.

"Give it up for Kenna O'Callaghan."

Several guys around the room called and whistled her name like drunken wolves howling at a full moon. Dayton drew in slow, steady breaths but felt as though his eyes were protruding out of his skull as he glared at the young men.

He pushed his empty glass toward the inside of the bar, signaling for Sasha to mix another round.

Kenna strummed a single chord with her thumb as if to find her rhythm before breaking into the first verse. Mouth close to the microphone, she delivered lyrics in a melancholic yet high-pitched voice that had the dark hairs littering his forearms standing on end. The song was familiar to him, but it was so stripped down it was near unrecognizable.

Dayton was so captivated by his mentee, he didn't notice when a third vodka lime materialized on the counter. Kenna's thumb caressed the strings a final time, at which point she offered a shy smile as she walked off stage to the tune of the night's loudest applause.

Crossbody guitar case strapped to her torso, she sauntered toward him with swaying hips and he was seeing double, no, triple. Kenna times three approached the bar.

"You made it." A sultry edge corrupted her usual sweet voice.

Or perhaps the vodka had Dayton imagining things.

Yes, he wanted to watch her hips sway and for the edge in her voice to be real rather than imagined but one look at Kenna's face reminded him of who they were, *where* they were.

"Mumford & Sons, right?" He pounded back the rest of his drink. "Fantastic performance, by the way, though I don't think you need any affirmation from me after all of that fanfare."

The shy smile she gave set his chest on fire and it was in that look, so pure and addictive, that Dayton knew for certain this woman held the power to destroy him.

That smile was like a shot of adrenaline in his veins.

It had him heedless.

He lowered his voice, private airwaves meant for them alone. "I'd offer to buy you a drink but this place is crawling with people from school."

Dayton knew how to play this game and he played it well. She had invited him out to see her play but something more underlied this evening.

Her laugh came out timid yet artificial.

"It's probably for the best."

She wanted to accept. He saw it in the flash of crackling light in her eyes that had been snuffed out upon its ignition.

Elbow on the bar, he rested his head in the palm of his hand. A non-threatening pose. "Have you been to Purgatory? It's a block up the street. The crowd's generally older than this place."

Hesitance secreted from her every pore, emanating off her skin and making it difficult to breathe in tandem with his expectancy for her to utter an agreement.

The loud voices carrying in the bar and clanking of glasses disappeared. The smell of liquor and stale cigarettes neutralized. Dayton could only see her, hear her.

Kenna batted her thick lashes. "Let's go."

## Kenna

She didn't know the place, but she didn't care.

This was precisely what she had expected to come of the evening and Dr. Merino did not disappoint.

Curiosity blanketed her brain like a fog. Fearful as she may have been to be more or less alone in a bar with him, her desire for answers to the thousands of questions throttling her ability to think was far greater. In spite of the inner erraticism, she understood what she was doing.

Lucidity was a requirement, not a suggestion.

Kenna was fully aware of the night's parameters. She knew his history and yet dared him to repeat it, sacrificing herself as the next Charlee, Alex, or Erin.

The knowledge that those women were alive and well, not six feet under, was her lone consolation as she tailed Dr. Merino into the closet-sized Purgatory.

All of 12 seats lined the bar. Four two-person booths bordered the opposing wall. Half the seats at the bar were occupied, and a couple sat at one of the tables.

Overhead hung a pair of giant onyx crystal chandeliers, radiating the dimmest light known to mankind. Votive candles in frosted jars illuminated the bar as well as the tables. Black paint coated the interior: the floor, the walls, the ceiling.

No windows.

The space looked like a vampire's lair, not somewhere mortals gathered to socialize. Everything about the bar screamed alternative. Her and Dr. Merino's shared academic vibe-killing aura should have gotten them kicked out.

"What can I get the two of you?" the blue-haired bartender inquired. Her coffin-shaped name tag read, 'Olivia.'

A butterfly was tattooed on her middle finger.

Kenna reckoned she must have shot that finger off quite a bit if she'd deemed it necessary to give its viewers some art to browse.

"A vodka lime, and whatever she's having." Dr. Merino produced his card, imploring, "Leave the tab open."

She wanted to offer to pay for her share of the bill, but she didn't have much money to go around so she swallowed her pride and ordered a glass of riesling.

Not a drop of wine had passed over her lips yet a drunken dizziness held Kenna captive as Dr. Merino carried their drinks to a two-seater booth.

Alcohol, a splendid idea while in the company of her morally gray mentor.

Her fear had peaked and been demoted to dread. No longer did she fear his presence as she slid into the booth seat across from him but rather she doubted her ability to entice him, to lure him, to get closer in order to uncover the truth.

The confines of the booth created a more intimate atmosphere than the openness of the bar. Dr. Merino still sported his work clothes: a boysenberry button-down and graphite slacks. His attractiveness had not waned since she saw him at the office.

Kenna's fingertips quivered in her lap, preventing her from sampling the wine and acting casual.

She relied on humor.

"If this is your idea of keeping our relationship professional, you may need to reacquaint yourself with the definition."

His knees brushed against hers beneath the table and she involuntarily looked away, the slight contact dredging up unwanted memories.

Liam's hand on her thigh.

How Reid Emerson's absence of remorse had almost been worse than what he'd put her through.

The contact was so miniscule, it likely went unregistered by Dr. Merino. His sluggish movement upon retrieving his glass alluded to the fact that he was at least tipsy from whatever he'd consumed at the previous bar, and that made it easier to write off the contact as accidental.

"It's the weekend. I don't think anyone here is binding us to any degree of professionalism." His lowered voice contradicted his words.

He stared into her eyes, seeming to study other details of her face. The way his dark, lifeless gaze concentrated on Kenna sent her heart racing.

Shoulders going slack, his head lolled. It was the same easy-going intoxicated demeanor she had observed every week at trivia. "How long have you played guitar?"

Talk of their personal lives was something she should've been prepared for but the election of the topic hit her like a ton of bricks. She had built a life of her own in Oregon, a testament to her independence.

Any reflection, however small, of her 18 years in New York overshadowed that progress.

"Since I was 9, 10? Something like that." She shrugged, finally tasting the wine if only to dissolve the truth welling on her tongue. He didn't need to know what her childhood had actually been like. "I would play at get-togethers after Mass, sometimes, growing up. When I was in high school, I played at weddings, cafes, anywhere that would have me, really."

"Your voice blew me away. I have to say, I never would've expected it. Ever think about L.A.?"

If Kenna's parents caught wind of even a hypothetical conversation about her venturing out to snake-infested Los Angeles, they would have demanded she return to the farm. That was something she loved about being so far away.

The distance made their demands empty threats.

"No, not for a second. I'm where I'm meant to be."

He inhaled a considerable portion of his drink. Forehead wrinkling, he asked, "Why so on edge? It's just a question."

Her hands slid across her tights. She needed a lie, quick.

"I'm not used to this." Kenna gestured between them. "Being out with … someone like you."

"Someone like me? Well, I certainly hope you don't have a habit of going out to shoddy bars with university staff. I'd *hope* this is the exception."

The moment her empty glass hit the table, Dr. Merino signaled two fingers to Olivia. Kenna was one pour of wine away from wrecking her bike into a bush on the way home.

"Would it make you more comfortable if I shared something?" A trace of a smile flashed on his face and she found something comforting, something safe in that illusory warmth. Now, as Dr. Merino's eyes settled on her, she didn't feel scrutinized by their gaze, but protected. "Why don't you extend the question? You've always had a penchant for inquisition."

**Dayton**

"What were you like in high school?"

"I was quiet. Read a lot. Those two qualities didn't do me any favors with my teammates."

"You were an athlete? Which sport?"

"Lacrosse."

'Lacrosse player' rolled off the tongue a lot easier than 'sex addicted son of family medicine doctors.' And, to his credit, it was the truth.

Kenna shuffled her feet and her boot collided with his dress shoe. An unspoken apology came in the fluttering of her lashes from her glass to him and back down again. He couldn't tell if his extra beats per minute were a precursor to an alcohol-induced arrhythmia or a side effect of her company.

For weeks Dayton had observed his delicate flower from afar and here she was, within reach. However shy she may have been in some of their interactions, he felt her petals loosening, blooming, becoming more receptive to him. Kenna leaned into the table, toward him, as if he were the sun.

How he wished he had light to give her.

"Lacrosse? Were you any good?"

"I must have been alright. I made team captain junior year." Dullness invaded his chest. "But I had to quit."

She traced the base of her wine glass, glancing between him and the tabletop. "Would that have anything to do with why you were in the hospital?"

"Turned my life upside down for a bit. I wanted to play in college. I almost tried out, but I know if I had, my mom would've driven all the way to L.A. to beat my ass." Dayton laughed, polishing off his vodka.

Kenna wasn't laughing.

Neck tensing, she whispered, "Are you sick?"

"What do you care?" he fired back with more venom than he'd intended. "No, I'm not sick. Not exactly."

"What do I care? I spent three days with you in the hospital. I barely left your side. Call me crazy, Dayton, but after something like that, I think it's only human that I'd care about you."

"Yeah, well, you shouldn't care about me beyond kissing up to me at the office. It's unwise."

Kenna clasped her hands on the table, a chess master declaring checkmate. "Then why are you knocking back drinks with me on a Saturday night?"

Her tone was even, confident.

She deserved a response that was even, confident.

"Because maybe I care just a little bit, too."

2 1

# INTERVENE

**Dayton**

Monday morning had them stumbling through awkward hoops as they attempted to reacquaint themselves with the roles that Dayton continually hoped would, by some merciful accident, be rendered null and void.

March had nearly run its course. Final exams were slated for the first week of May.

A month.

That was all the time Dayton had left to add Kenna to his box before he was on to his next subject.

The amount of alcohol he'd consumed during their outing had taken him to dark places and he considered that, for the first time, his game of seduction may end in failure.

She'd go on with her life and he would be relegated to his office awaiting the arrival of a suitable replacement 'K' all the while pretending that the stunning prospect of Kenna O'Callaghan had never existed.

Her intelligence was likely the saving grace keeping her at arm's length from a volatile affair.

Dayton observed that instinctive reservation in her deliberate, languid shimmying out of her thin coat as she trained her eyes elsewhere, like one look at him might be enough to sully her life.

Expression stony, he unlocked the filing cabinet and retrieved four blue folders. "We have appointments at 7:15, 8:15, 9:15, and 10:15. You can hang the walk-in sign after we clear the last session." He used more muscle than necessary to shut the cabinet with the aim of startling Kenna into sparing him a glance. "Busy morning."

Her eyes burned him like a summer sun.

They were crystal balls of apathy, but he declared victory in being their momentary audience.

She broke the staring contest. "One appointment shy of a full morning." Dayton had been too distracted to notice the attire gracing her body. It was the exact outfit she wore on her date with Liam. His heart thumped as she raised the paper to-go cup in the air, saying, "Thanks for the coffee."

"No problem."

He wanted to ask a simple, 'Are we good?' An innocent question which would force her to remember the weekend, who they'd become, if for one night.

"Jeremy Haines is first on the docket. His visits are usually straightforward." Dayton skimmed the documents within the patient file to avoid skimming his protege. "Looks like he's due for a medication refill."

"That'll be quick. 10 minutes tops."

Kenna dragged her chair to the right of his desk, her post during appointments that he let her occupy without complaint. She laid out her coffee, lavender notebook and DSM-5. Catching glimpses of her hands and sleeves as she went about the routine did little to satisfy him. Dayton stole a glance in his peripheral, unable to manage a full-on look, and for those two seconds relished in her shape and nearness.

"What's wrong? You're acting weird."

Dayton planted the tip of his pen atop her diagnostic manual. "I understand I never gave you a dress code, so I'm not faulting you, but trust that the next time you show up to my office dressed like this, I will send you home to change."

She blinked in rapid succession. "Are you joking?"

Chest fluttering, he lifted his chin.

"Only half joking." A mischievous smile played at his lips but it was dashed as he called, "Come on in, Mr. Haines."

### Kenna

Red danced across her line of sight when Dr. Merino commented on her outfit but she snuffed it out. Kenna had been mouthy with him in the past and it hadn't gotten her anywhere, and while anger had been her initial reaction, another part of her swooned at the nonsensical demand.

And so began her descent into madness.

She had damning evidence stacked against him; cold, hard proof that should've nipped any chance of emotional attachment in the bud.

So, why did she feel this pull toward him, this incredible if not disturbing ache in her heart that could only be soothed by his presence?

Regardless of how inclined Kenna was to explore it, the smart thing to do was to take everyone else's word about Dr. Merino and believe that he was a despicable monster.

But she'd seen him at his lowest and they could never come back from that.

Jeremy shut the door as he left the office. Paper in hand, Dr. Merino turned to her, "Would you—"

Kenna pressed her lips to his. They were warm, smooth, not at all what she'd expected.

Her stomach contorted at the brief contact, at being this close to him. Close enough to smell the coffee on his breath, to inhale the mint in his cologne.

A single purse on her part and it was over.

Dr. Merino handed her the folder labeled 'Haines.' Indifference cloaked his face and when he spoke his demeanor was calm. Steady.

"Will you file this?"

She accepted the task and flew over to the filing cabinet, opening the drawer marked 'F-J.' Kenna's ribs tightened as she combed through the expanse of folders in search of Haines' spot. Dreading the thought of returning to her seat, she slowed her search. Cold sweat broke out on her forehead.

This man held in his hands the power to make or break her impending grad school career and she had kissed him based on nothing more than a gut feeling, an undeniable tug of intuition combined with the somewhat reassuring knowledge that he had crossed lines in the past.

She was banking on the fact that he'd cross it again.

Releasing an almost inaudible sigh, she slid the folder into its rightful place. She kept her gaze downcast upon returning to her seat and pretended to review notes in the margin of her diagnostic manual.

At least her busy facade was in character.

Dr. Merino reviewed the file for the 8:15 appointment. She tried to ignore his presence, his movements, but it was hopeless when seated less than two feet apart. The ruffling of papers preceded by the grotesque moistening of his thumb filled her ears.

"We can't do this. Here," he said, eyes never straying from the paperwork.

Kenna coiled her legs around those of the chair until an ache rang out in her ankles.

He didn't say they couldn't do this, period.

It couldn't be done here, in his office, on campus—where she was a student and he an employee.

"I understand."

An insistent knock came at the door. Dr. Merino braced his hands on the edge of his desk as if to stand but halted upon consulting the time. Until it came again and forced him on his feet, the sound thundering in the small space. If it was the next patient, they were considerably early.

"I'm expecting a patient in about 20 minutes. If you'd like to speak with me I'm afraid you'll have to wait until walk-ins begin later today or schedule an appointment."

"Please, it's urgent." A brunette wedged her way into the room. Her eyes were bloodshot and she wore a blue Phi Sigma Sigma hoodie.

"Okay, we'll play by your rules this morning, Ms.?"

"Lacey Greene."

"Well, come in and have a seat, Ms. Greene. Is it alright with you if a student observes our session?"

She said nothing, nodding as she sunk into the designated patient chair, tears already welling in her brown eyes. A plaid scarf covered her neck and the accessory struck Kenna as odd. It was commonplace to remove cold weather layers upon entering any of the buildings.

"How are you doing today?" Dr. Merino asked.

Perhaps the worst question to have used as an opener on a patient who was on the verge of crying.

Lacey peered out the window from where she sat. An hour seemed to have passed before she said anything. When she spoke, her voice was hollow. "Not great."

"What exactly are you referring to when you use the phrase 'not great?'"

Slowly, her eyes moved between the two of them and Kenna felt uneasy beneath the gaze of the girl she didn't know.

"My boyfriend."

"So, you're experiencing relationship trouble? Because if that's the case, I have a reputable couples therapist I can refer the two of you to. Off-campus, of course."

"We don't need couples therapy." She laughed. It was ugly, broken, like she had forgotten how. "I came here to get help."

"And what kind of help do you suppose you need?"

"I'm scared." Her jaw trembled and she looked out the window once again, shifting the scarf slightly askew from its previous position. Kenna's attention flocked to the exposed skin. Dark purple and red bruising. Swallowing, she whispered, "I'm scared that, one day, I won't wake up."

Kenna glanced at Dr. Merino and she noticed his eyes flicking to the contusions. "Are you familiar with IPV?"

Tears rolling down her cheeks, Lacey continued looking out the window. Kenna was well-acquainted with the view from that vantage point. The tops of the dead trees and the gray sky, waiting for a spring that it seemed would never come.

A landscape of desolation.

It pained her to think that within the town that had become her safe haven, people were being beaten. Raped. Killed. That, for some, Branch Spring was a hell from which they may never escape.

"Ms. Greene?"

Her head snapped in their direction and she adjusted her scarf. "What?"

"IPV. Intimate partner violence."

Lacey flinched, horror glinting in her eyes, and Kenna made herself look away. It felt invasive sitting in on a session of such severity.

She sprang from the chair, shaking her head as she bordered on sprinting toward the door. "I shouldn't have come, really, this was a huge mistake. I'm sorry to have wasted your time."

Sighing, Dr. Merino stepped into the hallway, momentarily

staring down it before retreating within the office and shutting the door. "Her problems must not have been so urgent, after all."

"Why did you let her leave?"

"Just as I can't force people to come into my office and talk to me, I can't make them stay any longer than they're comfortable."

"You let her in here during your appointment block. Why?"

Dr. Merino raised his dark brows as if she'd posed the most naive question possible. "She seemed to be under a great deal of duress, did she not?"

"We have to help her."

"It isn't that simple, kid. She didn't ask me to intervene in any way on her behalf. Slippery slope."

"Are you honestly going to look me in the eye and tell me she didn't need help? When she came in here sobbing with a bruised neck talking about how she's afraid that she won't wake up one day? Excuse my language, but what the hell was that if not professional negligence?"

He restated his position calmly, "She didn't ask us to intervene."

The woman's unexpected presence evoked something within Kenna. No one had intervened between Reid and herself. No one had intervened between Dr. Merino and his victims.

She was hard-pressed to call them victims. The encounters had been consensual and they were alive, however unwell.

Broken hearts still beat.

"If you're satisfied with your little interrogation, it'd be wise for us to get back to work."

# April

2 2

# DEVIL IN THE FLESH

**Kenna**

Desolation was the library's parting gift to her on the last day of classes ahead of spring break. In the two and a half hours Kenna had been stuck behind the check-out counter, one student had come through to return books. Not that she blamed the collective avoidance of the humdrum building.

She, too, was eager to kick off the week-long vacation.

While her peers were off hitting the slopes at Big Bear or flying out to music festivals, Kenna planned to stay cooped up in her apartment compiling and organizing any and all information she'd collected on Dr. Merino.

She performed a routine scan of the room to be sure no one had snuck in under her nose before deeming it vacant and pulling out her phone to send a message to Erin and Charlee.

Though it required heavy-duty convincing, Kenna had gotten their permission to create the group chat in the end, citing tired phrases like 'strength in numbers' and 'three heads are better than

164

one' whose banality she needed to look past and believe for herself.

> K: Did you guys know he played lacrosse?

> C: Never heard a thing about it.

> E: He probably made it up.

Erin had a point. Lying didn't seem out of character.

A quick search for 'Dayton Merino lacrosse Oregon' produced an article in *The Register-Guard* from 1998. It detailed the game that had catapulted his school's team into the state playoffs. Kenna pasted the link in the group chat and waited for an influx of what would surely be dissenting comments.

Eleven agonizing days had passed since she kissed Dr. Merino, and though he'd indicated interest on his part, nothing had happened since. His determination to not breathe a single word about their awkward peck incited further puzzlement.

Had he decided he wanted nothing to do with her? She thought perhaps she'd inched closer to figuring him out.

Cue new complications arising and overshadowing all of her progress.

> E: Did he tell you or did you find it on your own?

> K: He told me when we had drinks a couple of weekends ago.

> C: Please tell me 'drinks' was a typo.

An echo bounced off the vaulted ceiling as the front door creaked open. Kenna chucked her phone into her bag, pretending she was wrapped up in reading the nearest book and fighting to ignore the way her pulse flickered in her throat.

Discussing Dr. Merino carried an inherent danger, even with no one around.

"We're closing in five," she announced.

The dark, teasing remark that followed from a familiar baritone tightened her shoulders.

"You look awfully busy. I'll come back another time."

Her gaze snapped up from the pages and there stood the devil in the flesh, resting his forearms atop the high counter. She willed her features to soften.

"Shouldn't you be heading home?"

"I wanted to see you." Dr. Merino's brow furrowed as if he'd been put off by his own honesty.

Kenna forgot how to breathe, a fish reacquainting itself with water after it had been stranded ashore. She distracted herself by powering down the computer system and gathering her things, delaying her unavoidable addressing of him until she exited through the partition. "I kiss you and then it's radio silence. How do you suppose I'd react to that?"

Bag slung over her shoulder, she barreled past Dr. Merino toward the double doors. Kenna shoved the metal bar to force one side open.

Neither her speed nor disinterest fazed him.

"I needed some time to process what happened."

"I don't have time for this."

Truly, she didn't. Her brain was supposed to be warming up for her week of sleuthing, not fixating on the soap opera grade love subplot unfolding between her and Dr. Merino. Their seed of a relationship was just as fictional.

She turned and, met with an empty bicycle rack, chewed the inside of her cheek until the metallic tang of blood spread in her mouth.

The clinking jingle of keys cut through Kenna's fury.

"Want a ride, kid?"

## Dayton

His original plan in seeking out Kenna had not included stealing her bike, but when he spotted the chained Beaumont City he capitalized on the opportunity. The deed reeked of childish despair.

It was an impulsive attempt to deny the undeniable.

Spring break would prove excruciating. Dayton had come to expect her presence. Not having her around felt foreign. The absence of her company took a backseat to his chief concern: what, or worse yet who, would she be doing during their week without contact?

Several students whispered in passing at the sight of them together but Dayton could not bring himself to care.

Dean Raza had plenty of chances to fire him over the years, and this act brimmed with innocence when compared to his other transgressions.

An earsplitting silence filled the walk from the library to the parking lot. Kenna wasn't one to fall mute. In his experience, she had no shortage of topics to conjecture on.

Her first comment did not come until they'd departed the university's gates.

"I told you to stop calling me 'kid.'" It came out soft, lacking the defensive edge she often employed with him.

"So you did. I'll work on that."

He glanced at the clock as he turned onto the main road.

Nathan and Charlaine had invited him for dinner at 6:30. He could afford to be a few minutes late with his little prize in tow. Any repercussions were worth the temporary bliss.

Oh, just having Kenna there beside him.

Even if she was reluctant to speak to him. Even if she was possessed by hostility after the way he'd handled her tame display of passion in the office.

Euphoria raced through him as he fantasized what it might be like to snake his fingers between hers, the feeling of validation when she gave his hand a gentle squeeze.

Presently, Kenna's hands were in her lap, wrists crossed.

"What are you doing over break?" he asked.

Only a few weeks of classes were left after spring break. Every question he posed and move he made were critical. Not a minute more could be wasted.

"It'll be a miracle if I leave my apartment."

He caught her sheepish smile as he parked in front of Building F. Kenna made no bid to get out of the car and he did not dare tell her to.

They sat together and hotboxed the forbidden.

A small part of Dayton hoped they would forever remain in those seats. She could say everything or nothing at all while he reveled in the simple pleasure of her proximity until they decomposed and wore away to skeletons.

Reality always seemed to be less romantic.

"Should I expect you at trivia this week?"

"I never miss it," Kenna said, reclaiming her bag from the floorboard.

As she reached for the door handle, Dayton grabbed her wrist. He'd not intended to lay a hand on her. It was his brain's automatic response to her departure.

Her head whipped around. "What?"

What, indeed. His aim had been to keep Kenna in the car for a few more minutes but he'd frightened the poor girl. Subtle terror eclipsed her beautiful face. Overly bright eyes and trembling lips.

Yet she did not ask him to let go.

She allowed Dayton to hold her frail wrist in his hulking hand. Her skin burned into his as her pulse *thump, thump, thumped* against his palm.

He retracted his hand with haste as if the burn had been fourth degree when he realized he still held her. Someone else in her position may have bolted from the car, shouted a slew of obscenities. Not Kenna.

Thumb rubbing her wrist, her gaze locked on him.

"Your eyes," he said. "I've always found them striking."

She licked her lips and shifted in her seat so that the tips of their noses nearly brushed. Her complexion had gone ashen but she let Dayton see past the fear in the slow shutting of her eyelids and quiet breathing as she leaned closer. Anticipation electrified him and though he angled to meet her lips, he pulled back.

His heart shrank, brows drawn together.

Kenna stared ahead at the glovebox. "Can I have my bike back?"

"It's in the trunk. I'd unload it for you now, but I'm late for a prior engagement." He reached across her and pushed open the passenger door. "I'll bring it by later. Scout's honor."

## Kenna

She didn't know if Dr. Merino planned on setting foot in the apartment but she did not leave anything to chance.

Kenna stashed anything pertaining to her research on him in a corner of Alex's closet. Between hiding things and tidying up, she peered out the window in excess, on edge due to his vague distinction of *later*.

He would either show up unannounced or not at all and her nerves were shot at both possibilities.

Inspecting the fridge and the cabinet where they kept their dry food yielded embarrassment when she could not find a single edible item to offer him. Alex's bedtime tea sat in a jar by her electric kettle. It would have to do. Kenna set it to boil and ducked into her room to trade her school clothes for terrycloth shorts and a fitted t-shirt.

The shirt slipped over her head as the teakettle beeped and a firm rapping sounded at the front door. She gathered her hair into a messy ponytail on the way to answer it.

"Hey." Her smile came too easily and did not align with the paranoia-fueled sweep of her home.

Dr. Merino gestured behind him. "I put your bike under the staircase. Hope that's all right."

In one hand, he clutched a brown paper bag. He wore the same clothes from earlier. The standard dark slacks and a light pink button-down that complemented the swooping scar on his collarbone.

Kenna stepped aside. "Would you like to come in for a bit?"

He looked past her into the apartment.

"What about Alex?"

"She's visiting her family in Phoenix."

She knew she couldn't trust him, not completely, and here she was inviting him into her place and brewing him decaffeinated tea. Dr. Merino gave an imperceptible nod and came inside.

Adrenaline ricocheted through her chest. She'd dumped herself into open water with a great white. No cage.

"Have you eaten?" he asked, setting the brown bag on the counter as if he lived there.

Kenna wanted to lose herself in his sweetness, to fully surrender to his charm, and she'd come dangerously close in his station wagon. Logic had not abandoned her.

"I haven't, actually." She took a seat at the island but he remained standing. A thank you didn't come naturally in this situation. She didn't force it. "There's tea. It's decaf."

He mumbled his thanks and made himself a mug.

Neither of them spoke as the spoon clanked and clinked in its rotations. At the office they had built a natural rapport, but unknown variables and unresolved romantic tension reigned supreme in the new setting.

Dr. Merino stood directly opposite her on the other side of the counter, hunched over with arms braced on the faux epoxy granite. He watched a little too intently as she took the first bite of the saucy, bright green curry.

"Where were you?" Kenna did not care if the question echoed that of a suspicious wife.

It was her home. He would play by her rules.

His lips clamped together before they met the mug. "Cool it, Velma. I had dinner with some friends."

"*You* have friends?"

"There's a lot you don't know about me, a lot we don't know about each other, for that matter." Dr. Merino brandished a bemused smile, the parenthetical lines on either side of his mouth deepening. "Where are you from, anyway?"

"You should know. You raided my file. I'm surprised you don't know the name of my first pet and my Social Security number." Heat rushed to her cheeks. He may have been in her apartment but he was still her mentor and therefore deserved a modicum of respect. "Sorry."

"That's alright. I deserved it. Your file listed your high school, but no location."

"Syracuse. I'm from Syracuse."

He pushed his sleeves up to his elbows. Kenna distracted herself by identifying the types of vegetables in the curry lest she stare at his exposed forearms.

"As in New York?"

"That'd be the one."

"What the hell are you doing all the way out here?"

She was supposed to spend spring break poring over her notes on Dr. Merino and now they were having what seemed to be a heart-to-heart in her kitchen.

Maybe logic *had* abandoned her.

"Same reason everyone moves far, far away for college, to get away from my family. Things were pretty stressful at home. I was responsible for my siblings most of the time and I think they saw me as a third parent instead of a sister." Kenna swallowed the guilt creeping along her throat while the faces she hadn't seen in years flashed through her mind. "What about you? Was Los Angeles far from home?"

Google had already informed her that he hailed from Eugene. She also knew that, funnily enough, his high school mascot had been the Fighting Irish.

"Far enough from Eugene. My parents begged me to stay in-state and go to U of O. I was ready to go my own way."

Her gaze locked on Dr. Merino and did not falter. She took in the familiar empty, black eyes. The scar that cut precisely through the hollow of his left cheek. He was both handsome and frightening, and she likened the time she spent with him to exposure therapy.

"Why didn't you kiss me in your car?"

He turned away and put his half-empty mug in the sink, shooting Kenna a darting glance over his shoulder that stung her chest. "It's getting late. I should go."

23

# ALEX

Kenna

Thursday morning, Kenna wandered into the kitchen and found Alex seated at the island smashing avocado into slices of sourdough toast. The bread flattened in the center beneath the force of the fork.

Smashed may have been an understatement.

Had she any caffeine flowing through her, she may have been more concerned with her roommate's aggressive breakfast preparation. Kenna needed coffee stat or she'd be retreating back to her room and sleeping through her birthday.

She had stayed up until 3 a.m. sifting through search results relating to Dr. Merino.

Many of the pages rehashed the same basic information she had on him—the dull but vital facts of one's existence that could be dug up on the web for any living person. It was infuriating that his internet presence blended in with the sea of everyday people.

How it wasn't decorated with wanted posters or confessional

style diary blogs from his who knew how many former lovers was hard to believe.

She wasn't willing to take it at face value. Hours of fruitless searches whittled away Kenna's sanity and led her to a seedy corner of the web, a site that offered what they advertised as 'extensive' background checks and thirty bucks seemed a negligible price for the intel it promised.

On March 19, 2007, in Los Angeles, Dayton E. Merino was arrested. For what, she was unsure, but the details wouldn't have made a difference. Kenna could not have been any more sated.

She'd had an awful feeling about him from the start, and while the women's accounts somewhat solidified that point of view, she now had concrete proof of his malefaction.

"Happy birthday." Alex displayed a cold smile.

"Thanks," she replied just as flatly. Kenna poured a mug of coffee, accidentally adding too much half and half in her bleary state. "When did you get in?"

Alex took a ridiculous-sized bite of the toast, speaking despite her full mouth. "Last night."

"Did something happen while you were gone?"

Kenna was too exhausted for these kinds of theatrics.

She wiped her mouth with the back of her hand and produced an ugly laugh. "What are you talking about?"

"Alex, we've lived together for almost three years. I know when something's up with you. So, what is it?"

"Something came for you. It's on the mat outside."

When was the last time someone remembered her birthday? Flutters erupted in her stomach as she sprinted to the front door and a quiet gasp left her lips as she opened it.

She knelt to retrieve the massive pot of garnet roses positioned in the dead center of the doormat. Kenna didn't need to look at the note. They couldn't have been from anyone else. Still, she peeked at the tiny placard staked into the arrangement. *Happy 22nd -Dr. M*

The familiar illegible scrawl sent her into a tailspin that she was, for once, not desperate to escape. She did not view the flowers as a symbol of a line being crossed. Insatiable curiosity coupled with human fallibility had brought her here.

Dr. Merino's dark pull held no more blame than her meddlesome brain. They had crossed the line together.

Heart thumping, Kenna carried the roses to her room. Though she admired the bouquet as she set it on her dresser, the knowledge of his arrest precluded her joy from reaching its maximum capacity. He was dangerous.

The beauty of the flowers did not negate that.

"Did you sleep with him?" Alex demanded the second Kenna swept into the common area.

"Don't be ridiculous. I'm studying under him."

"I pray to God that's the only thing you're doing under him." Her elbow dug into her hip as she scrubbed a plate in the sink.

"Why? Are you jealous?"

The scrubbing stopped.

Alex's hands covered one another over her breastbone. "Excuse me for trying to save you from what he put me through."

In the shrill words and wild eyes, Kenna identified a brightly burning fear that Alex had been passing off as resentment.

She brought her coffee into the living room and nestled on one end of the couch. Kenna felt a growing—and quite frankly, sickening—allegiance to Dr. Merino, but the loyalty did not run so deep as to keep Alex in the dark. "You're not the only one."

"What does that mean?"

"Other students are involved in this. I've tracked down and spoken with two. You'd be the third, and I'm pretty confident there are others."

"Others?" she echoed, joining her on the couch.

"Alex, I know you want me to stay away from him, but I'm already in way over my head. You have to tell me what you know."

. . .

"I was miserable when I moved here for school. I missed Phoenix, I missed my family, my friends. Homesick barely covered how I felt. I was a scared freshman who hadn't found where she fit in. To top it all off, I was living with a dormmate I hated."

"So, that's when you started seeing Dayton?"

Alex nodded, continuing, "He was nice in the beginning. He made me feel safe, secure, especially since he spoke Spanish, but our sessions ended after a few weeks. He said he couldn't see me as a patient anymore because he'd gotten too social."

"Social how? What did he say to you?"

"That he'd moved here from L.A. a few years earlier. That he knew how I felt. Alone. I didn't think it was enough to justify ending my treatment."

"Even being privy to small details about your psychiatrist can …" Kenna shut herself up in a hurry.

Now was not the time for rambling.

"I started hanging out in his office. After hours. It's not like I was attracted to him. He's no Channing Tatum, you know? But damn if there wasn't something alluring about him. He called me Lexi, which I hated, but the way he said it always gave me butterflies."

The faintest trace of happiness resonated in her tone. Was it possible they had some good memories despite whatever Dr. Merino had done? Kenna knew better.

This wasn't a fairy tale. There would be no filter glossing over whatever Alex had yet to say.

"He took me to this cultural festival in Portland. It felt like a date and I was young and naive enough to believe he was my boyfriend. There was a firework show at the end of the night and … he kissed me."

Alex's teary eyes transported Kenna back to her conversations with Charlee and Erin. She was struggling to identify any commonalities among their emotion-rich retellings beyond the obvious: Dr. Merino had hurt them.

Were he a sadist, she was certain there'd be more to these stories than breaking hearts. Kenna registered the likelihood that he was setting her up for the same, inevitable heartbreak. However senseless, however unwise, she yearned to be his anomaly. She wanted to canonize herself in the church of his love and be the one to put an end to his cruelty.

Remembering the call with Charlee, Kenna asked, "Did you give him a book? One of the girls mentioned it."

"Yeah. He'd done a lot for me and it was a small way to thank him, and he'd mentioned learning photography for some project he was working on so I thought it'd be useful. That was before I knew he was a whackjob."

"What?"

Alex drew her knees to her core, arms wrapping around her legs. Her throat bobbed in response to the sobs trapped within. "The first time we slept together, he cooked dinner for me. He bought me lingerie. I thought it was the sweetest thing, but looking back on it now makes me sick." She wrung her wrists. "One time, in the middle of things, he grabbed my hair and said I needed to repent for my sins. Then he recited a fucking repentance prayer in my ear. I can still hear his voice. *'Lord Jesus Christ, you are the Lamb of God,'* like something straight out of a scary movie."

Kenna's scalp prickled.

Days earlier, he had been in their apartment. The man who made Charlee move across the country. The man who rejoiced over Erin's miscarriage. The man who humiliated Alex during sex. And now he pulled Kenna's heartstrings like a puppet master.

"A few days after that, I told him it was over, but it wasn't that simple. He said he had compromising pictures of me, and if I ever told anyone what happened between us, he'd send them to my family."

Blackmail, another piece to this unsolvable puzzle.

"Did you see the pictures?" The slight hope Kenna exuded was ridiculous, even to her own ears. "What if he was bluffing?"

"I'd already witnessed his insanity on full display. I thought he was capable of anything. I was more concerned with him dumping me in the woods. I didn't have time to worry about pictures."

She recalled having the same fear ahead of the run, but the looming possibility of death did not dissuade her from disappearing into the pines alongside Dr. Merino.

Perhaps that had been the point of no return. The moment in time when her obsession could not be quashed.

"When you two were seeing each other, did he ever mention any health issues, maybe heart-related?"

"He'd have to have a heart to have heart problems." Alex rose from the couch. Her voice shook but her eyes were steel. Cold and unflinching. "And if it would've been me on that 5K, I'd have left him on that trail to die."

## 24

## IT'S ALL TRUE

**Dayton**

"Who said, 'The only thing we have to fear is fear itself?' Again, the answer was FDR."

Nathan gestured to the trio of men on the far end of the bar who were facepalming and shaking their heads. "I can't believe those idiots put Churchill."

The finer details of the trivia game were the least of Dayton's concerns. While he was accustomed to the icy greeting from The Barenaked Philosophers, he was dumbfounded when Kenna followed along in their lack of cordiality. Days ago, he had been invited into her apartment for the first time. He'd stood in her kitchen and watched her eat. They had practically kissed in his car and now she acted as if he didn't exist. Had the flowers turned her off? The florist had assured him it was a tasteful choice for a colleague—okay, technically they weren't colleagues and perhaps the florist would've said anything to make a sale.

Despite it being her birthday, Kenna seemed in no mood to celebrate. She scarcely passed a comment to her teammates. Her standard wildflower honey cider was absent from the table, a sweating glass of water in its place. Her impassive expression gave nothing away but she rubbed her chest as if in pain. The shaggy-haired Ingmar Bergman son of a bitch, Liam, seemed to ask if she was okay but Kenna shrugged him off.

Noticing the path of Dayton's hardened stare, Nathan nudged his arm. "You can't do this, man. Not with her. It's not right."

Michael's voice boomed throughout the bar. "When a group of this type of bird gathers, it's referred to as a murder. Need the name of the bird, folks."

"Honestly, Nate, I'm in no mood for your holier than thou speech."

"You're a psychiatrist. You should know a thing or two about ethics." Nathan scribbled the answer on one of their slips of paper and passed it to Dayton. "A month from now, you won't be responsible for her grade. Just ride it out."

He snatched the paper from the counter, insisting through gritted teeth, "I've got it under control."

Kenna was turning in her team's answer as he approached the trivia table. Her eyes danced around him, like she wanted to look at him but wouldn't grant herself permission. Dayton caught hold of her wrist long enough to get her attention but not so long as to cause a scene.

Craning down, he nearly missed her ear, mouth almost colliding with her forehead. That would've been prime gossip material for the throngs of students there that night. He'd had far too much to drink and yet could not stop. The way Kenna blatantly ignored him was simply unbearable.

It was a frightening peek into how she would treat him once he'd had his way with her. That had a sobering effect, if only a little.

In an almost unintelligible murmur, Dayton instructed, "Meet me around back during halftime."

At last she looked at him, eyes wide as if he'd been a spectre and not a man of flesh and bone. He tried to account for the terror but came up empty until a possibility crossed his mind, one which made him ill.

*Alex*, he seethed.

Dayton returned to his seat and terminated his half-empty vodka lime, head swimming. He should have foreseen this situation. He'd figured out from the start that Kenna was inquisitive at best and persistent at worst.

The two traits were a dangerous combination.

Still, he didn't know whether to be impressed or enraged that she'd managed to pester the truth out of her roommate.

"Hey, our tuxes are out of final alterations on Tuesday. You free that afternoon?" Nathan asked.

"Yeah, sure," he answered, hardly listening.

His friend could have alerted him that the bar was burning down and it wouldn't have registered with Dayton. His sights, his thoughts, his soul were locked and loaded on mending the rift jeopardizing his acquisition of Kenna.

## Kenna

Most Thursdays, a pen had no hope of keeping pace with Liam's brain as he scrawled the answer to the halftime bonus. Three whole minutes had elapsed and he was still cogitating on which five '90s films had the most Oscar wins. Kenna had to restrain herself from signing the cross as he dotted the i's on his final entry, *Titanic*.

"I'll take it," she said.

Liam glared at her, surrendering the paper. "Alright."

Her pulse picked up speed with the index card in hand. She and Dr. Merino would be alone together, outside, under the shadowy moonlit night in the alleyways of downtown. Not another soul would be around, save for the stray smoker.

Why, after everything Alex said, had she agreed to this? She hadn't, technically, but she assumed he read her lack of response as agreement.

As Kenna headed toward the host's table, she heard Will's steadily fading voice, "And this is why you shouldn't fraternize with your trivia teammates."

She slipped Michael the paper and wandered down the hallway that housed the bathrooms. Her steps seemed to slow, feet reluctant to carry her away from the safety of the bar. Kenna emerged into the breezy darkness, slumping against the brick. Waiting. Watching. Wondering.

The conversation with Alex had affected her more than she let on. Brandi and Erin were a few years older, and had involved themselves with Dr. Merino on their own accord. But Alex had been a freshman, a terrified girl getting her grip on college life. No familial support. What he'd done to her had been sinister.

Every time Kenna looked at her birthday bouquet as she was getting ready earlier that evening, she thought of the repentance prayer, the manipulation, the trauma and string of heartache for which he was responsible. She should have chucked the flowers into the trash, but she left them on the dresser, untouched.

The way she stood little chance to remain.

Paranoia had her in its chokehold as the backdoor shut with a snick. Dr. Merino approached, placing a hand on the brick and leering over her. "You're ignoring me."

"I talked to Alex."

Had Kenna uttered those words in a deserted alleyway, while the man she accused pinned her against a wall? Or had it been a nightmarish slip of consciousness?

"Whatever Alex told you, it's all true." A haunted look crossed his face. "I was in a weird place when I was seeing her. I'm not proud of it."

His ownership of the situation took her by surprise and left her unsure of how to proceed. A change in subject seemed like the logical route.

"Thanks for the flowers. They're beautiful."

He cracked a wide smile, the widest his lips could stretch without baring teeth. Dr. Merino's hand slipped to her waist and her stomach turned to cement.

For whatever reason, she craved his touch, despite the arrest, despite his potential psychological instability. He was an intelligent, unconventionally attractive man. A licensed psychiatrist. And she was just his understudy, a student.

But with his fingertips pressing into her skin, the insistence that their connection was something unique and set apart from his reprehensible history fired on all cylinders. Kenna had peeked behind the curtain and caught a glimpse of his real life in the hospital. On the darkest days, when she thought her mission was futile, she held onto the version of Dr. Merino confined to Owens-Adair.

He'd been alone, sick. Human.

That flicker of humanity buried within him attracted her far more than his credentials, than his looks.

The pad of his thumb outlined the right side of her jaw, to her chin, and around to the left before sliding up to stroke her cheek. He brought his lips close to hers, hovering so near it felt as though they were touching. "Happy birthday."

The hardly detectable, stinging odor of vodka and a hint of lime seeped from his breath, and Kenna turned her head as he motioned to meet her lips, causing his to collide with her ear. Dr. Merino either did not mind the misdirection or was too plastered to notice. Something hot and wet met the helix of her ear. A chill crested like a wave throughout her body when she realized it was his tongue and she shut her eyes, breathing in the moment of pleasure. His mouth dragged from her earlobe down to her neck and left a trail of goosebumps in its wake.

"I want you so badly, Kenna. My need for you, it's terrifying."

His speech broke her spell. Her eyes fluttered open and she saw the filthy alley, the broken glass glinting on the ground, the man towering above her who reeked of alcohol and temptation.

"You're drunk." Kenna shook her head. "You don't know what you're talking about."

He straightened. "I shouldn't have put my hands on you, I'm—"

"Don't apologize. I want this, but not *like* this, not when you're out of it and won't remember."

She'd managed a drunken confession without the alcohol. Dr. Merino slunk into the bar without a parting phrase and she hoped that the ringing wrath of his hangover the following morning would be loud enough to drown out the faint echo of her words.

The chatter of a hundred conversations and stench of hops and greasy food assaulting Kenna's senses ushered in a sense of familiarity and made it easier to forget that, moments earlier, her mentor's tongue had coasted along her neck.

Any attempt to ignore what transpired outside became impossible as she rejoined her trivia teammates. A table full of people who knew precisely who she and the man at the bar were to one another.

Will wasted no time chiding her. "Where were you? You missed the first question of the half. And what was the category, you may ask? Religion. Right in your wheelhouse."

Was it in her wheelhouse? She had not attended Mass since Christmas Eve. Her determination to decode Dr. Merino had drawn her away from the light and into an inferno.

An inferno from which she was still reeling, his hot breath and wanting lips blistering her skin like hellfire.

"Earth to Kenna." Will leaned over the table, waving a hand in front of her face. "Where were you? You were gone for like, what, 20 minutes? You can't keep up with the time, suddenly, or?"

Rebecca and Brandi eyed the far end of the bar, and dread constricted Kenna from head to toe as she trailed their line of sight, where Dr. Merino was reclaiming his seat.

"Oh, gross," Rebecca said.

Though she did not speak, Brandi fixed Kenna with a hostile gaze and she knew if they were alone, she'd have no shortage of things to say.

She could only imagine what Brandi must have been thinking, that Kenna was playing both sides. It spelled betrayal.

"What?" Will asked.

"She was off sucking face with Dr. Strangelove during halftime, that's what."

"Don't be ridiculous," Kenna said.

"You have a sick mind, Rebecca." Will scrunched up his face. "And no proof."

"Is that why you didn't want to go on a second date with me?" Liam demanded coolly. "Because you have the hots for the school shrink? This is bullshit."

"I didn't go on a second date with you because you tried to put your hand up my skirt."

Their table was a chorus of 'oohs' and expletives.

Liam muttered, "That's an exaggeration."

But no one cared about his weak defense. Like buzzards, they had circled back to their prey.

"Are you sleeping with Dr. M?" Brandi snapped.

In her eyes, Kenna saw Erin. The day at the diner. How pained she had been to recount her affair with Dr. Merino and further by the revelation of her miscarriage. She stared dead at Brandi and let her imagination wander. Had the pregnancy carried to term, that child would be alive. She would be an aunt. A part of his family.

A reality worlds apart from the one they occupied.

"There's nothing going on between Dr. Merino and myself. Our relationship is strictly professional. Now if you'll excuse me, I'm leaving."

Ears ringing, she found herself on her feet, fleeing the table of her friends and bolting to the main entrance.

"Real classy, Kenna," Liam yelled as she went.

Her chest hitched as her phone rang within her bag. Kenna

stopped short of the exit and braced an arm with a shaking hand. Alex. She never called.

"Alex?"

"Hey, I know you're out, but I was just online and—" The speaker crackled as she exhaled. "God, you won't believe this. It's Reid. He's dead."

## Dayton

The heated scene between The Barenaked Philosophers had caused quite a stir among the bar's patrons. The joint didn't have a reputation for drama and even though the teammates' theatrics were juvenile, it garnered interest.

"What the hell was that about?" Nathan mused.

"No idea." He swirled the last of the vodka in his glass. "All I know is that they just lost their most valuable team member."

"I'm going to level with you." Nathan pushed aside his beer and the lines on his forehead gathered to create thin folds of skin. "I've got your back in any and all situations, but this? I don't condone whatever's going down between you and Kenna—but I'm not going to be the whistleblower who brings it to Raza. I'm a better friend than that. Now, on the other hand, if someone else were to stumble across your dirty little secret, they might not be as kind. Your recklessness will bite you one day."

Dayton tipped his head back, inhaling the rest of his drink that, regrettably, diluted the taste of Kenna's skin.

He should have been grateful to have someone like Nathan. Someone who was concerned with the choices he made. Effects and consequences.

God knows he wasn't.

2 5

# CONFESSIONAL

**Kenna**

While Kenna had hoped to never see Reid again, she would have preferred to see him alive.

An ivy-lined oval framed his smiling face on the funeral program that rested before her. The dates he entered and exited the world were marked beneath the photograph. A bleak timeline for a life that had hardly begun.

They had been the same age yet he was six feet under and she was full of life, breathing in another day.

How was it fair?

A hazelnut latte sat on the table, untouched. The nutty aroma wafting out of the lid's cutout turned her stomach. Dr. Merino sat across from her in the generic hipster coffee shop. He'd dropped everything to be there for her and Kenna had not given him any details beyond revealing that Reid had been her ex-boyfriend, which was a warped version of the truth. The minimal information had been sufficient enough for him to clear the day's appointments and drive them up to Portland for the funeral.

She longed to get home and be rid of her stuffy Peter Pan collared dress and itchy black pantyhose. Her Mary Janes pinched her feet. Every light and sound in the bustling shop furthered the discomfort. Guilt feasted on her.

She had never forgiven Reid.

"I realize this is horribly inappropriate to comment on in light of the day's events, and well, period, but you look beautiful," he said.

This was new, making a pass at her sober and in the daylight. Kenna did not play into his comment. She'd let herself be condemned to Hell before allowing Dr. Merino to take advantage of her while in a state of mourning.

"How can you stand to drink decaf? I'd go insane."

"I can't have caffeine."

"I'm sorry, I didn't even think. That was incredibly insensitive."

Shame flayed the tips of her ears. His health did not come up in their day-to-day conversations, but it was too significant a detail to forget even under the grim circumstances.

"That's alright." Dr. Merino sipped his Americano. "Were you and Reid together very long?"

The question was soothing. His tone, gentle.

"We weren't actually together. Not in a relationship, I mean."

One half of his mouth pulled into a weak smile. "Are you familiar with the term emotional contagion?"

Kenna shook her head.

"The hurt you're feeling right now? It's so powerful, I feel it as if it's my own. In my experience, any emotion that's strong enough to radiate and be felt by another means the person who's the source of it experiences it tenfold. There's a great deal of pain here, between yourself and this guy, isn't there?"

"You're not shrinking me. Not today."

His neck stiffened. "Kenna, please. That's not at all what I'm trying to do. This is a conversation between myself and someone I care for."

She played with the cardboard sleeve on the coffee cup and tried to talk herself out of the impending conversation, but her muscles tensed with understanding as she looked across the table and glimpsed into Dr. Merino's eyes.

Those eyes roared to life for the first time, no longer hollow and depthless but blazing with insistence and compassion. That was when Kenna understood, with absolute certainty, that his heart lay in his work. She may have been too distracted by her own studies to notice it in his office, but now it was impossible to miss.

Something fluttered deep within her. Identifying this felt as if she'd been handed a key that unlocked a hidden part of him. It instilled her with courage and perhaps a sliver of trust.

However misguided.

Kenna scooted to the edge of the wooden booth seat. "Do you remember when we ran into each other at the grocery store? The guy I mentioned?"

"The incident you described as 'not exactly stalking?'"

"Reid was that guy. He made a fool of me, and I was too naive to see what was coming."

She said she wouldn't let him shrink her though they teetered on the cusp of psychotherapy. The venue would have presented an issue had everyone in the shop not been consumed with themselves. They took no notice of her and Dr. Merino, sharp-dressed and forlorn and tucked away in a booth.

"When did it start?"

There was no way out, only through.

### Dayton

"Sophomore year, I went to a party at Delta Psi Delta. Reid accidentally spilled a beer all over me. Well, I found out later it wasn't exactly an accident." Kenna bit down on her bottom lip. "He apologized to me and I took it as sincere. Sincere enough to hang out with him until four in the morning. He walked me back to my dorm, like a perfect gentleman."

Something shifted in her eyes, a horrific twinkling, as she spoke of the dead boy. This was a side of her with which he was unfamiliar.

Gone was the fearless young woman cut from marble who refused to hold her tongue. Now, she tripped over her words as if they were forbidden. Silence, an evasive gift.

"We kept seeing each other. He'd come to my dorm when my roommate wasn't around. I'd hang out at the fraternity. I assumed we were dating, but we never discussed the specifics." Her gaze shifted to the window, and through the glass she watched intently as a series of cars passed on the street. "As soon as we slept together, Reid disappeared. He wouldn't answer my messages, my calls. I went to the frat house to see him, but his housemates wouldn't let me in, and basically refused to pass along any of my messages."

It was strange to hear the religious and studious Kenna casually discussing sex over coffee, in a public setting, no less. Dayton hid his amusement behind the lid of his lukewarm coffee.

Her skin appeared pallid under the track lighting. Not a trace of blood flowed through her veins.

"A few months later, I went to another party at Delta Psi Delta. I overheard a group of girls talking about this bingo game and how it was a show of allegiance for the new members. Hazing."

A bitter taste spread in his mouth independent of the coffee. Dayton had heard stories of the same nature from innumerable patients. Though he was familiar with Kenna's calculative nature, it seemed unlikely that her willingness to detail her romance with Reid was some convoluted form of retaliation after finding out about Alex. She wouldn't cause herself pain for the sole purpose of getting under his skin.

None of this was about him.

"I found Reid at the party and confronted him. He wasn't

completely rotten, as it turned out. Rotten enough to go along with frat shenanigans, but man enough to come clean about it. There *was* a bingo game." Kenna fiddled with her Saint Rose bracelet, tears spilling onto the varnished oak table. An empty laugh emerged but the sound was elongated and distorted. "'Red-head' was one of the spaces."

A fresh ache seared the inside of Dayton's throat as if he had swallowed a strand of barbed wire. Had he known about the trauma she carried inside, he wouldn't have ... the line of thinking was useless. From the moment he'd laid eyes on Kenna, it had never been a question of claiming her.

It had been an understanding.

Her revelation summoned a dormant feeling within him, a possessive edge which he had never harbored for anyone but his twin sister.

"After what this guy did to you, how was your attendance at his funeral even a consideration?"

"I guess I wanted to come because I feel guilty. I never forgave Reid for what he did to me, and I'll never have the chance." She rubbed her arm, speaking softly, "I have to go on living with the weight of that regret."

"*Forgive* him? Are you hearing yourself? Do I need to call in a 51/50 for you?"

That earned him a genuine laugh.

"Matthew's Gospel, you know? Aren't you Catholic?"

"How'd you arrive at that?"

"The tiebreaker at trivia. You knew the saint. The obvious conclusion seemed more likely than you being a closet theologian."

"I was Catholic. Once upon a time."

"But you still seek confessional?"

"How do you—"

"I saw you at St. James, Christmas Eve. I didn't know you at the time, but I recognized you when I proposed my mentorship."

Dayton understood that, rationally, there was no way she

could've known why he made occasional trips to St. James, but his adrenaline jumped as he fought to remain perfectly still. His eyes stung from a lack of blinking. He worried his mind had gone transparent and she could peer into it so clearly that she could see the guilt to which he was forever bound.

It was nonsense, all of it. Only under the veil of paranoia did the highly illogical become believable.

"My relationship with God is complicated."

"Whose isn't?" Kenna mused. "Who did you light your candle for that night?"

The blinking returned but Dayton's eyes now burned for a different reason, sodium-tainted pools rising behind his lids and draining just as quickly.

"Myself."

## Kenna

After Dr. Merino excused himself to handle a call with an unknown person she presumed to be Professor Scott, they hit 99W. Fifteen miles of pavement separated them from Branch Spring. Much of the drive from Portland had been silent.

The eerie confession he gave burned in her mind. He'd lit the candle for himself. It brought Kenna just as much confusion as it did pity. Was that how he viewed himself, someone who needed to be prayed for?

His cold stare fixated on the road ahead. Stoic, stone-faced and clad in a black suit, he was an amalgamation of paradoxes.

Handsome yet lonely. Strong yet broken.

Kenna's hand crept onto his lap, resting near the pocket of his dress pants. "Thanks for everything today. It means a lot."

He placed his hand atop hers in lieu of a response.

The platonic touch triggered a stuttering in her heart. She'd thought too often of the night behind the bar, the hot press of his tongue on her skin. She needed to forget.

In a few weeks, the semester would come to an end, bringing with it the end of their connection. Even though her attraction to Dr. Merino had grown beyond any hope of manicuring, even though he'd admitted his attraction to her without a drop of alcohol in his system, even though he cared for her, they were statistically and realistically unfit to be together.

His Adam's apple bobbed as he shot her a sidelong glance. "Kenna?"

"Yeah?"

"I would never do anything like that to you."

How could she refute those words? Tender and true. Reckless as it may have been, she believed him.

26

# RED FLAG

**Dayton**

The Portland trip stirred things between himself and Kenna in a way that Dayton never could have foreseen. Discovering what Reid put her through had brought them delightfully close. It should have been easy for him to accept that shiny new facet of intimacy but steel bars ascended and imprisoned him on all sides.

He'd become a prisoner of guilt.

Guilt, an emotion he had strived to snuff out after how things had gone off the rails with Jasmine.

Guilt, what Kenna somehow felt in response to Reid's passing. That boy was undeserving of her guilt or her empathy or her tears. He'd deserved none of her, yet had every part.

Dayton thought that perhaps he, too, was undeserving of her. All those months spent scheming and clawing his way closer to a young woman who had already been sought out and wrung dry by another's twisted idea of pleasure.

He and Reid, they were no different.

Her retelling of events haunted him. It clung to his conscience like an unshakable nightmare. His want for Kenna was equivalent to the burning insistence to stay away, some invisible warning buried within the patchwork of her trauma. Dayton couldn't focus at the office. He was all over the place and it hadn't escaped her notice. Despite that week being the final days of their mentorship, he'd called out sick. His condition was no better at home.

At night, he couldn't sleep. Clouds carrying dark dreams crept in, showing Kenna and Reid in a dimly lit dorm that reeked of cheap beer and manipulation. He'd shoot upright, bleary eyes stretched wide, drenched in cold sweat.

Though, presently, the possibility of sleep was hours away, he had already accepted the reality that it would not come. He'd just gone for a run and hadn't bothered to remove his muddied tennis shoes before sprawling out on the couch with his laptop. Slouching down, he scrunched up his legs, earth-dampened and mud-caked soles meeting waxy brown leather. No sooner than he pulled up his university email account, his heartbeat slowed, petering out to a weak rhythm.

Kenna's name rested atop his inbox like an unvoiced prayer. She was inquiring about the possibility of recording his thoughts as part of a cumulative project on acute trauma, the deadline for which was fast approaching. He found it curious that she hadn't yet completed the assignment.

He couldn't even respond to her email, this inanimate representation of her. The end of the chase was in sight yet he was second-guessing everything.

Perhaps it was time to retire the experimental form of treatment. Maybe he had been cured. The names and memories he'd collected over the last six years were rendered meaningless. And then, with a begrudging reluctance, it clicked into place. Kenna was more than a notch on his bedpost.

She was the fucking frame.

The idea resurrected something within Dayton that had eroded long ago. Hope.

In spite of her reservations toward him, she had been so caring when he'd been stuck in Owens-Adair, so attentive. Even if that ray of affection was only the result of the adrenaline and uncertainty that followed in the wake of his collapse, he wanted to believe it shone beyond. His mind stretched that beam, drawing it out until it illuminated a lifetime of possibility. Having someone to come home to in the evenings, someone to accompany him to his cardiology appointments, someone to love.

And what was that like? To love, to be loved?

His cell phone rang and his whole body flinched as it pierced the stillness of the evening. It was Kenna.

A sign from God to go forth and claim what was his.

"Hello?"

"Hey, it's me. Are you busy?"

Dayton glanced around at the empty quiet of the house, those four walls of inactivity, and restrained a laugh. "Not at all."

"I don't want to sound selfish, but I need a favor."

*Anything for you*, he wanted to say, but he stuck to his no-nonsense persona. "Go on."

"My hours track sheet was due yesterday, but I told my professor you'd been out for a few days. Luckily, he gave me an extension on the condition that it's in his box first thing Monday morning." She paused, her light breathing like white noise. Every follicle on Dayton's body rose in reverence to that sound. So gentle and unsure. "Could you, um, come over and sign off on it, or would it be easier if I went to your place?"

Bumbling filler words were not a typical part of Kenna's vocabulary though he welcomed her uncharacteristic anxiety. It was an indication, however small, that she was just as frightened by their interactions as he was.

Perhaps she felt something, too. Not with the same depth and fantasticism that Dayton guarded close to his heart, but he would settle for a fraction of interest.

"I'll be over in 20."

## Kenna

Dr. Merino was drenched in sweat when he turned up on her doorstep. His damp hair was tucked behind his ears, with several rogue strands hanging in front of his glistening face. He smelled of pine and rust, a pairing that was at once sweet and repulsive.

He stepped past her into the apartment and she shut the door. "When you said 20 minutes, I assumed you were driving."

"I wouldn't pass up a run in this weather, and I live on Fairbrook. It's not that far."

His sneakers stayed on his feet, a silent but certain proclamation that he didn't plan to stay longer than was necessary. His tone was oddly casual. Laid-back, even. Kenna brushed off the observation. Dissecting his behavior was pointless when he was one signature away from terminating their professional relationship.

"Do you want some water?" It didn't matter if Dr. Merino refused. Her mind insisted that she do something, anything to get herself away from the spot where she'd stood anchored in place, staring at him until that stomach plunging into feet feeling that only he could elicit took hold. "Not to sound like a stalker, but I love the houses on Fairbrook. The different architectural styles, all of the colors."

He accepted the water with a half nod of thanks before draining most of it in one go. "Oh, it's unique. Quiet, safe. Good place to raise a family."

An imaginary red flag billowed between them. No, Kenna had just put her infernal need to dissect to rest. She pushed aside the desire to compare his comment about raising a family to his history of relief over a miscarriage. She was reading into it too much and she knew it. He'd said it was a good place to raise a family; that didn't mean *he* intended to raise one.

She was doing it again. Moreover, Dr. Merino's intention to have a family or lack thereof was none of her concern.

"Did you get my email?"

"I did. I can set aside an hour to be your lab rat, just give me a day and time." She thought his pupils dilated but she couldn't tell, like a small pool of water overflowing into a larger one. Black mixing into black. He rubbed the back of his neck. "Where's this life or death paper I need to sign?"

Kenna pointed to the document resting in the center of the island. Without so much as reviewing the information on the page, he signed with a single, practiced flourish of the pen. Those mesmerizing strokes played on repeat in her mind while she considered the past week. Her slow acceptance of Reid's death. Dr. Merino's absence.

"Where have you been?"

He ventured a look at the ceiling. "I called out as a way of limiting my exposure to you."

Exposure. The word sounded dirty, as if she were something contagious or altogether undesirable. A quiet rage trellised Kenna's throat, trailing up, up, and latching onto its walls.

"What is that supposed to mean?"

His mix of hurt and regret was effortless. She wondered if he practiced this cocktail of vulnerability in front of the mirror each morning. She wondered how many other women he had played exactly like this and then understood with blinding surety that there was nothing special about her. Nothing that set her apart from the rest. And the only reason she was burning with fury and felt slighted was because Dr. Merino was a mastermind at his game. This moment felt like a breakup, despite them never having been together, because he'd orchestrated it to feel as such.

He lifted his chin and terror coursed through her like a paralytic. He was so much larger than Kenna. Stronger. It would've been nothing for him to curl his hands around her frail neck and demonstrate that strength until a final gasp of breath departed her lungs.

She didn't believe Dr. Merino was a violent man, but she believed passion inspired irrationality.

Rather than strangling her, he gently tipped her chin, forcing her to meet his gaze. "I hurt people. It's a pattern."

"What about what you said after the funeral? That you'd never do anything like that to me. You wouldn't hurt me."

The sentiment was laced with delicate desperation. A prayer whispered in the dark.

"I wish that were true." Looking at his face had become too much, the torturous twist of his features. Kenna shifted her attention to the sweat stains on his shirt. Instead, she pictured them as ink blots on cardstock; something to make sense of in this situation that made none. "Kenna, look at me. Please."

A softness had settled over him, replacing the well-crafted mask he'd worn moments before. Something visceral and raw had crept across his skin and taken hold, and she found that she could not tear her eyes away from this version of Dr. Merino. The actual man living within the shell of a no-fuss psychiatrist. Kenna had caught glimpses of him occasionally, but now he was on full, unadulterated display. The white hot pain of clarity sliced through her.

He wouldn't hurt her.

He came a few paces closer and she stepped backward in response but soon her lower back rammed into the counter's ledge, making her wince. His eyes darted back and forth as he searched hers. Her pulse beat within her throat. Could he sense that exhilaration? The thrill of having him near.

Dr. Merino planted his hands on either side of her on the countertop. His forearms became bars, a barrier meant to keep her in place. The pounding of her heart spread throughout her body, a constant jolting sensation that left her unsteady.

"Listen to me." He leaned in and their faces were much too close. There was no room for his words, no space for his breath, yet Kenna loved the warmth expelled onto her skin as he spoke to her, voice low and urgent. "I've tried to be good. I've tried to fight this, and I've failed, and it's because I don't want to stay away. I *can't* stay away. It's killing me from the inside out."

His confession hummed between her ears like a ballad written just for her. Even if it had been recycled from past lovers, she was disinclined to care. She and Dr. Merino were the only two people on Earth. The rest of the world had fallen away and thereby ceased to exist.

"Are you comprehending what I'm saying here?"

Kenna reached out until her fingertips connected with the pink scar that cut across his cheek. He flinched but did not recoil from her light touch, her fingers ghosting along the rippled line of flesh. Happiness coiled itself around her bones and she couldn't help but feel this was a small victory, the simple connection. She cherished the scene. Heavy but free of expectation.

Mouth dry, she retracted her fingers, slowly bringing them to the exposed skin near the loose collar of Dr. Merino's t-shirt. She traced the swooping scar that met both sides of his collarbone. That vanilla-spiked sweat scent intensified with him this close and Kenna let herself inhale without any internal admonishment. Her chest fluttered as she caressed his scars and breathed him in. He was in her apartment, letting her touch him, the space between them a scarcity.

"God, I want to kiss you."

"Do it." It was a meager dare, a weak command.

The fire in his eyes died down and they returned to neutral pits of black. "I can't. It isn't right. I haven't turned in your evaluation."

*The rules don't apply to me*, Dr. Merino had told her—but that had not deterred him from sleeping with Charlee during her mentorship. Why was he shying away from doing the same with her?

Her fingers fled from his skin as if she'd been burned, hand falling limp at her side. "Have you forgotten what happened behind the bar?"

"I had too much to drink. Still, it doesn't excuse my behavior."

Kenna's heart jackhammered. "I shouldn't have turned my head that night. I should've let you kiss me." Throat tight, she went on, "I think about it all the time, how I made the wrong choice."

Dr. Merino brushed the hair out of her face, sweeping it over her shoulder, and then withdrew his hand. "Often, the right thing to do is the hardest. You rejected my advance that night. You acted with your head instead of your heart. And I believe your ability to say no in that situation is the sole reason you then revealed your feelings. You denied yourself physical satisfaction, so you went another route to earn it."

"You shouldn't have been physical with me. I shouldn't have spilled my feelings. I get it. No need for a drawn-out speech."

He shook his head. "That isn't what I'm saying. I'm grateful for that residual want that led to your confession. Over the last few months, there were times I was sure you were interested but I guess I was waiting for verbal confirmation, and when I got it ..." Dr. Merino swallowed and the sound ballooned in the stillness of the room. "I don't know why I'm telling you any of this. None of it matters."

"Why would you say that?"

She remembered the candle he had lit in St. James. He'd prayed for himself. That memory alongside his present discouragement cinched Kenna's insides.

What kind of monster did he believe himself to be?

While she had heard some disquieting stories about him, she was not convinced that any trace of evil lurked within the stern yet soft man who stood before her.

Every story had two sides, and though he admitted to Alex's version of events being factual, she had not heard his side on things with Erin or Charlee. Not that Kenna could ask him anything relating to either woman without outing herself as a relentless snoop.

And then what?

He'd label her untrustworthy. He wouldn't let her trace the pink lines that ran across his skin. He wouldn't look at her like she was the reason the sun rose and set.

In the stringing together of those hypotheticals, Kenna arrived at a solution to a problem she hadn't been aware she was solving. Dr. Merino must have felt something for her. She couldn't glean the scope of his feelings nor did she care. To know they existed was enough and it left her heart undulating in delight.

He didn't answer her question, instead offering a reserved ghost of a smile. "Good night, Kenna."

2 7

# THE BLOCK

**Dayton**

"Thanks again for agreeing to this last minute," Kenna said as she set up at his desk, littering its surface without mercy.

A latte from Bigleaf, her barely-there lipstick marking a faint stain on the lid. Her cell phone with a voice memo app queued on the screen. The strap of her bag hung over the side of the desk, an array of notebooks peeking out from its opening. And the woman who made the mess, sitting in his chair and looking every bit like she belonged there.

Poised. In control.

Dayton absorbed the sight. It was something he was unlikely to ever see again.

While his signature on the hours track sheet had officially ended their mentorship, his procrastination in determining her 4960 grade left them stumbling in an ethically questionable limbo.

Not kissing her in her apartment had required more concentration than studying for his MCAT. He still honed that concentration, afraid he might swiftly lock the office door and draw the metal blinds. But he was done with that way of life.

This little lamb had seen to that.

Dayton sat across the room, occupying the chair designated for patients. "I have to admit this doesn't seem like you, the waiting. Finals are next week."

"We can't be our best selves all of the time, can we? Then you'd be out of a job. Is it alright if I start recording?"

He tipped his head and she tapped the phone screen.

"Kenna O'Callaghan for Professor Savas. Subject is male, between the ages of 20-39." Steepling her fingers, she released a quiet breath as if this were the most important project she'd been tasked with in all of her 22 years. In a way, he supposed it was. Another class standing between her and grad school. "Can you walk me through whatever you believe to be the most distressing event in your life?"

Those jade eyes bore into him, bone deep, and he ached to tell her everything. To lay bare every jagged fragment of the past.

Though Dayton had recently deluded himself into thinking otherwise, there was no denying they were on a fast track to nowhere. Revealing any part of his past would not change their trajectory.

But there was no harm in Kenna believing whatever story he fed her.

"Wait." He lurched forward in the chair, elbows stationed on his knees, and purposefully lowered his voice. "Will other people listen to this?"

She terminated the recording.

Fright flickered over her, shoulders tight one second and relaxed the next, as if he'd imagined the imperceptible shift. "We're supposed to play a highlight during our presentation. Something short. Why do you ask?"

"If someone were to recognize my voice, they may draw some wild conclusions."

"I had the same thought." A relieved smile pulled at Kenna's lips. "I'm going to use software to disguise your voice, and if Savas gives me trouble for it, I'll just explain to him in private that I interviewed a faculty member." She started a new recording but she didn't recreate the introductory commentary. Her eyes flicked to him and then back to the desk, where her notebook lay open. Waiting. "Whenever you're ready."

His thoughts raced a hundred miles a minute to weave a mostly fictitious narrative with a few truthful bits thrown in to compensate for his unimaginative right brain.

"It was the end of my final year of undergrad. Same boat as you. Exam week might be rough around here, but exam week at UCLA? It's something else entirely. I had a hysterical breakdown, to put it mildly, which led to a more severe incident than what you witnessed on the run."

She winced.

The run. Perhaps he shouldn't have mentioned it. He was already giving Savas and countless others information to piece together and figure out what was going on between Kenna and himself.

Nothing, yet.

Dayton had faith that would change. He'd peel back enough counterfeit layers to snag her heart.

"And following your incident?"

"I went home for the summer. That's when I got my ..." he trailed off. He would grant her one critical truth amid this fabricated tale, something not even Nathan knew about. His clothes seemed to disintegrate and he felt naked in that chair. Sweating, exposed. "It's congenital. A block. My heart beats slower than it's supposed to."

Her grip tightened, ever so slightly, on the pen she held and she blinked one too many times.

He watched as Kenna tried to feign some sort of activity that indicated she went unaffected by his words but she was all shaking hands and false starts.

She was a bundle of nerves and he knew she couldn't speak freely due to the recording that was in progress, the one that others would be privy to. Dayton supposed it was better this way, almost; telling her within the confines of a circumstance that prevented her from having a theatrical reaction to the news. And still he pictured Kenna's reaction, unrestrained. The shouting, the weeping, the inevitable interrogating. It was the antithesis of her current form, polished and professional behind his desk, holding herself together. She would do just fine in therapy.

"You said you went home for the summer, but after that I think you cut yourself off."

"I had surgery." His fingers twitched as he unfastened the second and third buttons on his shirt, giving the material enough leeway for him to pull it aside and show her the two-inch scar. "For a pacemaker."

With this revelation, her mask of neutrality slipped. It was there though it was askew. Parts of her face were hammered in cold, therapeutic apathy and the rest were awash in hurt.

Dayton wanted to grab her hand and guide it to that spot below the left side of his collarbone, to feel her fingers trace that scar like she had traced the others.

But she was across the room and they were collaborating for a finals project on campus.

He refastened the buttons and spoke before he did something worthy of getting them both thrown out of the university. "My parents, and my doctor, threatened me into surgery. They said I was being irresponsible, that I should've gotten one years ago."

He had, in fact, not gone home for the surgery.

He stayed in California and his twin sister, Carmen, had overseen his brief recovery. Dayton found it repulsive how easy it was to look Kenna in the eye and distort reality and bury the lifetime of truths he'd been dying to share with someone.

"When I went back to California for grad school, it all went to hell. I use an app to monitor my PM now, but that technology wasn't around then, so I kept a monitor in my bedroom. I lived with two other guys. It was college. I thought people would be more accepting. So I told them. Everyone on campus seemed to know within a week. People I'd never met were coming up to me, asking ignorant questions."

It wasn't his story but it was one he'd heard a hundred times from the lips of his patients. Victims of Ponderosa's rumor mill. They were a special breed who came around with the sole intent of burdening another with their plight, and they'd leave, never to be seen again, as if his office were a confessional. People who didn't truly want help but didn't mind flirting with the idea of it.

What he was doing with Kenna was hardly any different. He knew there was no future in store for them and yet he continued in his attempts to win her over, spinning a sob story with the hope of evoking enough empathy to spend one night with her in his arms.

One night, and Dayton could let her go. *He could.*

"It seems childish, discussing it so many years later. You have to understand, I thought I'd gained a newfound freedom when I moved to California. No one knew who I was. No one knew what was wrong with me. On the outside, I was just like anyone else. Then suddenly, overnight, I'm reliving my adolescence."

Kenna maintained a death grip on her pen but it never met the blank pages of her notebook. Dayton became hyperconscious of that pen and her lack of notes. Was there not a faraway look on his face?

Nostalgia was difficult to conjure on the spot.

The bullying narrative wasn't enough. He needed something grander, and above all else believable, something that would appeal to Kenna's sensibilities.

"Something strange happened during that swell of attention. This girl, Audrey Dresden, started talking to me. I'll admit, I had my eye on her for years. But it didn't end there. A ton of her sorority sisters were flirting with me, constantly. I didn't date much in college, so the whole ordeal made me uncomfortable."

"And did you and Audrey date?"

"No."

He admired her fixation on Audrey and her ability to tune out the sorority sisters as if they were nothing more than static on a radio station. Dayton also rightfully feared that keenness. Her beautiful, analytical mind that was a little too skilled in discerning fact from fiction.

## Kenna

She hung onto Dr. Merino's every utterance though she knew it was unlikely he was telling the truth, and even more unlikely that she would ever hear Audrey's version of the truth. His California arrest pressed against the walls of her mind throughout the recording. A fact that couldn't be argued or justified into dormancy.

And the city that continued to roll off his tongue, L.A., wouldn't let Kenna forget that the arrest overlapped with the time he lived there.

When he was in school. When he was in the 'same boat' as her. Like they were remotely the same type of person.

"We didn't date. We hooked up, once."

It was difficult to listen as Dr. Merino mentioned a past sexual encounter, no matter the absence of detail.

Her voice broke. A hairline fracture. "And would you say that experience was transformative for you?"

"No. It was what followed."

The notebook pages stared back at her, that sea of white. She hadn't written a thing. Kenna would have to play the recording on a loop if she had any hope of successfully composing the accompanying paper.

"She had a bet with her friends to see which of them could sleep with me first. To them, I was a joke. Of course, they would've never been interested in me if word had not traveled around about my surgery, that golden opportunity for humiliation. Though they viewed me as undesirable, under this new lens, it was overshadowed by the chance for bragging rights and a cash prize."

She listened as he droned on about the fallout, the mortification, and her doubts multiplied alongside the level of detail he interspersed in the obvious tale of fiction.

He had endured no such thing. She was sure of it.

Dr. Merino wanted to evoke some degree of empathy from her. He was manipulating her, just as he'd done with the others. What he failed to realize was that she didn't need to be manipulated.

She'd walk into his arms, unafraid.

She'd tread fearlessly into that ring-of-fire embrace and cradle his black heart in her hands and dust it off to prove that it was functional despite a lifetime of disuse.

Kenna knew that, somewhere along the way, obsession had consumed her. An adoration that had planted its roots and whose death wouldn't coincide with the end of the semester. Something pestilent that would live within her forever, slowly killing her.

"Do you think that was enough?" he asked.

"Hmm?"

"For your case study."

Dr. Merino's mouth twitched and she cursed herself. He knew that she had been on the velvet chaise in her mind, analyzing herself in circles when she should've been going through those motions with him.

"More than enough." Heat scaled her neck as she made quick work of clearing her belongings from his workspace. "I'll surrender your desk."

"Where did you go, just now? Because you weren't here."

She didn't answer him nor did she meet his eye. Why was he asking when he knew? Clutching her pile of books, the muscles in her arms tensed as she rounded the desk en route to the exit. Kenna was possessed by paranoia and was prepared to leave the office without so much as a farewell.

To cut her losses. To hell with temptation. To never look back on the five months she spent with one Dr. Dayton Merino, MD.

But her own curiosity had landed her here and it wasn't extending any mercy. Before she registered what was happening, he was out of his chair, forming a wall between herself and the door.

His voice lowered to an almost indistinguishable humming and she strained to decipher his speech. "I apologize if I upset you. That wasn't my intention." Forehead creasing, he went on, "I was wondering if you'd like to come over for dinner on Sunday. A little bird told me you love craftsmens."

Kenna wondered why he didn't project his voice when no one else was around, and then it hit her.

This was not to be overheard.

Silence enveloped the room. She gazed into Dr. Merino's dark eyes and caught the glint of a sunrise. Miraculous gold on the horizon. Desperation? Happiness? Whatever the case, she was overcome with an unfounded need to please him.

Though, perhaps in the back of her mind, she was fearful of what disappointing him may have brought about.

"I would love that."

2 8

# THE BOX

**Kenna**

The sun had begun its evening descent as Kenna biked to 673 Fairbrook. Blood orange and pink streaked the sky, melding with the remnants of blue and the sparse white of the clouds. She felt like a model mid-photoshoot in an eyelet tank and high-rise shorts, wild hair rippling behind her.

Dr. Merino hadn't asked her to bring anything and so she brought only what he wanted most.

Herself.

Weightlessness claimed her as the mailboxes whooshed by in her peripheral. 655, 657, 659. She stopped paying attention to the addresses and focused on the scenery. Tiny homes with RVs parked in makeshift driveways of grass and tire tracks. Cape Cod style homes even though they were thousands of miles from Massachusetts. Impossibly green lawns that must have been subjected to endless bags of supplements and fertilizers.

It was a street she'd long admired, a kind of non-comforming suburbia. Back in Syracuse, she was lucky to see something similar in passing during her family's monthly grocery trip. One of the few occasions she or her siblings were permitted in a car.

Kenna squeezed the hand brakes as she neared a black house with white tapered posts. The paneled station wagon was parked in the driveway. Modest gardens of salmon and eggshell azaleas lined the front of the home. Their presence was strange, and she was unable to picture the owner planting the feminine blooms. She eased her bike up the twin steps that led to the porch and propped it against the railing.

A warning whispered through her head but she ignored the pleading cry.

Footsteps approached from the inside as she reached for the bell. The door swung open and revealed a new version of Dr. Merino: bootcut jeans, a green and black flannel.

Her mind ventured all the way back to that bitter January morning when she'd first approached him, recalling how his disposition had mirrored what laid beyond the office windows that day. She remembered his cold and affectless gaze. It was hard to believe she was staring into those same eyes, reflecting only warmth.

A lopsided grin contorted his face, giving him a slight boyish quality as he scanned the length of Kenna and she felt bare before him, rooted to his welcome mat.

For one perfect moment, the memories of Charlee's tears, Erin's tragedy, Alex's anger, all subsided.

"You better come in before the entire street sees you standing on my porch."

Dr. Merino retreated within, branching off to the left, and she took a tentative step over the threshold and found herself standing, alone, in his entryway.

Entryway was perhaps a poor descriptor. It was a living room with a door.

Wooden beams lined the ceiling. The room was split between a traditional living area and an office. Bits of life littered the space and implied that he had not bothered to clean up. Mugs of tea on the desk, his muddy tennis shoes resting by the sofa, several stacks of books on the floor before their built-in shelves. Apples and cloves filled the air, a sweet yet spicy scent that made her feel at home in spite of her guest status. Kenna traced the scent to a candle burning on the coffee table.

Peering inside the frosted brown glass, she watched the flames dancing at the head of each wick, jumping at the sound of Dr. Merino's voice from the next room.

"I hope Indian is alright."

It was then she heard the sizzling of a pan. As she drew closer to the kitchen, the apple fragrance faded and was replaced with the smell of—judging by the array of shakers on the counter—every spice in the Merino household.

He looked like the host of some ranch-set cooking show in his flannel, at the helm of the gas stove, stirring and smelling and seasoning.

"You're cooking?"

"Were you expecting takeout? I wouldn't invite you into my home to eat out of paper boxes."

She wasn't expecting takeout. She was counting on it.

Whatever Kenna had done to dissuade herself from fearing their intimate dinner party vanished as Alex's words blared through her head like a siren. He had made her dinner the first time they slept together.

"I didn't know you could cook," she lied.

"Live alone long enough and you figure it out."

Dr. Merino winked at her and she marveled at the intimacy it held. Their lips had brushed but once yet within the span of a wink he'd convinced her that they had been lovers for years.

He nodded to a hightop table in the corner, nearest the window. "Have a seat if you like. I'll serve us."

Sweat emerged on the soles of Kenna's bare feet as he rushed around pouring glasses of water and wine and plating the food he'd prepared, as if it were their first date and everything had to be just so. She stiffened.

Was it a date?

Had she squinted, she could've seen light shining through the entrance of the rabbit hole from whence she'd made her darling descent. How had it taken this long to realize she'd reached the bottom, that cold and damp place she had sworn not to go?

Kenna wanted to dwell in that darkness, with this man, no matter if he was a murderer or a seducer, or was afflicted with some other perversion of evil.

He, too, was the captor of her heart.

Somewhere amid the haze of her mental calculations, Dr. Merino had joined her at the table. They were seated across from each other, having a meal together, in his home.

She was terrified of the scene, romantic and real. It conjured dread greater than supplying suppositions for patient diagnoses or listening to the women recount their tales.

He extended his wine glass toward her to toast. "I enjoyed working with you this semester, despite my initial resistance. I hope grad school is everything you expect it to be, and that you find something akin to happiness in general therapy, as much as I'd like to see you go into psychiatry."

"Six years of university is enough, thank you."

"Cheers to that."

They'd spoken little since digging into the food, a rice dish that had Kenna constantly suppressing threats of a coughing fit and refilling her water.

The silence flooded her mind with doubts.

Maybe nothing romantic lurked in the dinner invitation. Maybe it was a farewell, Dr. Merino's way of tying up their professional relationship with a neat bow before sending her on her way.

He was pulling away from her.

Though he usually left the top two buttons of his shirts undone at the office, the flannel was buttoned up to the collar. However minute of an observation it may have been, Kenna took it as a searing slap across the face.

She realized she'd never voiced the question that had lived in her head since they first met.

"Dr. Mer—Dayton." His eyes instantly flashed to her, as if he'd been waiting for her to speak. "There's something I've wanted to ask you for a while but it always felt impolite."

"Impolite?" he echoed.

"Your scars. How did you get them?"

"Car accident."

"That's what happened to your other car, the one before the Caprice? You crashed it?"

"It wasn't entirely my fault. There was another driver involved. Pouring rain. It was … complicated." He spoke into his plate. Either he was lying or he didn't want to discuss it.

Soon, Dr. Merino was pouring more wine and changing the subject. "I hope what I revealed to you during the case study doesn't change anything between us." Solemnity shaded his face. "I'd hate to lose you."

Her chest sang at the words, momentarily blind to their danger. Kenna had believed he'd meant to dismiss her that evening, but it was proving to be an arena for romantic admission.

Logic was quick in overtaking her foolhardy mind.

*I'd hate to lose you.* The phrase called to mind Charlee's allegation of his clinginess. It signaled an attachment.

Was she another pawn on his chessboard? Others had played him and lost. But she was privy to their secrets.

She would try her hand.

"Whatever was said during our interview was for academic purposes. I promise it hasn't influenced the way I look at you."


With multiple glasses of water and wine in her system, Kenna couldn't postpone her need to use the bathroom any longer. She slid from the bar height chair.

"Where's your restroom?"

"It's through the bedroom." Burning intent lit his eyes as they raked over her. "Hurry back. I have something for you."

Dr. Merino's bedroom was the absolute last place she needed to be and she ventured there purely out of desperation.

A lamp had been left on, casting a warm yellow glow, but she kept her attention trained on the hardwood until her feet met the cold tile of the bathroom. Kenna didn't flip the lightswitch.

She had an intuitive knowledge of the space that negated the need for light, this place she'd visited through the memories of others.

In the dark, her heartbeat thundered in her ears as she grew more and more thankful that she hadn't turned on the light. She wouldn't have to see her reflection in the very mirror the other women had seen themselves in. She wouldn't have to see the shower where they had scrubbed themselves clean after enduring whatever they'd mistaken for love.

Kenna stumbled to the sink and felt woozy traveling the short distance. The cold water rushing over her skin stimulated her thoughts. Her hands shook as she felt around for a towel.

Had she been drugged?

No one had mentioned blacking out, but she'd never doubted there were others. It was a question of how many.

Fear clung to every part of her as she stepped back into the bedroom. She'd consumed half a bottle of wine and with the possibility of a drugging on the table, her chances of returning to her apartment in one piece seemed grim.

A violent pain seized her stomach and she fell to her knees on the rug lining the foot of the bed. Kenna reined in the cries that were fighting to escape but it was of no use.

The home was small. She knew Dr. Merino had heard the thud.

She rolled onto her back and felt like a defenseless animal, waiting to be killed, not knowing if she was drunk or high but knowing without a doubt she had gone mad. Why else would she have entered the home that had been the center of endless romantic horrors?

She'd trapped herself with a man who was insatiable, predatory and, above all else, intelligent.

Excess alcohol blurred her vision as her head lolled to the side. The apple and clove scent carried to her, lying on the floor, as if urging her to remember where she was.

Kenna's eyesight focused once again and she found herself looking beneath the bed. There was no sound, save for her breathing. Precisely in the middle of the otherwise bare floorboards was a box. Clamminess enveloped her hands and feet as she contemplated its contents.

It was safe to rule out childhood mementos.

Footsteps creaked on the hardwood and she turned her head so that her gaze rested on the ceiling.

"You poor thing." Dr. Merino lounged against the doorframe. "Did I make you sick? I'll use a lighter hand with the spice next time."

She clutched her stomach even though the discomfort from moments earlier had passed. Sickness provided a plausible cover for lying on his bedroom floor.

"The food was amazing, really. Please don't feel like this," Kenna gestured to her body, "is your fault. I wasn't feeling that great before I came over. When finals roll around, I neglect my basic needs."

"I'll make you some tea. Why don't you try the bed? I promise it's more comfortable than the floor."

Though it was beyond foolish, she accepted Dr. Merino's invitation and settled in on the right side of the bed, burrowing under the covers. A quiet excitement overtook her at being wrapped in the same sheets that held him every night. She inhaled the floral lavender of the detergent and the woodsy scent that was a testament to all of the time he spent running—and, apparently, gardening.

Juniper paint coated the walls and gave the room a soothing ambiance. Kenna immediately cast her attention elsewhere upon spying the reflection in the full-length mirror and catching sight of the little box under the bed. The satchel he carried to campus was tucked to the side of a mahogany dresser, above which hung a collection of framed photographs, each of the same boy and girl at different stages of life. Playing in a backyard. Painted faces on Halloween. Then they were older, donned in business casual clothes. Smiles tugged at their mouths in every shot. She assumed the girl was his sister but they'd scarcely spoken of their families.

He returned through the doorway with a steaming mug in hand. "Chocolate mint for the non-tea drinker. It's pretty mild. The mint will help your stomach."

"Thank you."

The flavor was lackluster but she continued sipping the tea for its alleged curative properties.

Dr. Merino perched beside her on the edge of the bed. His palms came to rest on his thighs. "I'd say you could stay here and sleep it off but tomorrow's Monday. We both have our roles to fill."

"Why are you doing all of this? Cooking dinner and bringing me tea? Offering to let me stay at your place?"

She could've sworn his neck flushed with color, unless it was an illusion borne out of the room's uneven lighting.

"You are very important to me."

Important how, she yearned to ask. Important in the construction of a domestic cover story for another disturbed American male?

The Kendall to his Bundy.

No, she couldn't see it, and with the alcohol slowly leaving her, she was certain that she had not been drugged.

Gently, he took the mug out of her hands and placed it on the nightstand, his eyes never leaving her. Kenna pressed her back into the headboard though she wanted to lean into him. Her mind acted against her heart.

Dr. Merino wasn't offended by her reproach. His fingers ghosted along her arm, inciting a shiver, trailing to her shoulder and down again where his hand meshed with her own. Flesh on flesh, it was impossible to discern desire from danger. He leaned in closer, closer still, until their lips met and her pulse pounded and mouth burned from the soft yet searing caress. His kiss was slow and thoughtful, like he was mulling over a diagnosis. The tender manner in which Dr. Merino kissed her and held her hand left Kenna casting doubts on the validity of his former lovers' testimonies.

How could a man capable of inspiring this level of sentiment have also been capable of such malicious things?

His lips against hers electrified the air and stopped time. There was no room within him to administer such genuine love and to act without a heart.

Chest hitching, Kenna broke away from their kiss. She peered into his midnight eyes, blazing like a blood moon, and an ache spread through her that fractured her voice.

"I have to tell you something."

**Dayton**

He'd known the night had been an illusion, far too perfect to be real, and it shattered with her words. If Kenna's ashen complexion was any indication, she wasn't about to profess her love for him.

Dayton had gotten comfortable with the idea that she knew about Alex. Simply put, he had no other choice. Yet the idea that she possessed knowledge of anyone else had him balling a fist into the sheets.

How long had she known, and why had she waited until this moment to say something? Unless her discovery had been more recent.

The trauma interview. He plucked at his flannel and prayed Audrey Dresden didn't tumble from her mouth.

Paranoia summoned Dayton to his feet but he refrained from pacing. He faced Kenna, his arms crossed, and fought to ignore the sweat collecting at the nape of his neck as he fixated on her countenance, brimming with disappointment.

Hugging her knees to her chest, she whispered, "I know things about you. Things beyond Alex."

"What do you mean?"

"Please don't be angry."

"Tell me what you know," Dayton demanded, regretting his tone as she flinched.

Kenna fled the bed and stood on the opposite side. She mirrored his posture, arms crossed. Two feral animals squaring off.

Except when she opened her mouth to speak, eyes glassy, she bolted for the door.

But he was closer.

He was right behind her, forcing the door shut with one hand and bracing the other around her throat. He'd long awaited this, to feel the press of her body against his.

Though, the circumstances could've been better.

"Let me go."

She sounded calm but his palm detected her thick swallows and hammering heartbeat.

Dayton spoke into her hair, menacing, "I'll do no such thing until you tell me precisely what it is you think you know."

"When we started working together, I was paranoid. I thought I'd feel better if I asked around and did some research."

His nerves were raw, as if he'd scratched through every layer of skin. He put more pressure on Kenna's neck and her head thrashed into his chest.

"Give me a name."

"Erin Wright and Charlee Pender."

Some degree of relief flushed through Dayton. She didn't know about Jasmine. Her boyfriend. The *mess*. The extent of his research.

He released her but kept her pinned against the door, permitting just enough room for her to turn around and face him. Mascara bled beneath her eyes.

"How did you find Erin?"

"Her sister's on our trivia team."

"Brandi?"

"So, is it true? About Erin?" Kenna gritted her teeth. "You got her pregnant and then you *abandoned* her?"

His fist slammed into the doorframe, inches from her face. "It wasn't so simple."

"Make. Me. Understand."

She screamed the words at such a volume he feared the neighbors had overheard but the damage could not be undone. If things didn't pan out with Kenna, perhaps he could add 'domestic disturbance' to his roster of romantic memories.

And so Dayton shouted.

"There are things about me you don't know."

"You don't think I realize that? Why do you think I'm doing all of this? The truth is, Dayton, the more I uncover, the less I understand, and I'm terrified because I don't know which version of you to believe."

He put as much distance between them as the room permitted, migrating to the window. He didn't intend to cause Kenna further harm. Their heated exchange flipped a switch and called upon the darkest recess of his soul, the part that threatened Alex and betrayed Audrey.

"I am *every* version."

Shouting wouldn't aid in her understanding. It was all Dayton had. His lungs were on fire and he desperately wished for an easy way to explain the purpose of the life he led without explaining every damning act he'd committed along the way.

But Kenna's breathing had not yet adjusted from having his

hand curled around her throat and—any sane man would concur —she was in no position to believe him.

She was calm. Angelic and noble despite the smeared cosmetics.

Hand lingering on the doorknob, she looked at him, composed as ever. "No, I won't accept that. That's not who you are. The man those women described, the one you're claiming to be, that isn't the man I know."

"You can't swoop in with your Nancy Drew detective skills and alter a life already lived. Spare me your savior complex, kid."

Her chin trembled. "If I can't save you, no one can."

Kenna left the bedroom, the echo of her retreating footsteps soon replaced by the clicking of the front door. Dayton kicked his dresser and it disturbed the purple box atop its surface, the gift he'd meant to give her. His thoughts turned to the one beneath his bed, and though the evening had not gone according to plan, he remained determined to add Kenna's picture to the box.

Where she'd live, immortalized.

# May

2 9

# WHITE LACE

**Kenna**

*K*enna barely slept the following week. Studying for finals proved to be her saving grace amid the mess with Dr. Merino. The week had turned to the weekend and still she was at her desk, head bowed over an open textbook.

As she reviewed the fine art of somatic intervention, she forgot the way he'd shouted at her, forgot her lapse of judgment when she'd revealed too much, but she could not forget the crushing strength of his hand around her neck.

Kenna blamed only herself.

Had she kept her mouth shut, none of it would've happened. The question then became, had she wanted it to go on like this? Ignorance was far from bliss.

She flipped through the chapter on neuroplasticity, running the end of her pen along sections she'd previously highlighted. Something pulled at her concentration. Kenna glanced at the dead arrangement of roses atop her dresser.

Nothing had ever distracted her from coursework; not even

when Reid, God rest his soul, had broken her heart. Shutting the textbook, she buried her head in her hands.

All she fought to suppress flashed through her mind's eye in a horrific slideshow.

The feelings she had for Dr. Merino were forced into a different light since he'd pinned her against his bedroom door. Her fingers flew to the space where his palm had held her, flat and merciless. Kenna wanted to believe her feelings were merely a byproduct of her close study of him, the time spent in his company.

But her romantic inclinations were no longer strictly tied to research, and she was disgusted with herself for desiring someone who went from cooking her dinner to choking her all in the same night.

She jolted in her desk chair as a knock came at the door.

"Knock, knock. Sorry, I know you're busy in the final trenches," Alex said, flexing her thin brows in apology. A box was bundled under her arm. "This came for you."

She set the violet box on the edge of the desk.

Kenna eyed the package. Her throat constricted the longer she stared at it. "Thanks."

Alex gave a single, slow nod and shut the door on her way out. She returned to her biological psychology textbook in a weak bid to ignore the box. Its presence alone was unnerving when she knew full well who sent it. Dr. Merino should've been issuing an apology, in person, not sending along gifts.

Her pen fell into the book's spine and her hands fell limp on its pages as she recalled his words from dinner.

*I have something for you.*

Curiosity dominated her repulsion and she tore into the box. A note, only legible to her after months of being forced to decipher his handwriting, was nestled among the tissue paper.

*Kenna,*

*Words hardly suffice for the horror to which I subjected you. Know that I am deeply sorry, for everything.*

*Dr. M*

Lifting the layers of tissue, her toes curled, digging into the rough carpet as the contents of the box were laid bare.

"Oh my God." Face aflame, she examined the delicate items within. She reached out to graze the fabric but halted, calling, "Alex!"

"What's up?" she asked, reentering the room.

Kenna, incapable of speech, pointed to the open violet box. Alex plucked up the white hipsters and matching bra that had rendered her roommate mute. A huff escaped her lips as she let the items drop. "Hate to say I told you so."

Checking the tag on the bra's band, Kenna mumbled, "How did he know what size to get?"

She rolled her eyes.

"He's resourceful, I'll give him that. Are you still seeing him? Because I really don't think this—"

"He put his hands on me." She surprised herself with the admission. Anxiety swarmed her and she felt foolish for having said anything.

"He hurt you?"

"Not exactly. I don't think he meant to."

Alex's tone went soft, as if Kenna were a frightened animal she didn't want to scare off. "Well, what happened?"

"We had an argument." She pushed the box to the farthest corner of the desk. "I told him about Erin and Charlee."

"Why the hell would you do that?"

"I don't expect you to understand, but I feel close to him. I wanted to come clean about it."

Hand planted on her hip, Alex cocked her head to one side. "I felt close to Dayton, too. Look what he did to me. You can't live in this fantasy where you think you mean something to him. He's a monster, and he's manipulative, clearly. One minute you're saying he hurt you and the next you're saying you feel close to him. Do you know how messed up that is?"

"You don't know him like I do."

He was manipulative, of course. Dr. Merino had permeated her mind and lived there full-time, an unshakable fever dream. Kenna wasn't sure if they were on speaking terms and she was defending his honor.

"Cut the rose-colored bullshit. None of us really *know* him. He doesn't want to be known. He's charming long enough to have his way with you, and then he's gone."

"That statement is completely unfounded."

But it wasn't. It was the cold, hard truth and she had files upon files that supported as much. Redirecting her attention to her laptop, Kenna loaded the drafts of her acute trauma presentation and paper, figuring if she ignored Alex long enough she'd get the hint.

She was thankful when her roommate shuffled toward the door but that feeling evaporated when her hand landed, featherlight, on Kenna's wrist.

"I know it isn't what you want to hear." Her speech was gutted with a hurt they had come close to sharing. "But this won't end any differently for you."


Though Kenna had been dishonest about the recording being a requirement of the assignment, it provided a cover for what she really wanted.

Dr. Merino's consent.

If nothing else, she thought it'd be invaluable for her investigative records. The audio track played on repeat through her earbuds as she toggled between her presentation and composing her paper, occasionally scrawling cues on index cards. Late spring rain pelted the window but Mother Nature's calm couldn't be heard over the chaos whispering through Kenna's ears. Too often, she'd pause her work and listen with rapt attention to particular sections of the audio, convinced that some hidden meaning lay in his words but ultimately found none and blamed her state of burnout for producing the auditory phantoms.

Midnight neared and her gooey brain begged her to turn off the computer in favor of crawling in bed; her restless heart had other ideas and as the hour waned so, too, did her sanity. She restarted the recording.

The deep, familiar sound of his speech filled Kenna with infantile comfort, as though it were a lullaby.

Dr. Merino trailed off as he spoke about his heart condition and her lids shut, leaden with exhaustion and memory, remembering the way he'd met her gaze and revealed without fanfare the scar marking the device that kept him tethered to this life. A dog on its back, weak spots exposed.

At the first mention of Audrey, her comfort morphed into razor-edged anguish, not because she pitied him but because she knew he'd fed her lies during the majority of their mock session. The indisputable knowledge filled Kenna with a complicated mix of emotions she herself couldn't sort out.

His voice continued until she reached the part about him sleeping with Audrey. She ripped out her earbuds and closed the app.

It was then Kenna heard the rain, the soft pattering against the windows. The repetitive nature of the sound soothed her anxiety and in the quiet moment of serenity she was reminded the world was a beautiful place filled with ugly people. People who did awful, unspeakable things.

And she'd fallen for one of them.

Blood pounded in her temples as she regarded the box. She thought of lifting the lid, retrieving the note, tracing over the words he'd written for her alone.

But the obsession had gotten her nowhere, no closer to the truth. Finals would begin Monday and shortly after, she'd graduate. Grad school in the fall. Yet amid all of the accomplishment, failure festered at her core like a malignant growth. She had not succeeded in what she'd set out to do that semester.

To understand Dayton Merino.

The lone thread of connective evidence among the girls was that they were all students of the university. Beyond that, Kenna had nothing, no rhyme or reason to account for why Dr. Merino had engaged in the behavior.

Rereading the notes she'd collected felt like an optical illusion. Fine details that served as a distraction from the real picture. She wasn't willing to believe intimacy had been the sole reason for the short-term relationships. He had a purpose. What it was, she had no idea.

Brave in the face of the panic rioting within, she snagged the underwear from the box, rolling the lace between her fingers.

One thing Kenna knew for certain. She'd never truly understand unless she sacrificed herself.

## Dayton

The night sky wept beyond the walls of his home as Dayton fought and failed to concentrate on the digital documents before him.

Hours before, a call from Owens-Adair had snatched him from sleep. One of his patients—female, severely depressed—had fainted and gone unresponsive in the hall of her dormitory. She had not eaten in three days.

When she came to and saw him standing among the people gathered by her hospital bed, she'd only said, 'I told them not to call you.' Dayton had spent the drive home wondering if that was how he came across to most people, someone who couldn't be called. Someone to be avoided at all costs. He also found himself wondering if Kenna felt that way about him. It would've explained her lack of calls and absence of visits to his office, but he suspected her sudden exit from his life had more to do with the hand he'd had around her neck.

It was a slipup he replayed over and over, something he fervently wished he could erase.

Years of research populated Dayton's laptop screen and he couldn't bring himself to sift through it and make new connections in the face of his horrid mistake. Every muscle tensed with the breach of a terrifying realization.

Kenna may never forgive him.

A creaking came from outside and instilled him with a sense of calm rather than fright. The porch.

He meandered around furniture in the near dark of the living room on the path to the front door, opening it before the guest had a chance to either knock or break a window. A blur of red hair and pale limbs brushed past him.

"It's late," Dayton said, locking the door. Anything to delay turning around and beholding that magnificent face.

"I know."

While the blinding laptop didn't illuminate the entire room, it provided enough light to see Kenna seated on the couch, an angel glowing in the dark.

He thought the scene was an elaborate hallucination.

Droplets from the light rain adorned her hair like jewels. She was a princess of twig and stone, criminally beautiful despite being disheveled by the elements.

As Dayton stepped closer, he identified his favorite scent emanating from her body. A run in the rain. Damp earth and the vanilla of the pines.

Her cheeks were devoid of their usual flush of color. Hands clenched, trembling at her sides.

He wanted to speak but didn't feel it was his place and had a strong inclination that Kenna, who'd biked in the pitch of a rainy night, had something rather important to say.

Instead, he joined her on the couch, wordlessly enduring the excruciating, ensuing moments. An orchestra of breathing and bated breath.

"What you did last weekend was inexcusable." Dayton opened his mouth but she held up a hand. Tears gleamed in her eyes. "Let me finish. Please."

"I know you think you're irredeemable, but you don't see yourself the way I do. You can't. I look at you and I see someone who's confident, intelligent, so sure of himself. But I also see how lonely you are, how afraid you are of your sickness, and how, despite all that you've done, you don't *seem* like a bad person. You've made poor decisions, sure. Whatever happened with Charlee, Erin, Alex, and whoever else you crossed paths with before I walked into your office? I don't care about any of it. You insisted you were every version of the man from your past, but I only know this version. And he's enough."

How Kenna could stand in his home and speak to him with such ardor after their last encounter went beyond all comprehension. Lust didn't have a reputation for being logical.

She had glimpsed the vile and still wanted him. Burrowed into pockets of the past and uncovered ex-lovers.

But Dayton knew her. She could've exhausted all possible routes of research where he was involved and it wouldn't have satiated her.

What she wanted was to know him, completely, in a manner that couldn't be achieved via the internet or interviews.

The rain fell harder, pummeling the roof.

His hand covered Kenna's knee and she glanced at him through her lashes, letting his fingers trail along the warmth of her cheek.

"I don't want you to question who you are to me because of the things I've done. You're not just some girl. *You* are everything that's good in this world. You," he whispered, thumb skimming her bottom lip, "are my salvation."

## 30

## LAMB

**Kenna**

His salvation.

She'd intended the visit to be her last but Dr. Merino's words alluded to a degree of permanency. Still, they were just that. Words. And, coming from him, it required no effort to imagine them as transparent, easily punctured.

True or not, Kenna refused to let it weigh her down when he was on the verge of giving her what she had longed for since Brandi mentioned across a sticky bar table that he'd slept with a patient.

Clarity.

He dragged his thumb agonizingly slowly from her lip to her chin, tilting it and claiming her mouth. Fire barreled through her and swallowed her whole. Her heart danced and as she attempted to steal a breath Dr. Merino slipped his tongue past her slightly parted lips. Their mouths possessed little energy, their movement resembling the passionate persistence of a dying flame, fighting for oxygen.

His kisses were harrowing, as if he were unloading years of pain onto Kenna with each brush of their lips.

Tangling his fingers in her hair, possessive yet protective, he eased her down until her back met the arm of the couch. The position was far from comfortable but the arousal humming through her veins insisted she say nothing. Dr. Merino abandoned her long enough to discard his sweatshirt and returned with the cool press of his skin and a renewed hunger in his kiss.

Delicately, Kenna touched the surgical scar guarding his pacemaker. The small pink line that marked his entire existence as fragile. Handle with care.

"Don't put pressure on it," he said.

"Of course not."

She barely allowed her fingertips to graze the spot for fear of hurting him before her hand flattened against his chest, roaming over the plane of smooth flesh. He was solid despite his lack of visible muscle and beneath lay a natural strength that needed no definition. A shudder passed through Kenna as his hands found the hollow of her back, forcing them closer.

Her pulse was deafening in her ears, louder than the rainfall, and the heat in the seat of her denim cutoffs had become maddening. She needed every layer of fabric separating them to vanish, to feel his bare skin on her own.

As if he'd been privy to her thoughts, Dr. Merino slid the bra and tank top straps off one shoulder, his teeth following in their wake. They roved over her skin like the flat side of a razor, harmless.

Until they sunk into her flesh.

Blood surged through her, boiling, and Kenna couldn't separate her shoulder's piercing pulsation from the shock of pleasure surging through her like a current. The source of the bite throbbed as he peppered it with kisses.

His lips ghosted down, down to her chest, halting at the border of skin and clothing. She shuddered at the unexpected coolness of his fingers delving into her bra to cast the cup aside. His tongue outlined the curve of her exposed breast and Kenna's stomach rolled as a wild blush bloomed across her neck, her face, just at the thought of Dr. Merino performing such an intimate act. He captured her nipple between his lips and she squirmed beneath him, entranced by the heat of his mouth and sweep of his tongue.

They were practiced, delicate motions and, amid the passion, she found herself not caring who else had received this grade of his affection.

He reached to free the other breast and Kenna breathed his name, low and dripping with ecstasy, and he mumbled into the valley of her chest.

"I love hearing you say that."

A billowing roar of thunder shattered the still of the night and Kenna's entire body jerked in response.

It shook her from her spell, much like their moment of weakness behind the bar, realizing the scene was less glamorous than she'd envisioned. His bite had left her shoulder ablaze and an ache had spread through her back from being lodged against the sofa's arm.

She'd been too distracted to realize that the length of the furniture prohibited them from lying together, and as a result, Dr. Merino had been leaning over her in a seated position.

"Are you afraid of storms, lamb?"

Stomach knotted, Kenna went still and prayed she had misheard him. "What did you call me?"

"Lamb." He stroked her hair. "My darling lamb. Maybe it isn't the storm that has you trembling. Is it me you fear?"

"You know what I think of you."

"How can I be sure?" Dr. Merino caressed the spot he'd bitten and, though she wanted to recoil, her skin tingled beneath his touch. The laptop screen set half of his face aglow and, looming above her exposed chest, he looked every bit a villain pinning a maiden, his gaze wild.

His ability to charm was as flawless as his ability to conjure fear. Kenna supposed God couldn't bring himself to decide if Dr. Merino embodied good or evil and so it had been a 50/50 split.

Seductive and threatening.

He was doubting her. Even if he was playing games, she had to convince him she was in.

She vanquished the knot rising in her throat and drug her lips along his scarred cheek. "Take me, Dayton."

"Take you?" He laughed, a low sound that infected her with want, but his face grew serious in the same beat. "I've waited a lifetime for this. I intend to make the most of it."

Another thunderclap echoed in the sky and Kenna's limbs instinctively wrapped around him. The warmth radiating off his skin comforted her—a false sense of safety in a situation that was anything but safe. His arms encircled her and she became weightless as they traveled through the dark as one, toward the gates of Hell. Moonlight cast a faint glow on the hardwood in the bedroom and it was comical almost, she supposed.

Revisiting the very place she'd felt her life had been threatened in the name of satisfying some animalistic need.

Dr. Merino sat on the edge of the bed and she stood between his legs, leaning in, and tilted her lips toward his. But he made no move to kiss her. He studied Kenna with an intensity that had her heart turning over.

It was haunting, the way he looked at her, like he feared he may one day forget the details of her face. She was half-clothed but had never been more naked than she was in the silver, shadowy light, held in place by his eyes.

"One day, you'll hate me." There was a tiredness to his voice. It soothed her. The sound. Their proximity. "Maybe not today, maybe not tomorrow, but it will happen."

Her arms went heavy, dead weight at her sides, for she had resigned herself to be his for the night and he spoke of a forever that would never come.

Kenna cast aside the self-loathing and did the only thing that would bring her closer to her goal. She lied.

"I could never hate you."

Gaze locked on his, she took a step back and undid the metal button of her shorts. She released the zipper in a drawn-out manner, not aiming to tantalize Dr. Merino but instead to give herself a minute to process what was transpiring. Undressing in front of someone was a new experience—Reid had always yanked her clothes off the second they were alone—and she hoped she wasn't making a fool of herself. It wouldn't exactly further Kenna's research if the night ended with him laughing in her face.

He wasn't laughing. Far from it.

Her tank top and bra went, leaving only the gifted underwear, and Dr. Merino looked at her as if she were some beguiling object, something spun from gold. Too precious to touch but too beautiful to not be beheld. He was quick to transition from admirer to appraiser.

A fire burned through her, insistent and familiar, as his index finger trailed along her throat, sternum, and stomach, retracting before he reached the hemline of her underwear.

"Do you have any idea how beautiful you are?"

She stepped closer. Closer, somehow, than they'd been moments earlier. Close enough to feel the heat of his sex. Close enough for her breath to fan across his face as she said, "I do."

Those two words, her confident intonation, broke something within Dr. Merino. She thought she saw him cock his head, like he couldn't believe she'd said such a thing, before his arms locked around her and in one dizzying, fluid motion her back was flush with the mattress.

He stalked up Kenna's body, easily finding her mouth in the semidarkness, and it was sensory overload.

The faint trace of ginger tea and honey on his tongue. The lavender airing out of the sheets with their movements and the petrichor clinging to his hair as it brushed her cheeks. The heat of their bare skin, chests heaving against one another, competing for the right to breathe. The restraint of his subdued sighs mingling with their fevered kiss. And if she'd opened her eyes, just a bit, she would've seen Dr. Merino hovering over her, nearing the complete absence of clothing.

But she needn't look.

The suggestion alone had her pulse competing with the storm raging beyond the house's walls.

Her thoughts spun as his affection drugged her, slowing her down, making everything blur together. He'd been pressing one of her wrists into the comforter for a while, maybe worrying that she'd again flee in a panic. There was nowhere Kenna could've gone, even if she had wanted to.

Not when she was on the verge of overdosing on a lethal mix of oxytocin and the taste of Dayton Merino.

His hand freed her wrist and it slid along the inside of her thigh, higher, higher, and she released a sigh of her own, remembering what Erin had relayed to Brandi.

How he'd made her feel otherworldly, like they were the only two people who existed. How Kenna presently felt.

Though her want for him was terrifying, she could not rid herself of it. Had she not been courageous enough to turn up on his doorstep, that kindling of desire would've burned within her evermore.

He traced the patterns in the lace of her underwear. His touch was light yet scorching, branding her flesh. Dr. Merino didn't bother with removing the fabric nor did he venture beneath it. She swore her hips relaxed as he touched her through the material, applying a pressure so pleasurable it bordered on painful. The absence of light became disorienting with each flutter of her lashes as her body surrendered to him.

The lace had once moved with his touch but now it was plastered to Kenna, dampened with desire.

He planted a kiss between her breasts, dragging his mouth up her neck, up to her lips, where he spoke against them, "You're all wet, lamb."

A raging shade of crimson covered every inch of her skin and she was thankful for the anonymity of the darkened room. No one had ever spoken to her that way, and she didn't quite know how to respond. She leaned toward saying something but feared sounding like an idiot.

Her teeth grazed his bottom lip.

"Only for you."

"Fuck, Kenna."

It was something she had never heard him say and she was pleased with the way it sailed over his tongue. Harsh, sharp, so much passion packed into one syllable.

His election of the word led to an intense pleasure ricocheting from Kenna's core. The euphoria continued to roll through her body long after the initial high had passed. She blinked at the ceiling in the dark and felt pleasantly empty, like she may have floated away into the ether and maybe that wouldn't have been so bad.

She wouldn't have to face what she'd done in the morning.

A hand snaked around her back and came to rest between her shoulder blades, drawing them closer. His other hand covered her hip, thumb stroking the skin, and his mouth found her earlobe.

"I want you so badly. I've never wanted anyone like this," Dr. Merino said, breath hot in her ear. His hand abandoned her hip and roamed the length of her, familiarizing himself with every dip and curve, as if she were an apparition in danger of vanishing. "My body is on fire."

Outside, the rain slackened. The thunder lessened in frequency. Kenna registered the weight of him on top of her, as well as his arousal pinned to her thigh. It was like hot silk slipping over her and she inhaled sharply at the intimacy of the contact.

"Dayton, please."

With two fingers, he tore her underwear aside, far too ruled by desperation to remove them completely. The need Dr. Merino demonstrated for her in that moment was oddly thrilling. She felt powerful knowing she could conjure such a response from him.

The light press of him between Kenna's legs turned her mind into a sinkhole. All thoughts disbanding on the precipice of his love. All but one.

Her hand shot out and held his wrist. "You should know that I'm not taking anything."

"That's okay."

He pushed her hand aside as he pushed inside her.

She wanted to tell him to stop, that it wasn't okay. But her lips betrayed her and her chest felt as though it would burst from bottled breath and things left unsaid as Dr. Merino drove himself into her, his movements languid and measured.

"Don't worry," he mumbled, trailing kisses along her shoulder and neck, where his lips threatened to bare teeth. "I'm sterile."

Disturbed as Kenna was by the admission, her body and mind were far too relaxed to protest. A week earlier, she would've been disgusted. She would've run for the door. But now, drowning in the sea of his passion, a hot ache assailed her and she anchored her legs around his waist.

Wholly tied to their madness.

He stroked her hair as his pace grew more impassioned. She loved the juxtaposition. His delicate petting and the urgent bucking of his hips.

A thin layer of sweat coated their bodies as they gelled together, their choreography flawless amid an improvised scene. Kenna tried to stifle the moan clawing its way up her throat but he'd already noticed the slight arch of her back and arduous tilt of her head. He pulled out and his fingers sank into her not a second later, effortlessly mimicking their tempo.

"Relax," Dr. Merino said, his voice a seductive lull. "I know what you want. Let yourself have it. Let go."

Liquid heat pooled within her and spread like embers in a

forest breeze, setting every nerve ending ablaze. Kenna was granted no time to catch her breath before he filled her once again. He pressed himself to her, chest to chest, and their hearts beat as one, his electrical impulse-induced rhythm and her natural one.

His fingertips dug into her hip and made her wince but she didn't ask him to ease up. She was no longer afraid. And, as she met his deep thrusts, something new and enthralling alight in his eyes, Kenna wondered how she had so easily agreed to give up this earthbending affection.

To give him up.

Eyes closed, she put her hands flat against Dr. Merino's chest and attempted to memorize the fluidity of his movements. The sweat-slicken skin.

The fire that had burned inside of her all evening was reduced to ashes and, as a single tear dissolved into her hair, she realized that it may very well have been the last time she'd touch him. See him. Speak to him.

She'd understood it with all the clarity in the world when she had hatched the plan in her apartment but clarity was hard to come by with someone buried between your thighs.

His kiss became more demanding as he fell apart and a delicious warmth spilled within Kenna.

Breathing ragged, he pressed his ear to her heart, fingers skimming her side. She played with strands of his damp hair as his whispers dissolved into the dark.

"I want to get closer to you. No matter what I do, it isn't enough."

Hours of coursework and the physical exertion she'd imposed upon her body soon caught up with her and she faded into sleep, Dr. Merino's voice calling to her either in dreams or consciousness.

"Save me from this, darling."

31

# SAINT

**Kenna**

*A* stream of sunlight coaxed Kenna awake. The soreness of her shoulder became pronounced as she shifted in the bed. She rubbed the tender skin but was indifferent toward its accompanying ache when fragments of the previous night crept forth from her memory.

His bite. His kiss. His touch.

Lying in Dr. Merino's sheets, she found herself not caring whether it was morning or afternoon. Her studying and half-completed presentation faded into insignificance because laying beside her was a man who'd proven more challenging than any exam or paper. And she'd had him.

But the rush of triumph fizzled out as she realized whatever conclusion she penned on his character wouldn't satisfy her. Something would always feel incomplete.

No answer would've been enough where Dr. Merino was concerned. Their having met had birthed an incurable obsession within her, an insatiable creature clawing on her entrails. They'd slept together and still that obsession tore at her insides, demanding more. She echoed the sentiment he'd mumbled into her chest, '*I want to get closer to you. No matter what I do, it isn't enough.*'

Maybe that's why something tugged at her heart at the thought of walking away from him. Insufficient research.

She'd cheated the system. She'd had the pleasure without the pain. Maybe she didn't deserve answers because she had circumvented the trauma he was known to inflict. What she did deserve was eternal damnation for wishing that trauma upon herself, if only it meant she'd understand.

Kenna's breath hitched as he stirred. His lids fluttered open, irises dark as ever amid the day's brightness.

"Good morning." Sleep edged his voice.

Stretching, hands clasped behind his head, he regarded her with a smile so faint, she may have dreamt it. She tried to focus on anything else in the room but her eyes betrayed her and roamed over the sparse hair under his arms and the contrasting bareness of his torso.

"Is there a reason you've left a foot of space between us? Did you have FedEx overnight a restraining order? Come here."

Their night of passion had waned and Kenna felt a different kind of heat ensconcing her neck. She had more reservations toward the innocent invitation to sidle up to him than she had been writhing beneath him.

As she scooted closer, Dr. Merino's faint smile gave way to a genuine one and his arm corralled her, tugging her flush to his side. She breathed in the smell of his skin. Something about it was off. Foreign yet familiar.

It was her scent, still lingering on him like perfume.

"How did you sleep?"

Kenna almost laughed. All of the tension and animosity and uncertainty between them reduced to talk of their sleeping habits. She outlined the small mass below his left collarbone.

"Well enough."

"I promise, it's not as fascinating as it seems." Dr. Merino stroked along her spine and she thought she was in danger of falling under a trance until he muttered the wrong age. "I've had it since I was 26. You get used to it."

"Oh. I thought you'd said it was ahead of med school."

"Are you trying to catch me in a lie, darling?"

"No, I just–"

"If I told you otherwise, I misspoke. We won't be off to a great start if there's no trust on day one, now will we?"

He'd possessed her body for one evening and was now operating under the assumption that they were a 'we.'

Charlee had warned of his clinginess. Erin, of his coldness. Alex, of his propensity to be sweet and then suddenly rob you of everything. Even knowing this, Kenna remained nestled against him as if there was no imminent danger lurking on the horizon.

But what if Dr. Merino wasn't clingy? Perhaps he was lonely. The majority of his time was spent on campus and when he did go home he had to be on call for hospitalizations and other incidents. She had little clue what else his job entailed but surmised–solely off his general attitude–that it was both extensive and exhausting. Kenna knew what that was like, to absorb oneself in something so completely, one forgets to live.

She shut her eyes until they stung.

Why was she empathizing with him? She should've been gathering her clothes and brainstorming an excuse to leave the craftsman on Fairbrook and never look back.

He turned away from her to consult the time on his phone and then dropped the device like it had burst into flames, fleeing the bed. "Shit. I'm going to be late."

Sitting criss-cross in the middle of the sheets, she watched in mild amusement as Dr. Merino stumbled to the closet and retrieved a hanging garment encased in plastic.

"Late for what?"

"My friend's wedding. Some friend I am." He laid what she assumed to be a suit at the foot of the bed and returned to the closet, kneeling and rummaging around before snatching up a pair of dress shoes. "I'd let you tag along as my uninvited plus one, but a) I'm sure you have nothing to wear on such short notice and, most importantly, b) Nathan isn't too thrilled about the idea of you and I."

"Nathan being Professor Scott?" He nodded. "Gee, I wonder why. You're responsible for 90% of my grade and we just slept together. This doesn't look good for you."

Dr. Merino narrowed his eyes at her and, for once, they were backlit by something akin to playfulness rather than hostility.

"He's my lone social outlet in this town so I need to stay in his good graces. I'm afraid bringing a former student of his as a date to his wedding is out of the question."

He rifled through a dresser drawer and she noticed a new addition resting atop its surface, something that wasn't present during her inventory of the room when she'd fallen ill.

A vintage Polaroid camera.

Tension laced her forearms as she recalled Alex's mention of blackmail pictures and Kenna thought how very clever it'd be to use an outdated, instant-print camera. No cyber footprint.

She forged a sense of calm. Alex had never seen the alleged photos. Dr. Merino had merely made threats.

Tracing her line of sight to the camera, he swiped it off the dresser and his gaze swept over her body. "Could I take a picture of you?"

"I–I don't have any clothes on."

"Underwear constitutes clothing, does it not?"

Kenna wet her lips and stared at him for a moment before quietly conceding, "Alright."

"Turn your head to the side." She obeyed and was met with her reflection in the full-length mirror, revealing the state of her hair, trampled by sleep. She was in dire need of a shower and a toothbrush and in spite of it Dr. Merino treated her like a supermodel. "Tilt your chin down, just a little. Beautiful."

In the mirror, her eyes locked on that box beneath the bed and something tore at her from the inside out.

Glass, cold and sharp, cutting through her.

She'd almost forgotten. As Kenna regarded it with silent terror, she remembered lying on the rug in a daze and being put off by its presence amid all of that bare flooring. Alone and unsettling.

A blinding flash shot forth from the camera followed by an obnoxious clicking sound and Dr. Merino plucked the picture sliding out of its mouth, fanning it lightly through the air and placing it on the dresser.

He dropped down beside her, fingers inching up her leg as she was met with the soft touch of his lips and her stomach twisted at how effortlessly he slipped into this level of comfort around her. Kenna didn't temporarily lose her sanity over the kiss. She felt numb, frostbitten.

There was no heat left within her, only an iciness shooting through her veins and insisting that with each passing moment she stayed in the house, she was putting herself at greater risk. At risk of what, exactly, she didn't know.

But the feeling was powerful. The need to run without needing to understand what one was running from.

Dr. Merino squeezed her thigh, jarring her focus.

"Why don't you stay for the weekend?"

"You know I have to study for finals."

He kissed along the hollow of her cheek, as she had done with his scar. "Next weekend classes are out and I'm afraid that leaves you with no excuses. We'll go somewhere, wherever you want, just the two of us."

He'd had a sliver of her and now he seemed to want everything, all at once, and she hated the part of herself that wanted to give it to him, every last strand of hair and bone.

"I'd like that."

"Good because it's non-negotiable. Now, if you'll excuse me, I have to shower and get going before I piss off an entire wedding party."

He kissed her forehead and retreated to the bathroom, shutting the door behind him. Kenna's pulse accelerated, wild, out of control, as she restricted her breathing and sat perfectly still. An animal who sensed a target on its back.

Listening. Waiting.

The second the shower cut on, she sunk to the hardwood. Heart in her throat, she reached for the box, sliding it along the dust-coated floor. It sat before her with its tattered lid and faded retail stickers which claimed it once held tennis shoes. Whatever resided in the box was probably highly inconsequential. Otherwise, Dr. Merino wouldn't have left it out in the open, begging to be discovered.

Unless he wanted her to find it.

With violently unsteady hands, Kenna lifted the lid. Her throat tensed and it felt like someone was choking her, like the night she'd first seen him in St. James. It had been a subtle warning from God to stay away.

She hadn't listened. She'd gotten closer and closer. And now, sprawled on the floor of his bedroom, it was too late.

Black spots hindered her vision as she stared at a pile of Polaroids, unblinking. Fear slithered through her chest, her lungs, but her exterior was the portrait of tranquility as the shower continued to run in the foreground.

Maintaining her composure was imperative.

A different woman starred in each photo, every shot bordering on soft-core pornography. Names and dates were inscribed below them in Dr. Merino's signature, ragged penmanship. Her blood ran cold when she recognized Erin among them. Then Charlee. Then Alex.

Bella, the girl who had jumped to her death.

Kenna placed the Polaroids on the floor as she sorted through them. The remaining women were unfamiliar.

Until she came upon the final one.

Bottom lip quivering, her eyebrows knit together as she held a photograph of herself. One that had preceded their spontaneous photoshoot and had been taken without consent.

In it, she slept in Dr. Merino's bed, clad only in her white underwear. The caption was divergent from the others.

*'Saint Kenna.'*

Terror possessed every cell in her body as she let the photograph fall amid the rest but she fought to steady her breathing. She wouldn't surrender to the fear, no matter her clammy skin or state of near hyperventilation. She was a final girl, a survivor, and though she didn't believe her life was on the line, she felt her academic and future professional reputation was at stake with the existence of the picture.

Kenna refused to let him hold something so damning against her. Against anyone else.

She spotted her phone peeking out of the pocket of her discarded shorts and yanked it free, steadying the camera over the arrangement of Polaroids and ensuring they were all in frame before capturing them. With tremulous fingers, she scrambled to put the photos back in the order she'd found them and replaced the lid. She crouched on the floor and slid the box beneath the bed.

As she steadied its previous, precise position, a rusty creak sounded within the bathroom that made her arms go rigid. The shower had cut off.

In a whirl of movement, Kenna was on her feet, making quick work of tugging on her clothes. Her hand fumbled around to check that her phone was in her pocket as she tore out of the bedroom and her expedient strides broke into a jog toward the front door as she heard Dr. Merino emerging from the bathroom.

A dangerous weakness dominated her knees and nearly sent her tumbling down the porch steps with her bike. She mounted it as the tire hit the ground and sped away from 673 Fairbrook. Her legs burned and strained from the fervency of her pedaling and yet Kenna couldn't pump fast enough. Every second she remained on his street, her anxiety intensified, latching onto her core and radiating throughout her defenseless body like a lecherous disease. She imagined him chasing after her. Shouting. Snapping pictures of her escape.

Tears singed her skin as if they were tiny flames. She'd thought she was different. Some kind of exception.

She was one of many.

Kenna screamed until her throat was raw and lungs felt on the verge of collapse, filling the desolate roads and forests of Branch Spring with her gut-wrenching howl.

32

# BLIGHTED

**Dayton**

jarring slam erupted in the main area of the house and Dayton's hands stilled as he reached for a towel. He waited for more noise but there was no sound save for the water dripping from the showerhead.

"Kenna?"

Questions hammered at him while he dried off. Surely, she hadn't left. Again. Pressure congregated in the center of his chest. Had he not behaved like a gentleman? As gentlemanly as he could manage, anyhow.

Wrapping the towel around his waist, his hand lingered on the doorknob as he siphoned a breath and was met with a still scene. His wedding attire was where he'd left it. The sheets disturbed by sleep and passion.

Kenna was gone.

Her love had transformed him but its magic had been fleeting, sparks dying in the wake of her absence, and he hardened into the man he'd shaped over the last decade as he regarded the empty bedroom. Cold, detached, logical.

Dayton had foolishly believed her insistent acceptance of him. It was everything he'd wanted to hear from her lips. And she had played him. A novice had beaten him at his own game.

Jaw tensed, he slipped into his underwear, socks, slacks. Possibilities turned over in his head to account for Kenna's abrupt departure but a plausible explanation evaded him. He struggled with the buttons on the shirt, missing the slits by miles and cursing under his breath. Dayton migrated to the full-length mirror but soon forgot he was getting dressed as his eyes continuously darted to the reflection of his socks.

His hands fell away from the half-buttoned shirt. Sweat collected in the middle of his back.

The box.

The room spun around him amid his frantic collapse to the floor. On his knees, he peered below the bed. No relief came upon seeing it exactly where he'd left it. He pulled out the box and his heartbeat was an anthem for the paranoid as he tore through the contents.

Nothing was out of place, the image of a dormant Kenna resting on the bottom.

He disregarded the mess on the floor and buttoned the rest of his shirt, tucked it into his slacks, and threaded his belt through its loops, buckling it with a final flourish.

As Dayton swiped his cuff links off the dresser, he noticed the more recently developed Polaroid. He fixated on it as he wrestled with the accessory.

Rays of light streamed across her face and chest. Though her head was turned to one side, it was impossible to overlook the solemnity of her expression, mouth drawn in a tight line. There seemed to be an artificial wideness to her eyes as she looked down into the mirror.

Where he'd asked her to look.

## Kenna

Kenna was grateful upon discovering Alex wasn't home. The extent of her acting skills had been exhausted at Dr. Merino's house. She didn't want to be asked why she was sniffling or slamming cabinetry or throwing things. She had to handle the full scope of this breakdown, alone, and then she'd pick up the pieces, just as she had always done.

But she knew this time was different, that some of those pieces would never fit the same way again.

She tore off her clothes in hot pursuit of the bathroom. A shower was her lone hope of clearing her head, if only a little, before reevaluating the files on her computer. Kenna's eyes stung as she spun the faucet. It was as if someone had dumped teaspoons of salt into them. The strain made her drowsy.

Steam filled the room, blanketing her in warmth, and she was tempted to curl up in her bed and surrender to the rest her eyes demanded. She dismissed the idea entirely as she reached to unhook her bra and caught a glimpse of herself in the mirror.

A bruise, violet and ugly, bloomed across her shoulder.

Kenna let her fingers brush against it. She felt the familiar welling of tears but it was a phantom sensation. The reservoirs of her red eyes were rusted and depleted. Her heart ached for the girl in that reflection, no longer recognizable.

What kind of darkness had she surrendered to in which she'd even conceive of letting someone hurt her so?

Tearing the hanging bra off her form, she slung it into the wastebasket and did the same with the underwear, stepping into the shower stripped of everything but feeling. It was all she could do.

Replay the hurt. Harness the fury.

The scalding water provided a mild comfort through her cycling of emotions. Kenna hung her head and clawed at the back of her neck. Water trickled from her hair into her mouth as she opened it to shout but she was unable to manufacture a sound, like the pain had made a home within her and refused eviction.

With frenzied hands, she washed every crevice of her body over and over again. She fought to scrub herself clean of the memories of Dr. Merino's bed. His voice echoed through her head—*darling, lamb, I know what you want*—once sweet sounding but now antagonizing as she buffed her skin until the loofah felt like sandpaper and she looked down and saw that her arms were pink.

How could he have done this to her?

The man who'd once confessed after a few drinks that maybe he cared a little bit, too.

Kenna deconstructed that line while tucking a towel around herself, understanding that Dr. Merino hadn't cared about her nor their working relationship.

He cared only about the perverse pleasure of getting off on taking half-clothed pictures of women he'd manipulated.

And yet, amid her intense displeasure, she found it difficult to reduce him to someone whose existence thrived on the thrill of sexual exploitation. It seemed far too simple and doubt tantalized her curiosity like the inaugural hit of an amphetamine that seals one's addiction.

Feeling unsafe even in her own company, she locked her bedroom door. She took up residence at her desk and forewent clothing. Getting dressed would've been a useless exercise.

There weren't enough layers of fabric in existence to stop the spread of the chills seeping under her skin.

Kenna pulled up every file, note, and document she'd accumulated relating to Dr. Merino, palm bracing her forehead. Had she missed something? It was worth a second look, a third; but she knew if the search beckoned greater attention to detail, she wouldn't flinch. She'd review the information until her retinas short-circuited if it meant finding an answer. Her mission had once been singular—to understand—but Kenna craved retribution for what he'd done.

The thought of Dr. Merino's lifeless corpse rotting in Hell did little to lift her spirits. She signed the cross, ashamed of the fantasy.

Three separate files, one for each girl, filled the display and she contemplated adding a fourth for Bella's suicide. Nausea teased her throat as the words 'pregnancy' and 'miscarriage' stood out in Erin's notes as if they were three-dimensional.

The sterilization. The pictures. It was all so sick.

Kenna had been naive to think she could save him. He was a lost cause long before the first day she set foot in his office.

She zeroed in on Alex's column and her stomach lurched. Were the Polaroids the alleged blackmail pictures?

An urge arose to check her phone. Irrationality ran wild as she zoned out on the device, fearing that she'd opened it up as a vessel for demonic possession after capturing Dr. Merino's little box of horrors.

"Enough," she muttered.

She emailed the file from her phone to the laptop to examine it in greater detail. If she was going to force herself to look, she'd rather study it on a screen that exceeded 5.5 inches.

The message populated her inbox and she clicked it without hesitation, expanding the image to its maximum size. A car alarm blared outside and sent Kenna's heart pounding but her pulse grew sluggish and threatened to quit as she was faced with the chilling picture. It wasn't until the taste of copper spread in her mouth that she realized she had been biting the inside of her lip.

There were 11 photographs. Of them, every woman wore red underwear. Every woman except her.

The white fabric stood out like a scarlet letter among the collection and she wasn't sure if it was more appropriate to be disgusted or touched by what appeared to have been an intentional distinction. Pallor veiled her face as she stared at her white-clad body, an unnerving sight among that sea of red.

Being special to Dr. Merino felt like a death sentence. Though he'd hurt the others, he had eventually let them be.

She looked beyond herself and explored the rest of the pictures. Alex had been the earliest, labeled as 'Dec. 11 2014.' Their names rattled around in her brain: Ivy, Bella, Jasmine, Freya, Harmony, Dakota, Giselle. Her mouth went dry as she bounced around the names and dates and puzzle pieces slunk together like they were magnetized.

All at once, everything clicked.

A connection Kenna couldn't refute.

Alex in 2014 was followed by Bella, Charlee, and Dakota in 2015, and on it went, alphabetization falling in chronological accordance with time.

The largest gap was between Jasmine and herself, spanning almost exactly two years.

He had been waiting for her.

Pulling in a breath that strained her lungs, she bought herself a moment of calm. She ignored the tick, tick, ticking of her heart as if it weren't in danger of exploding and scanned the Oregon Medical Board's website for information on filing a complaint. The beating grew louder, faster, a band of horses galloping in her chest, as she queued up her inbox in another tab and composed a new email.

*To whom it may concern ...*


**Dayton**


Love songs played on a nauseating loop within the tent of the covered event space. The sun that had lasted through the ceremony shied behind the clouds and a light but constant plopping of raindrops could be heard overhead.

Dayton envisioned the rain escalating to a downpour, all of that water collecting on the tent's roof, the weight of it eventually tearing through the polyester and drenching everyone inside.

Attending a wedding in his current state felt like a challenge from God on his character. The dancing and kissing and 'I love you's were poised to inflict greater damage on his dual heart conditions than the Moscow mule he held. He sipped the gingery drink and glared at the cheerful young couples and those who had been together for an unfathomable number of decades. They all made him grind his teeth as he offered terse smiles in greeting to those who passed him by. His irritation at the parade of affection melded to longing.

With Kenna, he'd tasted forever.

But he was damned. Undeserving. Destined to spend his life waiting on a happily ever after that would never come.

Dayton downed the rest of the mule and the alcohol blazed through him. Drinkware clanked in a toast, pulling him to the present, and he joined in with his empty glass. The huddled circle of groomsmen took their turns patting Nathan on the back. That rarely employed but universally accepted male affection.

His best man speech was fast approaching and he knew he was in no condition to deliver it, but the maid of honor was mercifully delaying his demise by going on and on about a trip she and Charlaine took during college. Setting the copper mug on the bar, Dayton attempted to call Kenna for what seemed like the hundredth time since she fled from his home. A knife twisted in his gut as it rang only to go to her automated voicemail. He lingered after the beep, cramming everything he yearned to say into a succinct message.

"I'm sorry."

He dropped the phone into his pocket and motioned to the bartender for another drink but was granted no reprieve as Amy, the maid of honor, summoned him to the dance floor.

"At this time, I'd like to turn over the mic to the best man to share a few words about this wonderful couple over here." Amy gestured to the bride and groom's table.

An uncoordinated smattering of applause rose and fell as she transferred the microphone to him. She leaned into him in part-ing, whispering, "Loosen up, sugar."

He managed a conciliatory nod before she swept away in her flowing aquamarine dress and he was left alone, the center of attention at a wedding he was dying to leave. An entire party of eyes were on him as he cleared his throat and failed to recall any shred of the speech he'd prepared weeks earlier. Charlaine's hand was laced with Nathan's atop the table, conjuring memories of the way Kenna's hand had fit with his and their love had been the eye of the storm raging around them.

"Most of you don't know me, but I bet a lot of you know that guy over there," he said, pointing to Nathan. "It's all about him today. Them, I should say. Nathan and Charlaine are perfect for each other. Fated to be together. When I moved here from Califor-nia, Nathan and I clicked right away. I'll admit that I got a little jealous when Charlaine entered the picture. At first, I thought it was because she was stealing my friend for chick-flick marathons and furniture shopping, but I was kidding myself. I was jealous of what Nathan had, something I'd never had in any real capacity for myself: love."

A couple of 'aws' arose from the mostly silent crowd.

"Then I found it. Suddenly, my friend wasn't so supportive. I'll cut him some slack. It was a tricky situation. Most would call it unconventional, but you must understand, it felt like my life depended upon having this woman."

He'd had one drink and he was baring his soul to strangers, not as a result of the liquor but of the hairline fracture running through his body. Everything ready to shatter without a moment's notice.

Nathan pressed a fist to his mouth and Charlaine shook her head as she spoke into his ear.

"She bailed on me, by the way, and you'll be pleased to know I had some class. I turned in her grade before I fucked her. Guess I got what I deserved."

Dayton dropped the mic on the linoleum. A cacophony of gasps and shrieks erupted while some looked on in wide-eyed horror.

It wasn't until he locked eyes with Nathan that he registered the immensity of what he had done.

His gaze fell to his dress shoes as he headed for the tent's opening but no sooner than he'd felt the caress of the evening breeze someone latched onto his shoulder, jerking him backward. He spun around and stood toe to toe with Nathan, whose face was dangerously close to his own. He smelled of whiskey and Charlaine's perfume and Dayton hated that his olfactory impressions of Kenna were being overridden by these inconsequential scents.

"Have you lost your mind?"

"All mental health professionals benefit from a smidge of insanity, Nathaniel."

"Nah, you don't have a smidge of it. You embody it. You fucked the girl you were supposed to be mentoring and you admitted it to a quarter of the psych department. Or did you forget some of our colleagues were here today? Congratulations, you single-handedly ruined my wedding. My *wedding.*" He went quiet, shuffling one foot where the faux flooring met the grass. "I never expected anything like this from you, man."

Dayton knew an apology was warranted but the wound was fresh and pulsating. Smearing anything on it while it was open would only agitate it further.

Instead, he said softly, "I loved her."

His quiet confession was lost to the music and cheer pouring out of the mouth of the tent.

Taking a step inside, Nathan stopped short and glanced over his shoulder. "I'm glad Kenna got the hell away from you. She deserves better."

He stood staring after his friend until he disappeared among the crowd and then he stalked off through the parking lot. Dayton fumbled with the keys in his pocket, metal on metal scoring his walk to the station wagon as the noise of the reception receded.

There hadn't been anything out of sorts with the box but he knew Kenna had seen it. It was the only explanation for her abrupt escape and dodged calls. He had not hidden it on either occasion she'd been in his home. He'd asked her to look into the mirror. Perhaps the direction had come from his subconscious, begging her to uncover what he was capable of.

Then again, she already knew. The discovery had merely served as confirmation. He despised himself for being so careless. The landscape of their premature love blighted by a simple mistake.

He sat in his car with the engine cut, looking out the smudged windshield. The sinking sun wove threads of gold through the needled pines and he admired its beauty. A blinding halo ringing creation. But Dayton knew that anything beautiful was finite.

Sunsets plunged into darkness. The women he shuffled through like playing cards lest he get too attached and make a mess of things as he had done with Audrey.

As he had with Kenna.

His head fell against the headrest. How was he to remain at the university throughout the course of her graduate program without going mad?

Sitting in his office and picturing her scribbling in one of her notebooks in the vacant chair across the room. Walking from the faculty lot to Markham Hall every morning and passing the library where she worked. Seeing her blue bike from his third-story window. He imagined what it might be like.

To constantly be surrounded by reminders of a life he couldn't live with a woman he couldn't have.

The thought was unbearable. The reality would've killed him, and he was struck with the painful realization that he had no choice but to surrender his post at Ponderosa.

He had to get away from the university because, despite the

sudden uncertainty of his future, he knew Kenna had no part in it. He'd resign so she could live beyond the shadow of what he had done.

The vow to leave her behind weighed heavy on his heart, a deep ache that spread and compressed every part of him as he twisted the key in the ignition.

Dayton would've carried that ache for eternity if it allowed her to breathe easy.

To forget.

3 3

# THE PEOPLE YOU LOVE

**Kenna**

"Give me your paper and I'll return your packet. One for one, ladies and gentlemen," Professor Henrick said.

Kenna felt nothing but relief as she shuffled along with the line of students. Once her essay hit the stack, she'd be free for the summer. Free of campus and of the doctor lurking on the other side of it. She kept her head bowed as she drew nearer to the professor's desk. Exam week was a special kind of hell but paired with the processing of trauma? Gray rings hugged her eyes and gave them a hollowed appearance.

She had not slept in so long, she'd forgotten what it was like. The peacefulness of it all.

Every night when her head hit the pillow, she feigned sleep, willing it to come; and though her breathing shallowed out as if to ease into rest, she'd soon push herself up on her palms, the high-pitched clicking of a Polaroid camera ringing in her ears.

She perched at her desk all hours of the night, reviewing self-constructed study guides and triple-checking that her papers were

260

free of errors through a curtain of tears. The endless crying terrified her. Dr. Merino had wrung her mind and soul of everything she had to give and yet her body managed to scrounge up something more for him, paying tithe to his memory.

Betrayal usurped her feeling of emptiness. It tore at Kenna's chest. She had been naive to think they'd had a genuine connection at any point. They had both used the other and each of them had accomplished what they'd set out to do.

As she steadily advanced in line, control fragile, she felt as if she had come away with nothing in an exchange that should've been mutually beneficial. Somewhere along the way, her goal had changed. Riding through the rain to Dr. Merino's house. Knocking on his front door. She couldn't pinpoint it, but she knew that it lay on the timeline of that night when the research, the investigation that had mattered most to her had been overshadowed by something greater.

Her need to belong to him. To heal him and fix him and save him from his destruction.

She dropped her essay on the designated pile but rather than returning her internship feedback packet, Professor Henrick scrawled something on a sticky note and folded it in half before slipping it to her.

*See me after class.*

Kenna almost rolled her eyes upon reading the threateningly juvenile statement. It was ludicrous. Technically there was no class and almost everyone had gone.

Still, her ill attempt at analytical humor did not abate the dread that came over her. Worst-case scenarios flooded her mind. Had Dr. Merino failed to submit the packet? She doubted Professor Henrick would hold her responsible for his mishap, and, at the very least, she had submitted the signed paperwork indicating her hours had been met.

As her final classmate left, Kenna approached the professor's desk, crumpled note in hand.

"You wanted to see me?"

Professor Henrick folded his weathered hands in his lap and looked at her expectantly. Releasing a weighted sigh, he began, "Are you aware that there have been, ah, rumors, surrounding you and your mentor?"

She was aware but saw no reason to tell him as much.

"You know as well as I do there isn't much else to do in this town but gossip, professor."

"Yes but, in my experience, students don't casually gossip about something as … salacious as this. Miss O'Callaghan, this is a tough subject to discuss with you. I've enjoyed your presence in my courses over the last couple of years and it truly pains me to even entertain what's going around." He grimaced and made as if to shake his head but thought better of it. "I'm just going to come out and say it. Students, as well as some of the faculty, seem to have the impression that Dr. Merino and yourself were involved in a sexual relationship."

It occured to Kenna, then, that Professor Henrick wouldn't have held her back for the sake of discussing rumors.

There had to be something more. Consequences.

"You understand, given the gravity of this situation, that I cannot, in good faith, honor the passing grade Dr. Merino has given you?"

"Yes, sir, I understand."

"Now, I don't want you to panic. There's one section of 4960 over the summer if you'd like to go ahead and redo your mentorship. I really believe this would be your best option. I'd hate for my decision to delay your graduate studies."

He didn't want her to panic. Why panic? It wasn't like an entire semester worth of work had been chucked out the window. She responded evenly, "I don't have transportation."

"Should you enroll this summer, I'll arrange for you to work with the incoming psychiatrist."

"Incoming?"

"Dr. Merino tendered his resignation earlier this week. You weren't aware?"

Resignation. Had she heard him right? Ringing filled Kenna's ears, faint yet piercing.

She wondered if she had anything to do with him fleeing his post. It was useless speculation. Maybe, for one glorious moment, she had been the stable center of Dr. Merino's universe, but there was no denying he thrived amid chaos and she introduced the expectation of order.

She was disciplined and he was dangerous.

It was better this way, or at least that's what she insisted as she swallowed the lump lodged in her throat. And yet, her mind wandered to that office across campus, to the man who held her heart on a string.

Kenna ran before she realized she was in motion.

"Please inform me in a timely manner about—Miss O'Callaghan?"

Professor Henrick's questioning voice echoed in the foreground as her feet carried her out of the classroom, out of the hallway, out of the building, everything a blur of drywall and sound. She flew along the paved walking paths, that university highway. Her Mary Janes clacked as she went, heart jumping, and she ignored an inane passing comment.

"Where's the fire?"

Kenna burst through the doors of Markham Hall and breezed up the staircase. Her lungs were on fire and her breathing had turned ragged by the time she reached the third-floor landing. The urgency that had guided her died as she tiptoed through the hallway she'd come down twice a day for months, where she spent hours with a doctor who inspired both panic and awe within her.

Someone who had, briefly, held a great deal of importance in her life and who had gone just as quick.

She stopped short of Dr. Merino's office and stared blankly at the frosted glass window. It was the middle of the day and the interior was dark. A familiar voice startled Kenna.

"He's gone."

Professor Scott stood a few feet away, bundle of papers and thermos in tow. His expression bordered on apologetic and he channeled the nervous energy of a flustered father tasked with administering an awkward topic of conversation to his daughter.

"Shouldn't you be on your honeymoon?"

He raised the papers. "Have to make it through exam week first."

"But you knew the schedule when you set the date, right? Why didn't you push it back a week?"

Any other day, Kenna might have thought it impolite to ask a faculty member such a personal question, but she'd had her hard work revoked and figured she could risk flying closer to the sun.

"I wanted to, but the date was important to my wife. It was her mother's birthday. She passed on a few years ago. You do that for the people you love." His gaze flicked from her to the office door before walking away. "You make sacrifices."

# August

3 4

# SIGNATURE

**Dayton**

The steady hum of traffic whooshed by through the cracked window. Beads of perspiration rolled along Dayton's neck, cementing strands of hair into place.

He had unknowingly leased a unit with a shot A/C and could withstand the noise if it meant some degree of relief from the summer heat.

His new office wasn't much: 300 square feet awkwardly split among a waiting area, session space, and a private office. After eight years in psychiatry, he had ventured out as an independent practitioner. And though it should have been a moment of professional triumph, everything dulled in importance with his darling Kenna out of the picture.

She was gone but he thought of her endlessly.

When he arrived home every evening, Dayton was haunted by the scenes that had played out between them. He sat in silence and reflected on the pain—physical and mental—he'd inflicted upon her. He had toyed with the idea of selling the house, but he wanted only to distance himself from her and feared that in moving he'd slowly lose the pieces of her he guarded so dearly until there was nothing to put together.

He pinched the bridge of his nose as if to silence the unwanted thoughts and turned his attention back to the slim stack of applications on his outdated, industrial metal desk.

Dayton had quickly learned that he couldn't effectively manage his patients' care as well as reception duties, and had placed an ad online a week earlier.

He sifted through the applicants without having any hireworthy criteria in mind. Even so, the candidates were a far cry from impressive. A Midwest transplant. A former dog walker. A retiree.

Distinct, clean print writing froze his hand in mid-reach of the next application.

His mouth slackened but he regained composure and cracked a smile as ineffable disbelief coursed through him. Kenna O'Callaghan graced the line marked 'name of applicant.'

A delusional hopefulness engulfed him while reviewing the form, but that hope eroded as her responses to the answers progressed.

Special skills? *Excellent at keeping secrets.*

Experience? *Hands-on with the employer.*

References? *Alex Guerrero, Charlee Pender, Erin Wright. Shoot, I have plenty more, but I'm out of space.*

All these months, Dayton had been certain she'd looked in the box but a most dreadful confirmation came with the sinking of his heart as the signature resting innocently at the bottom of the application stared back at him.

*Saint Kenna.*

If you enjoyed the first installment of Confessional, please consider leaving it a review on Amazon, Goodreads, or your vendor of choice. Reviews help indie authors gain visibility and expand their readership.

Sign up for my newsletter to stay up to date on new releases, cover reveals, beta opportunities, and more!

# ABOUT THE AUTHOR

Leighann Hart is the author of the Rosenfeld duet and the Confessional trilogy. She is a huge mental health advocate and this sometimes—okay, oftentimes—bleeds into her love stories.

She consumes heinous amounts of espresso and pays tithe daily to the New York Times Spelling Bee. Her biggest regret is that she probably will not meet Rick Moranis before he dies.

Leighann lives with her husband, daughter, and Sugar the Shetland Sheepdog in a convection oven—er, Georgia.

**Connect with Leighann Online**

www.leighannhart.com
leighanniswriting@gmail.com
Goodreads @ Leighann Hart
BookBub @ leighannhart